Two Sides of the Mirror

Mary L. Byrne

First Stillwater River Publications Edition
Library of Congress Control Number: 2020924373
Paperback ISBN: 978-1-952521-73-7
1 2 3 4 5 6 7 8 9 10
Written by Mary L. Byrne.
Published by Stillwater River Publications,
Pawtucket, RI, USA.
Publisher's Cataloging-In-Publication Data
(Prepared by The Donohue Group, Inc.)

Names: Byrne, Mary L., 1946- author.
Title: Two sides of the mirror / Mary L. Byrne.
Description: First Stillwater River Publications edition. |
Pawtucket, RI, USA : Stillwater River Publications, [2021]
Identifiers: ISBN 9781952521737 (paperback)
Subjects: LCSH: United States. Attorney-General--Fiction. |
Prejudices--United States--Fiction. |
Race discrimination--United States--Fiction.
Classification: LCC PS3602.Y7636 T86 2021 | DDC 813/.6--dc23

Also by Mary L. Byrne:

Only Children Hear Me
(Jake is a Friend You Can Talk To)

The Many Faces of Child Abuse

Tax Season from
the Spouse's Perspective

Dedication

I dedicate this book to all people who have ever suffered abuse of any kind. I hope you find your way to this book, and it provides you with peace of mind and heart.

Table of Contents

Foreword i

Acknowledgements iii

Introduction v

Chapter 1 - Run 1

Chapter 2 – Race to the Hospital 10

Chapter 3 - Reality 18

Chapter 4 - Truth 23

Chapter 5 - Fallout 39

Chapter 6 – Phone Call 47

Chapter 7 – Not So Fast 55

Chapter 8 – Healing 67

Chapter 9 – Laura's Project 78

Chapter 10 - Progress 84

Chapter 11 - Renewed 91

Chapter 12 – Trip Home 98

Chapter 13 -Getaway 101

Chapter 14 -Moving On 106

Chapter 15 -United 117

Chapter 16 -Meetings 128

Chapter 17 -Press Conference 138

Chapter 18 -Requests 142

Chapter 19 -For Laura 145

Chapter 20 -University Presentation 151

Chapter 21 -Revisit the Past 160

Chapter 22 -Extended Family 169

Chapter 23 -Actual World 175

Chapter 24 -A Step Back 184

Chapter 25 -Finally 187

Chapter 26 -Abe's Call 190

Chapter 27 -Moment of Truth 195

Chapter 28 -Forgiveness 200

Chapter 29 -Plans 202

Chapter 30 -Deja vu 206

Chapter 31 -Truth Is Stranger Than Fiction 212

Foreword

This book originated in the author's mind, upon awakening at 5:00 a.m. The details were sketchy at first but became apparent within five minutes. Once she had the title in her mind, she had to write the book. She would never have chosen it as her next novel, not knowing the subject; it picked her.

As you progress through the pages, you will realize *Two Sides of the Mirror* is more real than fantasy. Not defined as fiction, but a dream come true, a world without racial barriers.

Through research, the author has developed a new and more in-depth understanding of racial issues and the pain caused by racism and discrimination. Limiting friendships within just our race can restrict our growth.

Since the author was not familiar with the proper terminology for all ethnic groups, she turned to the people who knew best. If any term is incorrect or misused, it is through oversight and not meant to insult or offend anyone.

Acknowledgements

I am profoundly appreciative of the following people.

My granddaughters Sienna and Milan Byrne, and my son Dennis Byrne. Thank you for your never-ending support, encouragement, love, and interest as I wrote this book. I will always be grateful.

Thank you, Jacqueline Steele, for being the very first person to read my manuscript! I truly appreciate it.

You stated –

"You could not put it down; it was amazing."

Michaele Colizza, somehow you managed to read the entire manuscript on your phone, which is a fantastic feat in itself. Thank you for your persistence in completing it.

You stated -

"Thank you for this story of hope, inspiration, and love. May God bless you and help this story's message spread across the world at light speed."

Introduction

Two Sides of the Mirror is literary fiction written to explain how our actions affect others. Words can burn through to the soul and change the heart of the receiver, forever.

Shouldn't you weigh the power of your words? To realize before your conversation or confrontation with another person, they were a gentle, sweet soul? After, the pain that gripped them was permanent. You then continued on your way, never knowing or caring how you left them.

Before picking up this book, were you aware of what racism does to the heart and soul of the receiver? Do you understand we aren't responsible for our height, the color of our eyes, or our skin, any more than where our birth occurred or from whom? You already knew these things, didn't you? Stop for a moment and ask yourself: Did this person ever do anything to me, or did I base my bias feelings on the opinions of others?

May this book enlighten you and open your eyes and heart to the possibilities. We are all more similar than we are different, regardless of our race, sex, origin of our birth, or nationality. We have the same desires and goals for love, appreciation, and value. Imagine the possibilities if we all respected each other's differences.

* * *

Gregory Hastings was the United States Attorney General. He discriminated against people of all races his entire life with insults and ignorance. He was the ultimate bigot. Only his immediate family knew his genuine feelings, and it sickened them.

Greg did not judge people based on their merit. He drew his conclusions based on their skin color, profession, financial standing, or level of education. One day, the tables turned.

Two Sides of the Mirror will enlighten you. It will leave you with a better understanding of being degraded, insulted, and belittled. Your skin color is something you are not responsible for and cannot change.

This book contains descriptions of how racism and discrimination can affect a person.

Clarification: Within this book...

People that are black and born in America are referred to as black.

People born in Africa preferred to be referred to as African American.

Every effort was made in the writing of this book to address all people adequately.

Any errors made are accidental.

Chapter One

Run

Laura's entire being screamed, RUN! As fast as you can and never look back. She shuddered at the mere thought of disappointing her father, who never settled for less than two hundred percent of everyone's ability. She spent most of her time studying, seldom allowing herself the luxury of just relaxing and having fun. Somewhere deep inside herself, she thought if she didn't, she would fail.

Laura and her mother, Sylvia, enjoyed a very close relationship. That was not the case with her father; theirs became strained. She never thought she measured up to his unrealistic standards. He judged everyone by their accomplishments. Laura could not be herself. She did not dare show her beautiful personality, sparkling eyes, or a great smile. Thinking she must keep those parts of herself hidden or endure her father's never-ending ridicule.

He behaved cruelly for years. Upsetting and embarrassing Laura, many times saying whatever he chose to people he did not see as being like himself or his equal. Laura hesitated to invite her friends to her home for fear of what her father would say with no concern for their feelings. To protect them, she kept them away from him.

Laura and Ellen had become best friends at school. They were like sisters and spent a great deal of time studying together when they were able to.

Ellen expressed a desire to meet Laura's family many times. She wanted to see where her best friend lived. Even though Laura made Ellen aware of how cruel her father could be, she finally decided to take Ellen home with her for the weekend. After clearing it ahead of time with her mom, then explaining to her father that Ellen was Nigerian. Laura wanted to ensure her father would say nothing cruel.

"Ellen is my very best friend here at school. Assure me you will be kind and welcoming to her, or I will not bring her home."

"I want Ellen to be comfortable here with us; we will get along great."

"Dad, then why were you so cruel and insulting to so many of my friends and acquaintances? I shouldn't have to struggle like this to be assured that you will be on your best behavior with my best friend while she is in our home."

"I promise you, there will not be any problems, you'll see."

Laura finally agreed to attempt it, but an enormous part of her feared something would go wrong. Her history with her father had shown her the evil side of him.

Laura lay awake most of the night before. In the morning, she nervously drove over to Ellen's dorm to pick her up. Ellen seemed excited to meet Laura's parents and see where she grew up. The girls talked through the entire two-hour trip. They drove over the winding roads, laughing and joking all the way. They had gotten along well from the day they first met.

It surprised Laura that two young women from unfamiliar countries had so much in common. They focused on their education, studying together much of the time. Their dream of running a clinic together in a rural area was a driving force for both of them. They wanted to bring medical care to people who otherwise could not afford it. Their goals grew closer with each passing day.

When they arrived at the house, Laura reiterated, "Here we are, I hope it goes well, but let me apologize now, in case it doesn't."

Ellen attempted to ease Laura's concern with, "Don't worry, everything will be fine. What could your father possibly do to upset me?"

Laura hoped everything would go well, but could not get beyond her concern. It proved to be a nightmare from the minute they walked through the door. Laura's father didn't even greet Ellen. Instead, he insulted her clothing. He yelled to her from his chair without getting up, "Hey girl, where did you get the outfit, a yard sale?" He laughed at her, then added, "I did not expect you to be so dark skinned."

Laura tried to make light of her father's behavior, telling Ellen he had a strange sense of humor; he did not mean what he said.

Greg interrupted and told Ellen, "I meant every word. I wish you, and all the rest of your people, would go back where you came from."

Ellen was heartbroken. The girls raced out the door, with Greg following. Yelling, "Please stay. I am sorry; I did not mean it."

It was too late! Greg could never undo the pain he caused Ellen.

Laura thought it must be a nightmare, but unfortunately, it was real. Laura apologized and cried right along with Ellen.

Ellen told her, "You must, eventually, forgive him; he is your father."

"You are my best friend; I love you like a sister. I will never forgive him for hurting you! I have no idea what caused him to act like that and say those things to you. I am sorry from the bottom of my heart."

Laura did not understand how he became so nasty. His family was nothing like him, just warm and welcoming people. Where did this evil spawn originate? Her head ached, thinking about everything as they drove the two hours back to school. The thoughts entering her mind were just dreadful. She had to separate herself from him!

Ellen became silent and remained so for the rest of the drive. Laura's mind wandered. She wondered why her father was so difficult. He was nothing like the other fathers she'd met. Her heart was breaking. How could her father have done something so cruel and unforgivable, and to her best friend?

Her thoughts were all over the place. She hoped she and Ellen could somehow maintain their friendship after this painfully bad experience.

Ellen walked into her building without a word. Laura experienced a strange chill watching her friend disappear inside. She might never see Ellen again. Just the thought made her heartache.

When Laura awoke the next morning, she had forgotten about the previous night. Suddenly, the memories resurfaced like a tremendous slap in the face. What had her father done to her dearest friend?

She called Ellen. Her phone was off. She left a heartfelt message, hoping Ellen would get back to her soon.

Laura called her all day long, then stopped by her dorm to talk to her roommates. No one had seen Ellen. Laura panicked; where would she go? She shared with one of Ellen's roommates what had happened the previous night. Ellen's roommate, Jessie, told her about the harrowing experience Ellen had at her last school involving prejudice. She'd never recovered. She sought therapy, but very few people were aware of the incident.

A group of female bullies attacked Ellen at her first university in the United States. Her injuries were so severe they hospitalized her. She believed it was because of her race. The experience left her emotionally fragile. She transferred to their present school and attempted to address her feelings through therapy. She never told her best friend, Laura.

"If only I had known. I would have kept Ellen far away from my father and never invited her to my parents' home. I would never have taken the chance of exposing her to his hatefulness. I wanted her to be part of my family."

Laura wanted to understand the cause and result of prejudice.

The following day many of the students, along with the police, formed a search party. They looked everywhere for days. But still no word. Laura called her father and told him what a rotten human being he had become for what he had done to Ellen. She informed him they all participated in a search party in an attempt to find Ellen. She prayed nothing had happened to her dear friend. He tried to apologize, but it was too late for apologies. By the time she finished her conversation with him, he was sobbing. It changed nothing. Laura hung up and cried while she prayed for Ellen.

* * *

Ellen heard that everyone was searching for her and called the police. Telling them she needed to get away and had told no one. After apologizing for any problem her absence had caused, she then called Laura.

"I am sorry I left without letting you know I was going. It was a desperate reaction on my part. I had to get away. I am back in treatment and will be in touch when my condition stabilizes. I do not know any more than that at this time."

Laura told her she was sorry, and her father was too. However, she knew it was too late for his change of heart.

"I promise to be in touch with you, Laura, when I am better. It will take me time to process everything that has happened."

Laura sensed they might never recapture the depth of the friendship they had shared, considering her father was the one that hurt her so much. She feared there would never be another call from Ellen, breaking her heart on many levels.

Months flew by. Laura stayed busy with her studies, which gave her less time to indulge in the sad memories of her father. He called her every week, apologized, and asked about Ellen. She was beginning to believe perhaps this had been one of the few hateful acts he ever committed that he regretted.

After many months, Laura found it necessary to go home for a few hours. She dreaded it and drove very slowly to the entrance. Her mom was aware of her need to come home, but her car was not in the driveway. Laura did not want to talk to her father alone. She got out of her car and approached the front door. Her father opened the door, looking beaten and drawn. His coloring seemed to be off. Laura asked how he was doing.

"Why do you ask?" he responded.

Before she answered, he said he would be seeing his doctor that week, sensing something might be wrong. It seemed safer for her to concentrate on his health than rip him apart for his behavior toward Ellen.

Her dad brought it up himself, saying, "I do not know why I misbehaved toward Ellen. I am tormenting myself over what my treatment of her led her to do. It is heartbreaking to think I have been so vicious toward all the people I thought were so different from myself. Thinking it gave me a license to be abusive. I now regret my actions."

Laura stared at the man who looked and sounded like her father. She never imagined hearing those words come from his mouth. She always hoped and prayed he would come to realize what his viciousness had created.

It broke her heart, knowing it took him destroying the heart and soul of her dearest friend for him to understand. It appeared to be a transformation. Laura sensed he seemed honest. His words appeared to be coming from his heart.

It confused but pleased her. She needed to talk to her mom. Who might explain what happened to her father? He went to take a nap, something she never remembered him doing.

It wasn't long before Laura's mother came home. They greeted each other as always, with hugs and kisses. Her mom asked if she had talked to her father. She said she had then asked her mom, "What happened to him? He is not the same person!"

"Your dad is heartbroken over what he did to Ellen. His behavior has improved since he began seeing a therapist."

"Mom, he doesn't look like himself."

"You need to sit down while I explain this to you." Laura listened as her mom explained, "Your father has been going through blood and genetic testing. The doctors believe his genetic makeup is changing."

"What do you mean, changing?"

"The doctors say he is showing all the genetic signs of becoming black, as strange as it sounds."

Laura answered her mother between sobs, "Mom, it's not possible; he is one hundred percent white."

Laura sat, shaking her head, wondering how such a thing had happened. They had to wait until all the test results came back to gain a full picture of his current diagnosis and prognosis for the future. She refused to believe the situation that was presenting itself, along with the changes in her father. He appeared to be a different person, with a kinder demeanor. Where would this all end?

"Why didn't you tell me?"

"You were devastated over what your father did to Ellen. We didn't want to upset you even more. You needed time to process to show any kindness or concern for him."

Laura could not have found any empathy for him when it first happened. She became consumed with the pain he inflicted on Ellen. Laura remained at home for a few hours to spend some time with her mom before heading back to school. Her head ached!

She had hoped for so long her father would change his feelings about people he did not see as equals. She still did not understand how he had developed his attitude. His sense of entitlement nauseated her. He wasn't any better than anyone else, but for some unknown reason, he didn't see or believe it.

Laura and Sylvia talked for two hours. They caught up on the latest news regarding the family and Sylvia's work. Her mom told her that since being admitted to the hospital, her dad's color had changed. Strangely, no one seemed to notice. People did, however, say he looked drained and appeared thinner. He was about six feet tall with a broad build, but his weight loss was noticeable.

Greg's staff handled most of the work during the brief periods when Greg had to be out for testing. His assistant, Alan Harrington, being astute, realized something serious appeared to be going on. He asked many times, but Greg had, or so he believed, deflected the questions. Whenever Alan asked about his health, Greg claimed the fatigue was stress. As soon as he got some definitive answers, he would bring him up to date.

"Honey, you are facing a two hour drive, but I would enjoy having you here for breakfast in the morning. Will you consider staying overnight and going back in the morning?"

"I have an early class which I should attend."

Laura asked her mom to say goodbye to her father for her. She wished for a way to reach Ellen but had no way to contact her. She hoped Ellen's condition would improve, and she'd someday be able to return to school, even if they were no longer friends. It appeared their friendship never happened, except for the constant reminder of what Laura's father had done to her.

The following day Laura stopped again to see Ellen's roommates, hoping one had received news from her. They tried to reassure Laura she did not cause it. They all agreed they had to continue to work hard, get the best grades possible, and wait. They admitted Ellen to a competent hospital, and she continued receiving outstanding care. She had an excellent chance for a full recovery.

Laura thought if your best friend struggled with such grave issues, you would know it, but she didn't. Ellen seemed to be active, healthy, and happy. No one had a clue she was so troubled. It devastated her to be attacked at her first school in the United States. Laura wished Ellen had discussed it with her.

Laura tried to imagine being a different race in a strange country, then treated with hostility. She wanted to learn the effects of discrimination from the hearts of people themselves. Laura decided on a study to honor Ellen by interviewing minorities from all backgrounds. She wanted to understand the effect it had on them. Someday, she would help ease the pain people endured when confronted by a bigot like her father.

Laura rushed to the campus library to begin her research. She read article after article until her eyes would no longer focus. She wanted to experience discrimination for herself. What would it do to a person's heart and soul? How would a person deal with it long-term? Her need to learn as much as possible had become a driving force. She needed to understand as though it were happening to her. Just research wasn't enough. She wanted to explore their feelings. It wasn't just a racial issue, although that came to mind when one heard the word discrimination.

She would ask people of many races. Could people ever embrace their differences and their similarities? It seemed the closer they got to resolving the issues the more distance developed between them.

Laura called Professor James Williams, one of her former professors, to ask his advice on finding people willing to be interviewed for her report. He was interested and asked her to come by his office that afternoon to discuss her project. She was pleased and agreed immediately.

Professor Williams greeted Laura with an enormous smile. He had always been one of the most cheerful professors on campus.

"I haven't stopped thinking about your project since we spoke earlier today. It is an exciting idea. I would love to help you if you would allow me to."

Laura loved the idea. Since the professor was much more knowledgeable than her, she welcomed his input.

"It would please me to work with you Professor Williams, to study all facets of racism and prejudice."

Laura shared her father's history of nastiness with the professor, who found it fascinating after the physical changes her father experienced.

"What happened to Ellen is terrible. I hope she will recover a much stronger woman."

Laura thanked him for his concern.

"Things can start in a joking manner and turn serious and be very damaging."

"You are so right, Professor, you can find yourself in the middle of such a destructive situation in a heartbeat, still shaking your head and wondering how you got there."

They both agreed! It would be a fantastic project, which might take them to places they did not even imagine.

Laura walked back to her dorm full of excitement and anticipation, just about able to contain herself.

She needed to talk to her mom to check on her dad's progress. Ellen might have been right; someday, Laura would have to forgive him. He was her father! She wondered whether she would have been able to arrive at that point had her father not made some enormous changes. Thankfully, he did, for his sake and everyone else's.

* * *

Laura poured a glass of water and sat down to call home. She expected the phone to ring a few times, but her mom answered on the second ring.

"Hi, Mom."

Laura had hoped her mom would sound more cheerful; she sensed something had happened. "Laura, can you take two days off? Your dad is not doing so well; they've admitted him to City Hospital."

Laura wondered what was wrong. "What does that mean? Where is Dad now?"

Her mom told her, "They just took him to the lab for more blood testing; his doctor is very concerned. His blood counts are off, and his coloring has changed. He is getting darker."

Chapter Two

Race to the Hospital

She called Professor Williams to inform him she had to go home due to her father's condition then notified her professors they had a severe illness in her family. She would return on Monday and get her assignments online in the interim.

She left to begin the two-hour drive home. The night filled Laura's mind with thoughts of her childhood, remembering time spent with her dad. They took trips to the lake and fished from the old rowboat. She loved those times before her dad became impossible. It seemed the longer he was the United States Attorney General, the more arrogant he became.

Laura's stomach got the best of her. She'd get a sandwich and drive the last hour to the house. She never stopped in at night. Everyone at the restaurant realized something was wrong.

Laura ordered a sandwich and a bottle of water before using the ladies' room. Her reflection in the mirror showed her fatigue. She ate while driving and wondered what she would learn when she got home. Laura called her mom to let her know what time to expect her.

"Laura, I am distraught. Your dad is not himself at all; he looks terrible. I am at home. We can drive back to the hospital together."

They both hoped the doctors would find an explanation for Greg's unusual symptoms. Laura could not imagine their lives without her dad. He had been challenging to deal with for years, but there was hope as long as he was alive. She was not aware of anyone having anything even similar to what her father had developed. Would it be fatal?

After pulling into the driveway, she grabbed her bag while running into the house. Her mom was waiting for a hug, which she needed.

"Mom, I missed you! I drove way too fast, but I am here. I will change quickly, and we can leave."

Her mom smiled and said she would wait. Laura ran off to the bathroom and put some chilly water on her face, brushed her teeth, and changed her clothes, all in about three minutes.

The doctor would meet them as soon as they got to the hospital. They almost ran from the parking lot to the entrance, then to the room on Two East the doctor had reserved for their meeting.

Doctor Mathew Berkin was waiting for them when they arrived. "We conducted extensive tests to confirm what we suspected. No one has ever experienced this before. We have contacted many infectious disease specialists, which is what took us so long. We have the final results. I must tell you no doctor has ever given a family a diagnosis like this one."

Laura and Sylvia held onto each other, holding their breath as the doctor continued.

"Greg has become a black man. It is permanent and irreversible. We are building him up with high doses of vitamins. The anemia was due to the strain on his system caused by his changing DNA. It had a tremendous effect on him, but he should be as healthy as ever soon. We project keeping him here for four to five more days.

"I am sorry to deliver such a diagnosis. I cannot even imagine what your thoughts and feelings are at this moment. I wish I had better news for you. The only saving grace is his condition will not be terminal, but it is permanent. We believe his skin color has reached its maximum depth, but we cannot be sure.

"Greg is healthy. We suggest all of you work with a therapist to help you adjust to the changes life has in store. He is aware and very concerned with your reaction to the news. Doctor William Laden, our top psychiatrist, has spoken with him at substantial length. He took the report well, considering how life-changing it will be."

"Can we see Greg?"

Dr. Berkin said, "You can."

They thanked him and walked down to the elevator. Their minds were a maze. They saved their conversation for later at home. Both Laura and Sylvia wondered what they would say to Greg. How would they convey their concern, yet tell him they loved him? Then assure him everything would be okay when they weren't sure themselves what the future held?

"It's all so confusing, Laura, no wonder the doctors took so long to offer us their diagnosis. I wonder how Greg will inform the public about what's happened to him. He must inform them soon, before word gets out."

Sylvia had considered ending their marriage many times because of Greg's nastiness and cruelty. He belittled anyone he didn't see as his equal. It seemed to be karma, watching him become a darker race. She wondered how he would handle being discriminated against, as he had discriminated against others all those years. She did not rejoice in seeing it happen to him, although it seemed fitting. The issue for her now would be to remain empathetic.

How would she adjust to being married to someone of a race other than what he was when they married? They would all need the help of an excellent therapist to learn together.

Laura wasn't able to stop thinking of Ellen. Her father was so cruel to her, and his skin now approached the shade of hers. He might soon face the same cruelty he inflicted on others. They called it racism. Greg would experience it firsthand.

Laura saw something different inside this man she had known as her father. The changes were more profound; they seemed to reach his soul. It would have far-reaching effects. It would touch everyone in his life, everyone that had ever known him. Laura realized since her father was a public figure, it would require more of an explanation than for the average person. A press conference involving the doctors, their research, and then someone to make sense of it.

When Laura and Sylvia arrived at Greg's room, they said nothing, walked in, and smiled.

Greg smiled back at them and said, "Well, ladies, life has thrown us a major curveball. We can either catch it and go with it for all it is worth, or let it fall. So, what should we do? I already know how I plan to attack it."

Sylvia responded, "We just spoke to your doctor and are still trying to digest it all. I know we would both like to hear your thoughts."

"Well, I've given this serious consideration. As my color changed, I wondered if it might become a permanent situation. If it did, how would I handle it? I will just say it. We are all aware I haven't been a pleasant person, ever. I do not deserve your love or loyalty, but I am so thankful you have both continued to give it to me. Somewhere inside, I knew I had no right to belittle and degrade people I seemed to believe differed from me. I wasn't able to stop myself. I enjoyed such a sense of superiority. As a public figure, I became unapproachable and indestructible. No one could touch me. I continued, and it just got worse. How I hid it from my constituents, I will never understand. It breaks my heart, knowing how I hurt you both. I am truly sorry.

"Only after I hurt Ellen did I see the error of my ways. It bothered me to realize I had destroyed that lovely young woman. My concern for her has always been real. I am sorry it had to take something this serious for me to turn myself around. Can you two ever forgive me, and do you think someday Ellen might see me for who I am now?

"Before you respond, I would like to finish, if that is okay? It is important to me to know whether my being black might change either of your feelings for me. It will put me into a unique situation dealing with various races, since I am now another race myself. I am hoping to bring about more positive changes since I relate firsthand. There is an impressive amount for me to learn. But first, I need to know whether my wife and daughter can handle going on with me in this new role, as a black husband and father?"

Both Laura and Sylvia remained speechless. Neither of them expected any of what Greg said to them. He apologized for his past behavior, asked for their forgiveness, and wanted to be sure where they stood in his future. They needed it to penetrate. They both loved him, but there would be many changes. Could they handle them?

Sylvia responded, "This is all just beginning to penetrate. We realize there will be many changes in our lives. No matter what color your skin may be, we both love you."

Laura added, "Mom is right, Dad, we love you, and we will be by your side every step of the way. Your apology and acknowledgment of your past behaviors have made a world of difference for me. I can only imagine it did for Mom too. Thank you for sharing your feelings with us."

Greg told them he had been considering how he would inform his staff and the public of his diagnosis. He would first discuss it with Alan. He had been avoiding him for weeks. It was time for that honest talk.

They left the hospital in silence. When they reached Sylvia's car, they turned and hugged each other and cried. It was such an emotional experience; they weren't able to hold it in any longer.

What they learned they would not have imagined before meeting with Greg's doctor. They were still having trouble comprehending it. Greg had become a new, kinder, more decent, gentler, and compassionate man of a unique race. Soon they might live their lives together as everyone had always wished they would. Greg's former meanness had not allowed them to before. What a night!

Sylvia and Laura arrived home exhausted; they would get some rest and discuss the changes in their lives in the morning.

If this had happened to their lives, what else might not be as it appeared? Sure, her dad had been a monster. But had he changed so much that now he wasn't the father she had known her entire life. She would need therapy to sort it all out. There would not be a quick, easy fix, no simple solution. Laura wondered if her entire life had been a complete lie. She needed sleep and hoped it would all seem more doable in the morning.

Sylvia brushed her hair, as her mind wandered over all the years she had known Greg. His moods, the pleasant times, and the awful times. One constant throughout all those years: he was white. She wondered how she would experience it on an emotional and intimate level. They had responded, telling Greg she and Laura loved him. Would it take time to explore?

She would need therapy, just to come to accept it. Never mind making lifelong predictions and promises. She did not have any answers; she needed some rest.

Laura woke up very early and put on the coffee. The sun had just risen and cast shadows into the kitchen, the time of the morning she always enjoyed. Laura took her coffee out to the sunroom and sat down to watch the sunrise.

Sylvia surprised Laura as she entered the room with a cup of coffee and the morning paper. Laura became engaged in her thoughts, but a sense of relief settled over her to see her mom and end her rambling concerns.

"I imagine you thought of nothing else but your father, and what this situation will mean for all of us, as we go forward?"

Laura told her she was right.

"It will all work out. You know, honey, you cannot make this stuff up."

Laura looked at her mom, and they both broke into laughter. They laughed until they cried. Laura found it so appropriate since they needed to lighten the mood. That did it!

"Let's go out to breakfast. We haven't done that for a very long time, and Dad is having his breakfast served to him."

"I would love to."

The ladies showered and drove to their favorite breakfast restaurant, Hot Chocolate, a quick drive from their house. It seemed so right for Laura to be alone with her mom. With Laura in school, two hours away from home, and Sylvia with a busy pediatric practice, there wasn't much time for meeting up. When Laura came home for summer break, they would spend more time together.

"I wonder if, when Ellen hears what happened to Dad, she might consider forgiving him. When she realizes how sorry Dad is, it may be different for both of them."

"You might be right. Perhaps it may help Ellen heal, and you may get your best friend back."

"We keep each other sane."

Sylvia laughed; Laura could not have been more right.

They drove to the hospital in separate cars to visit Greg before Laura returned to school.

When they walked into his room, Greg was on the phone with Alan, his best friend and assistant.

They overheard him say, "Alan, I would like you to come to the hospital as soon as possible. I need to talk to you about something of the utmost importance. I am in Room 328 West; see you soon."

When Sylvia and Laura walked in, Greg asked, "Did you hear me talking to Alan? He is coming right over to discuss my condition. We must choose the proper way to inform President Mitchell and everyone else. It is such a delicate subject."

"My transformation will enable me to gain a better understanding of the issues faced daily by all people of color, not only those that are black. I must not forget when I became the Attorney General, I was white. I am now a black man. To us, it may not seem significant, but it may be for some people, which we cannot foresee at this moment."

Laura and Sylvia stared at Greg for at least two minutes, then Sylvia spoke. "It is a lot to consider and very complicated. However, as the Attorney General, you have always earned respect for the man you are. It has never been about your race."

Laura agreed with her mom; they were treading unfamiliar ground.

"Dad, I must leave to go back to school. I will see you soon. I am so proud of you."

Greg wiped away tears as he smiled and waved goodbye to his daughter. Sylvia walked out with her to the car, telling Greg she would be right back.

Laura and Sylvia walked to the parking lot without a word. They were both trying to process the events of the last couple of days.

When they reached Laura's car, Sylvia turned to her and gave her an enormous hug; she told her, "I love you, girl, with all my heart. I am amazed at how you handled the last couple of days with your dad. I feared you would never forgive him. You stepped up and amazed me at every turn. I am so proud you are my daughter."

Laura cried as she tried to respond. "Mom, I love you too, I always will. Dad hurt me, but I cannot go on being angry with him. I think he is sorry and has changed."

Sylvia was so proud of the lovely young woman standing before her and so grateful she could forgive and love her dad at the same time.

Sylvia smiled as she watched Laura drive out of the parking lot. They would be okay; with the love they shared, they would all survive the future. When Laura had gone out of sight, she returned to Greg's room. Her mind wandered as it had done for the past couple of days.

Alan Harrington arrived to visit Greg. He was keen to hear what Greg had to share with him. Alan and the rest of Greg's staff stressed about him for weeks, although no one had said anything to Greg. They had all been talking among themselves regarding what might happen with Greg. They had noticed his fatigue, lack of energy, and his coloring. Not one person said anything to him beyond, "How are you doing today?" His staff had an impressive amount of respect and concern for him. Realizing when the time came, Greg would inform them. Until then, they carried on day-to-day duties required when working in the Attorney General's office.

Chapter Three

Reality

Alan and Greg had not met for about a week. When Alan walked into Greg's room, he had shock written all over his face. Greg's coloring had deepened since their last meeting. Alan previously remained neutral and did not usually show his sincere feelings. Not this time! He stared at Greg, not knowing what to say.

"I am sure you have questions, and I have a lot to share with you. I am sorry I did not explain what had happened, but we were not sure ourselves. The doctors conferred with infectious disease specialists before they gave us their diagnosis last night.

"They are now all in agreement: my DNA has changed to that of a black man. It is not terminal, but it is permanent. We are all learning about this together. The strain caused weakness in my immune system. The doctors think I will regain my strength and be as healthy as I've always been within a brief period. However, I will live out the rest of my life as a black man.

"Since this has never happened to anyone else, it will be difficult for most people to comprehend. We must consider the reactions of the president and the public. How will the public view me as a black man, since I was appointed as a white man?"

"Greg," Alan managed through his shock, "I am at a loss, in total shock. Your transformation is overwhelming. We had all noticed the changes in you. The fatigue, your lack of energy, and your coloring had changed.

"My sense is to hold a private meeting first with President Mitchell and your closest constituents, then plan from there for a press conference, but subject to change as we go forward with our planning.

"Greg, we need to ensure that the doctors and researchers are on board. They can respond to questions regarding how they think this may have happened and what the state of your health is now. I am pleased it has not gotten out to the media yet. We are both aware it will, with you in the hospital. You are too well-known; it is a miracle no information has leaked."

"Alan, this is such a big issue for medicine the doctors all agreed they must keep it confidential. They can reveal nothing until we arrange for them to speak with the president. They bear an obligation to me as their patient, and all the physicians involved. I am here under an alias. Even the nurses caring for me here are skilled in assisting with confidentiality. I will give you the contact information for the lead doctor. You can complete all the arrangements with him; he will make his group available to the president."

Alan responded, "President Mitchell, members of Congress, the Senate and House of Representatives, the doctors, researchers, and your immediate constituents, besides all usual press and our overseas correspondents, will be present. Your doctors and I will discuss the meeting and prepare for scenarios. I will need three days to arrange everything; does that sound reasonable to you?"

Greg thought it reasonable but realized speed would be of the utmost importance. He was well aware of the tremendous undertaking it would be for Alan to organize the press conference.

"Alan, how do we convince the public my ethnic changes will not sway me one way or the other?"

"Greg, only you can answer the question from your heart; no one else can do it for you. Be honest and explain your feelings since going through this change. You can now relate to racism and discrimination on a different level than ever before."

Greg had the advantage of knowing he could trust Alan with his life. He took a deep breath. There was a lot to be done, so Alan prepared to leave.

Sylvia returned just as the men wrapped up their meeting,

She smiled as she told Alan, "I am so glad to see you. Now you will be beside Greg through this ordeal. It will not be a simple task. If there is anything Laura and I can do to help, please call us."

Alan said he would be in touch before he disappeared down the hallway.

Greg told Sylvia what they had decided, and she agreed with everything.

"Imagine," Sylvia said. "Three more days and our secret will be the main conversation with everyone. Then you can ingratiate yourself into the good graces of ethnic groups everywhere. Just ponder on that for a bit!"

"We may experience rough times ahead, but it will never be because I was a racist or bigot. It will only be because of external issues when there are any, I promise you!"

Sylvia smiled and kissed Greg. She was experiencing a multitude of emotions, but the strongest was love for her husband.

* * *

The entire drive back to school, Laura had not stopped reminiscing about her father. She thought about what life was like before he became the cruel man she'd known in recent years.

Laura wanted to discuss the latest news with Professor Williams before it became public information. Almost on the first ring, he answered, "Hello, this is Professor Williams."

"Hi Professor Williams, this is Laura Hastings. Can you meet with me today?"

"Laura, since there are no classes today, I am flexible. How soon would you like to meet?"

"Can you make it at eleven o'clock this morning?" she responded.

"Yes, I can see you then."

Laura needed to get out of the shower and prepare to meet the professor. Their meeting would be one of the most surprising and unbelievable ones he had ever had.

Sylvia called Laura to share. "Your dad is being discharged tomorrow and will meet with the president on Wednesday."

Laura told Sylvia, "Mom, I am not sure whether I want to attend the press conference, as long as you will be there. I hope it is ok with you?"

"Honey, I understand, and I am sure your dad will too. Whatever you decide is fine with us."

Laura thanked her mom, and they hung up. Now she had to hurry to get to the professor's office by eleven o'clock. She had a strange sense of excitement building up within herself, subtle but unmistakable.

As Laura walked, she could imagine several responses from Professor Williams, unsure of what he would say. She opened the door and walked into the outer office to be greeted by her favorite professor.

"Let's go into my office where we can speak."

Laura had to be careful. She must allow no one to overhear them talking until her father met with the president, and they held the press conference. She followed the professor into his office, where he motioned for her to sit down. Laura took a deep breath while Professor Williams waited for her to speak.

"So much has happened since we last met here in your office. My mom and I met with Dad's doctor, which turned out to be both frightening and enlightening. Before my last visit, they determined Dad had become anemic, weak, and his coloring was changing."

"Do they know any more now?"

"Yes, my father's doctor explained they had reached out to specialists from all over the world. When the final test results arrived, they realized he is okay. He will regain his strength, and the anemia will reverse itself. They are also one hundred percent sure his DNA has changed. He is now a black man, no longer white. They think his skin color has reached its maximum depth, but they are not sure. They also think we should all see a therapist. It will be quite a change for everyone."

"Is the president aware of anything yet?"

"No, my father will meet with the president on Wednesday to inform him of the changes he has gone through. Then they will all attend a press conference to announce it to the rest of the world."

Professor Williams sat for a while before attempting to respond to Laura's statements. He was trying to grasp everything they had just discussed.

Laura told him she would love to work on their project together and go forward as soon as possible.

"It would thrill me to get started on our project. Let me make some calls this afternoon, and we can begin the interview process right away. Your plan is even more important now than we realized. Who thought anything like this might happen? It will be good for you to stay busy with the project and your classes after the media announcements."

"I am pleased you are ready to go forward with this critical study. I expect we will learn an impressive amount while working on this together. Thank you so much. Please keep in touch."

Professor Williams said he would call her as soon as he gathered some information.

Chapter Four

The Truth

Laura could not decide. Part of her wanted to be there with her father at the press conference. The other part wanted to stay at school and learn about it after it happened. It would be life-changing for everyone involved. Laura called home. Her dad had left the hospital in the morning; he would probably be expecting her call.

Greg answered on the second ring and sounded cheerful as he said, "Hello."

"Hi, Dad, I wondered, would you like me to be there when you speak with the president, to show support for you?"

"Honey, it means so much to me for you to ask, but stay at school for now. Your mom is not going either. When the need arises, I will ask both of you to join me for at least one conference if you are okay with that? It will be fine with me."

Greg promised Laura he would keep her informed every step of the way.

"Dad, how are you doing? You've been through a tremendous amount since this all started. I am concerned about you. You seem to make such efforts to hold us up; how are you weathering all of this?"

"Laura, you can't imagine how happy you've made me. To know you care, love, and support me, means everything. I believe the three of us can weather anything now. You are an amazing young woman."

Laura could guarantee they would always be a family, no matter what race her dad became.

"Right after Ellen disappeared, I began a project which involved interviewing people from various races. Those who had experienced discrimination to determine how it affected them physically and in their hearts.

"I did not realize my father would end up being a black man himself. You may remember Professor James Williams. He consented to work on the project with me and is very excited about doing so. We've met a few times to discuss the details."

"Yes, I remember Professor Williams. He always seemed honest and down-to-earth."

"It is strange, Dad, I'm working on this project because of Ellen, and this happens to you. I guess we never know what twists and turns life will take."

"Honey, I cannot tell you how impressed and amazed I am right at this moment. I could not be prouder of you if I tried. This project should have far-reaching effects when combined with everything else that has transpired. I am thrilled to know you are working with Professor Williams. I trust him to be honest and to work in your best interest. Please keep me up to date on your progress. I love you, Laura."

"I love you too, Dad."

"I'll let you go now; I must speak to Alan to plan our strategy. There are only two more days. Goodnight, sweetheart."

"Goodnight, Dad."

It was an incredible price to pay. But she had her dad back. It pleased her knowing her father wanted progress reports on her project. Laura didn't enjoy working on it without his knowledge. Now it was unnecessary.

Greg reflected on the conversation he and Laura just had. Their relationship had all but ended because of his stupidity and belligerence. He had been a total bigot and became so wrapped up he couldn't stop himself. It almost cost him his daughter and his wife, too.

Since the transformation, he became grateful for its having happened. It opened his eyes and enabled him, in every sense of the word, to become a different person. He smiled, thinking he must be the luckiest man in the entire world.

He would help create some alternate possibilities for all ethnic people along the way. He needed some rest, but first, he had to call Alan to discuss his meeting with the president.

"Hello, Alan. We should discuss the meeting we will have with the president the day after tomorrow. I must admit I am tired of having to be careful of being seen in public. It will be wonderful to dine in a restaurant with Sylvia and Laura and not worry about being seen and sending shockwaves across the nation."

Alan laughed. "Sorry, Greg, I am not laughing at you; it is unbelievable. So, this is how I believe we should proceed. We will take my car; go in through the rear entrance and up to the Oval Office. I informed Steve Garrison, head of security, we will meet with the president and need the utmost privacy. He assured me of his full cooperation. If anyone sees us, they will have to accompany us to the Oval Office. We must ensure they will not speak to anyone before we meet with the president. After we complete our meeting, the president will be beside you when you inform the rest of the world at the eleven o'clock press conference."

"Alan, it sounds excellent. You addressed everything it will take to get us into the Whitehouse and up to the Oval Office. How about the media and everyone else necessary to be there for the press conference?"

"I contacted all of your doctors and arranged for them to arrive at ten. Your constituents and our local and international media, should come at ten thirty. The international press has all contacted their US media connections to ensure they will be present to provide coverage for them, so we should be all set. If you are aware of anything I missed, please let me know."

"Should we ask him if there are any foreign heads of state he would like to inform, rather than them hearing it through the media?"

Alan reflected about it for a moment and said, "You are right, but I cannot imagine him contacting anyone before the conference. He will make any calls necessary following the press conference at eleven in the Briefing Room. It should give us enough time to complete everything we need to accomplish."

"Alan, I appreciate you and all you do for me. There were times over the years when you must have wondered what my problem was and even wondered if I had lost my mind. Not only did my DNA change but also my old attitudes. Today, I am thrilled to live the rest of my life as a black man, along with all I can bring to society."

"I've noticed some unexpected changes in you, which I think are permanent. It is great to see. I am sure you will make some tremendous contributions to your fellow man. You and I have been friends for years, but sometimes you were a horrible human being. It sickened me. I tried to be patient, telling myself you would come to see the error of your ways and change your reasoning. There may be some people who will require convincing, such as Laura's friend Ellen. I won't say anything else on the subject."

"Alan, I too am excited about the possibilities of us working side by side wherever this takes us next. We should get some rest. We will talk many times tomorrow, goodnight, Alan."

Greg hung up and sat for a few minutes reflecting on his conversation with Alan and the events of the last few weeks. He had his wife, daughter, and Alan with him every step of the way. He could not ask for more than having them by his side.

As soon as Alan and Greg completed their call, Alan called Sylvia and Laura to ask them to come to the Whitehouse to be with Greg. He informed them they needed to arrive by 9:45 a.m. They had been procrastinating, but both agreed when they received Alan's call; they would get to the Whitehouse by quarter of ten with Greg's doctors. Sylvia declined the offer of a car to drive her to the Whitehouse, as did Laura. They both believed it would bring less attention to themselves, instead of having cars arrive at their home and Laura's school. Until the president met with Greg, they planned to keep everything very low-key, not alert anyone.

Imagine what everyone would say when they realized what happened to Greg! Laura and Sylvia had many discussions over the previous few days regarding whether they should attend and what to wear. Realizing they would stand next to Greg to support him through the most surprising day of his life thrilled them both. Laura regretted not sharing the news with Professor Williams, but was sure he would understand why she could not even tell him.

Laura woke up at 5:00 a.m., too nervous to sleep. Tomorrow they would all be getting ready to go to the Whitehouse. She took another deep breath without getting out of bed. She made a last-minute decision to call her mom.

Sylvia started talking before Laura even said hello. "Laura, I knew you would call. You are planning to drive home and go with me in the morning, aren't you?"

Laura laughed before answering her mother's question. "How did you figure that out?"

"Now Laura, how long have I been your mother, and who knows you better than I do?"

It relieved her so much to be talking to her mom. "Mom, I will drive home this afternoon if you agree?"

"It is more than ok. I have been hoping you would come home this afternoon. Remember, your dad still is not aware that we will be there with him tomorrow. We will tell him we wanted to spend a nice quiet family evening together."

"Sure, Mom, like it will be a lovely quiet family night, but we can tell him that," Laura choked out.

After telling her mom she would be there at about three o'clock, she closed her eyes and imagined what life might be like beginning tomorrow. She wondered what Ellen would think when she found out what had happened to Greg.

Laura smiled, perhaps because, in the oddest way possible, she and her parents had become so much closer than they had ever been. It only took a complete DNA change to accomplish it.

She remembered her mother's words; you cannot make this stuff up. No, you could not, no matter how creative you were.

She perceived her excitement, so she called her dad to say hello.

"Hi Dad," she said, when Greg answered the phone. "I just wanted to say hello and tell you I love you."

Greg responded, "I love you too, honey, it is so nice to hear your voice and receive this message. I have been thinking about you too. Come home so we can spend the evening together before all the craziness starts."

"Dad, what a splendid idea! It will be fun to enjoy some special time together before tomorrow begins. I should be there at three o'clock. I will see you then."

She hung up, knowing her dad would expect her. Laura called her mom to inform her of their conversation, then began putting her clothes in the car.

Laura sensed the excitement building within herself. Imagine, by tomorrow night, the entire world would know about her father. She hoped they would not be judgmental.

She knew the drive so well. Before long, she had reached home and pulled into the driveway. Laura grabbed her bag and headed for the door, leaving all of her more formal clothes in her trunk.

She walked in the front door. Greg was waiting to greet her with a hug and kiss, which was as she always dreamed it would be.

"Hi, honey," Greg said as he greeted her. "It is so great to see you."

"It is great to see you too, Dad," Laura answered. "I missed you."

"I am a little nervous. Knowing morning may end my beloved career forever, I did not sleep well. It could also be the start of an amazing new chapter. Too bad we must wait until tomorrow."

"Yes, Dad, we do. Nevertheless, it is exciting. What a tremendous change."

Greg received a call from Alan and took it to his office. They would talk for a while, which gave Sylvia and Laura a chance to discuss what time they would leave for the Whitehouse in the morning, and what they would wear.

Relief settled in. Sylvia and Laura were both happy they were attending, knowing it would thrill Greg when he realized they were there for him. Alan arranged for them to meet in the Briefing Room before the press arrived and informed security to expect them.

"I am so glad you came home this afternoon to be here with us for dinner this evening. It will be perfect for us to be here to discuss tomorrow and enjoy dinner together. Your dad will be up very early to drive in with Alan, which will give us time to get ready and drive there ourselves."

"Mom, you are taking a lot of time off, how are you managing to do that?"

"Laura, a doctor who is a dear friend has been filling in for me, which has allowed me to take a month-long leave of absence. We needed it. I told them it was a personal leave. They will all know soon why I needed the time."

An impressive amount of laughter ensued that night; they joked just like the old days. They never mentioned the following day's meeting.

"Laura, I just realized how close we are to your graduation. My baby girl is going off to medical school, it's amazing!"

"It is Dad. I am not sure I am prepared for it either, even though I've been waiting my entire life to become a doctor."

"Since you and Ellen have not worked toward your goals together lately, you may be a little off track."

Alan would be picking Greg up at six for their drive to the Whitehouse. After hugs and kisses, everyone said goodnight.

"I love you, Dad. No matter what happens tomorrow, we will always be together and happy. We can deal with whatever happens as long as we face it together as a family."

Greg had tears in his eyes, knowing Laura was right.

He tossed and turned all night, needing rest, but sleep would not come. All he could do was hope and pray he would continue being the United States Attorney General and maintain the trust of the president and the people. Knowing he would never revert to his old self again. The old Greg was dead and gone forever.

After shaving, Greg got into the shower. It was relaxing to have warm water flowing over his body. Reality struck him right in the face. Why had he thought he had done something wrong when he hadn't? He had gone through a physical and emotional transformation which he had no control over. People would understand and be in awe. Guilt had overwhelmed him, causing him to bear responsibility for something that was not his fault!

Greg got dressed and headed down to the kitchen for his first cup of morning coffee. Sylvia and Laura were there waiting for him. They heard the shower. He was eager to tell them what had just occurred to him.

Sylvia and Laura got up, and both gave him an enormous hug. They smiled at him in a way that he knew everything would be okay.

"A bolt of lightning hit me while I took my shower. I had been behaving almost as though I were responsible. I realized I had no control over the happenings of the last few weeks. A transformation occurred within me, changing my personality from evil to kind. That part I will omit. The change is overwhelming, as is my pride to be the only human to have experienced this."

Sylvia and Laura had such enormous smiles on their faces. Greg now had the right attitude. Together they shouted, "Yeah!"

Greg allowed himself to exhale and enjoy his coffee with his two favorite ladies. He realized he might like a little something to eat before Alan picked him up. Sylvia suggested French toast since it had always been one of Greg's favorites.

He expected a quiet breakfast alone, which became a delightful time with his family. Sylvia and Laura enjoyed the time with Greg before he left with Alan for the Whitehouse. Before they knew it, Alan had arrived. Greg ran off to brush his teeth and get ready for one of the most important days of his life.

Sylvia and Laura each kissed and hugged Greg and wished him luck. He promised to call them when it was over. They both smiled, knowing they would be right behind him. Then with him, for everything after he met with President Mitchell. The minute Greg walked out the door, they got moving. They both had to shower and get dressed, not wanting to run late or need to rush.

They both looked lovely, dressed for the occasion. During Greg's tenure, both women had become familiar with what to wear for each event. They dressed and were ready in plenty of time. Both Laura and Sylvia were beautiful women. Sylvia had light brown hair, lovely blue eyes, and stood five feet four inches tall, with a slender figure. Laura was five feet two inches tall, with beautiful long blonde wavy hair, her mother's blue eyes, and a slim figure. They would make Greg proud standing beside him at the press conference later that morning.

"Ready? Let's go," announced Sylvia in a loud voice.

The women held hands as they walked out to Sylvia's car and got in. They did not talk much for the first fifteen minutes of their drive, after which they never stopped talking.

Greg and Alan had a lengthy discussion on their way to the Whitehouse. Greg told Alan what he realized in the shower.

"Right, Greg. No one was responsible for what happened to you. You were the victim of the rarest DNA change known to man! We have been attempting to keep this all quiet until you informed President Mitchell, and it got carried away. I am so sorry."

"It hit me this morning and turned me around, realizing I had been attacking it from the wrong direction. Wondering if people would still accept me when I should have thought, I am quite the medical miracle."

"Since we were both thinking along the same lines, we got caught up in all the secrecy we had to maintain until we could advise the president. Somehow it translated into something negative when it was quite the opposite. You are a medical phenomenon.

"We are approaching the Whitehouse. I informed Steve Garrison we would come in early this morning. He should let us right in. Here's hoping, Greg."

They were on the list. The guard recognized Alan and saw Greg from a distance and let them in. They both breathed a sigh of relief. They had gotten past the first hurdle. Alan drove around to the rear door of the Whitehouse. There were no other cars there yet. They were in luck.

Alan parked as close to the building as possible. They both got out. The men could not help but laugh. They were sneaking into the building they had worked in for several years. This time they could not risk being seen before the president met with Greg. They used Alan's keycard. They had not considered the cameras. Alan motioned to Greg to put his head down and follow him. They made it to the stairway and climbed the twelve steps to the upper floor. Greg's heart pounded; now, they might run into someone in the hallway.

No one there either! They heard someone coming down the corridor. Alan pushed Greg into a closet. After about five minutes, the janitor continued on his way. Alan knocked for Greg to open the door. Making it to the office leading into the Oval Office, they walked in and locked the door behind them. The president would arrive in fifteen minutes; it seemed like two hours. Alan and Greg reviewed the plan one last time. As soon as the president entered the room, Alan would lock the door leading to the Oval Office to ensure no one would disturb them, and call Greg to join them. No matter what the outcome, Greg would soon discuss the details with President Mitchell, then the world.

When he arrived, Alan motioned to Greg to move away from the door so no one would see him. As Alan opened the door to the Oval Office, he gave Greg a thumbs-up.

Greg held his breath, not knowing what type of reaction to expect when he walked through the door himself. Alan walked into the Oval Office and smiled at the president, reached out his hand and said, "Good morning Mr. President, how are you doing today."

The president responded with, "I am fine Alan, what is all the mystery surrounding this meeting with you and Greg this morning, and where is Greg?"

"He will be right in. He is in the adjoining office."

"I am puzzled," he responded. "Will Greg be joining us?"

At that point, Alan tapped on the door, and Greg walked into the Oval Office.

President Mitchell just stood and stared at Greg for the longest time, then he said, "Well Greg, either you've been vacationing in the tropics, or there is something different about you we should discuss."

"Yes, Mr. President, we will discuss it at substantial length. The doctors needed to complete their testing before I told you or anyone else. They met with Sylvia, Laura, and me, just two days ago to present us with their findings.

"I have experienced a complete DNA transformation, from being a white man to a black man. Their tests are conclusive. I am healthy but weak, caused by the changing DNA affecting my immune system, but I am recovering my strength.

"I am sorry we could not share this with you sooner, but we had to be sure of the facts before I told you. I checked into the hospital under an assumed name, and the doctors brought in nurses that work under the strictest rules of confidentiality. I have not left the house since my color deepened, so other than Alan, I have seen no one."

"Wow," the president's responded, "I would never in a lifetime imagined anything like this. I am in shock, so please forgive me if I do not make good statements. One thing that strikes me is it will put you in a unique position. Although it has been a shock to you and your family, it may have a positive impact on you and the world if you can all adjust to this. Whatever you need, I will be here for you, Greg, please remember that.

"So, we will attend a press conference. I would like to speak with you and your doctors here in the Oval Office before we go into the news conference. Alan, thank you for the work you have done to bring comfort to Greg and his family and this project to inform the rest of the world. Your organization of this event has been exemplary. Thank you both for your determination to keep all of this confidential until you could inform me. I will inform none of the heads of state before the press conference. I will contact them when we conclude."

Greg smiled and breathed a sigh of relief as he shook President Mitchell's hand. He said, "Thank you, Mr. President. I am relieved to have this conversation. It made me uncomfortable keeping it from you. I am so glad you understand everything that has transpired, or as much as anyone can comprehend this situation."

At that point, President Mitchell asked Alan, "Please bring in the doctors and any other medical staff that are waiting so we can begin this once in a lifetime conversation. Greg, please stay here with me. You have done such an excellent job, and no one has seen you who might contact the media or anyone else."

The president then turned to Greg and exclaimed, "Greg, you realize your life will never be the same after this press conference."

"Yes, sir, I do. Sylvia, Laura, and I discussed the changes at substantial length. For instance, how will people react? Will they accept me as a black man? Sylvia and I discussed the fact she married a white man, and her husband is now black. Will it bother her to the extent she would no longer want to be my wife? We believe we can work it all out, but we also realize we will need to work with a therapist for guidance to do so. Mr. President, that leads me to a question. You appointed me as your Attorney General as a white man."

"Greg, I possess the utmost respect for you as a man, which is why I appointed you as my Attorney General, not because of your race. That will continue to be the case. We are all fortunate you are our Attorney General and will be for as long as you will stay."

President Mitchell's response thrilled Greg, and he told him, "Mr. President, you cannot imagine how relieved I am with what you said."

Alan introduced the president to all of Greg's doctors and nurses. He stated, "I am grateful to every one of you for the excellent care you provided to our Attorney General, Greg Hastings, and for affording him the benefit of protecting his identity until today, when we can announce it to the world. You are all true professionals. You accomplished your goal. Thank you all."

Everyone agreed it was the most puzzling case they had ever had in all their years in medicine. And for the doctors, they conferred with those from other countries. They would continue to search for answers, leaving nothing incomplete.

The president was interested in speaking with the nurses who worked on Greg's case. He was curious. "How did you maintain confidentiality, yet not alert the staff as to the identity of your patient?"

Their head nurse responded, "We told everyone we wanted to help since another tough case would have overloaded them. The staff nurses were so thankful they thought nothing of it."

He asked everyone to stay for the press conference then invited them to remain for lunch.

At that point, Alan entered the Oval Office with Sylvia and Laura, to enable them to walk into the press conference with Greg. He had cleared it with the president.

Greg had tears in his eyes. "I am thrilled you are both here with me, you look beautiful!"

Sylvia and Laura beamed, both happy they had attended. "It pays to follow your heart," Sylvia told Greg. "We love you, Greg, not much would have prevented us from being beside you today."

As long as his wife and daughter stood by his side, everything would be okay.

Alan continued taking the lead for Greg on this important day for him and his family. When the time came for the press conference, Alan led the way and announced the president's arrival. Next, the doctors and nurses took their assigned seats. Last, Greg entered the room with Sylvia and Laura, one on each side of Greg. He didn't know for sure how many of the media realized his skin color had changed, but cameras appeared.

Alan responded, "Please refrain from taking pictures. It is very distracting while such an important discussion is taking place. We will allow you ample time for photos."

The press honored his request.

President Mitchell announced, "You are all here today to cover a once in a lifetime story, for the local population and national news, and to share with your worldwide media outlets."

Everyone looked confused; what did the president mean?

President Mitchell continued, "I will now turn the mic over to Greg Hastings, to enable him to explain why we are all here today."

"Mr. President, Mr. Vice President, my valued constituents, honored guests, and members of the media, I want to share with you the incredible experience of my family and me over the last few weeks. It has been an arduous journey that began with fatigue, weakness, and a slight color change. I was not sure what had happened. My primary care physician referred me to Dr. Mathew Berkin. He and his staff ran many tests. They also contacted many other physicians, including infectious disease specialists from all over the world, before informing me, my wife, and daughter, of their findings. The doctors concluded I experienced a total DNA transformation from white to black. Since I am otherwise healthy, I'll live out the rest of my life as a man of color, learning firsthand what it is like to live as a man of a unique race. However, it will be necessary for me to seek help from many sources.

"I've worked to develop programs for all ethnic groups. Now, I will be more able to understand the feelings of being a black man, since I just became one. Besides the rest of my duties as Attorney General, I am concentrating on developing more understanding and new programs, meeting the needs of all races. My goal is to improve our country in significant ways if you will allow me and support me in doing so. Thank you. Dr. Berkin, would you now please address our audience?"

There were no interruptions between speakers, just silence.

"Good morning, Mr. President, Mr. Vice President, honored guests and members of the media. I am here today, along with many of my colleagues, to explain, to the best of our ability, Greg Hastings's DNA transformation. When his primary care physician contacted me, I figured there might be a simple explanation for what he had experienced. That happened two months ago. There was nothing simple about this case!

We now know based on our pervasive research, which included checking health information in all databanks known to the medical field, Greg is the only person ever to experience a DNA transformation. We still do not understand how or why it happened to him. Greg is now part of the black race and will remain so for the rest of his life. We will not stop searching to answer the question regarding how this came about. I can assure you based on the number of tests we ran. Greg is a very healthy man. Now, are there questions? Thank you."

The most intense feelings turned out to be from a black female radio host from a local radio station. She asked Greg how he intended to learn to be a black man. Stating, "You truly are an anomaly."

Greg told her, "Having given this an impressive amount of consideration over the last few weeks, I must gain most of my knowledge from people who have lived their lives as part of the black race. It is important to learn from your heart and soul how to be a person of color. I am not interested in statistics, or I would research it on the computer. Would you be willing to sit down and talk with me and tell me how you matured to be a black woman in our society? I hope you will all be patient with me if I ask a tremendous amount of questions. First, please tell me your name."

"I am sorry I didn't introduce myself to you. I am Grace Keeland, I host WLVO radio mornings from six to ten. I am happy to be here."

"Yes, I guess I am an anomaly; how else would one describe this journey? There should be many positive changes ahead; we will all learn together. I expect some people will not embrace the changes I experienced. In time they may come to accept it. I will leave you with these thoughts then we can adjourn for lunch. We do not receive advance notice of what the future holds for any of us. My changes are just more pronounced than most. Thank you all for coming. Alan will meet with all of you to guide your press releases."

Alan expressed, "This is the most comfortable I have seen any of you in weeks. You have not even imagined the excellent feedback yet to come, once the media reports your story. You will be the headline on the six o'clock news, then at eleven o'clock. By tomorrow it will be on the tip of everyone's tongue. Greg, perhaps you could make notes on minority groups you desire to meet with in the near future to solicit their input, and keep things going."

"Thank you, Alan, it is an excellent idea."

Sylvia and Laura looked forward to having the freedom to spend time with Greg in public once again.

Laura said, "I am excited about what is coming, but I hope you do not get overwhelmed trying to do everything at once. Dad, you will need to pace yourself. I wonder if Ellen will hear."

"She will learn about what has happened. I am confident you will receive news from her, but I do not know when. I hope it is soon for your sake, Laura; it will make you happy to talk to her. Maybe someday she would share her life story with me and discuss what she experienced growing up in Africa. That might be a stretch, but I hope she can. So, honey, how do you think things are at school?"

"It must be nuts there," Laura answered. "I'll call Professor Williams to make him aware before I go back to school. Hopefully, I can reach him before he hears it on the news, or I should say before he hears about it. The media will not waste time. They are like a dog with a bone when they have some important news to share."

Alan smiled as he listened to them talk and responded, "You are all right, but there is also an element of excitement that will be different. If you need anything at all, please call me. I love you guys; I hope you are aware of that."

"We are," Greg responded. "It is comforting to know we can count on you for anything, and it goes in reverse too, you can always depend on us. Never forget. We all love you!"

Alan smiled. He was sure of how much they all cared about him.

Greg and Alan said goodbye to Laura and Sylvia, then made their way over to the doctors to thank them and President Mitchell before they disappeared into the depths of the Whitehouse. Sylvia and Laura smiled at each other and breathed a sigh of relief. At least now they could get on with their lives. They said goodbye to the medical staff, hugged the president, and thanked him for everything before making their way out of the building.

As soon as they were outside the Whitehouse, Laura exploded with, "Mom, what an incredible day! I am amazed! Between sneaking into the Whitehouse, hiding until Alan came to get us, and walking in on Dad— it was like a fairytale! I am floating! We would never have forgiven ourselves if we had declined to attend this press conference today. Now actual life begins with Dad as a black man. Mom, you cannot make this stuff up!" Both women broke into hysterical laughter.

"Mom, how are you doing? Are you having any problems being the wife of a man of color? I realize you did not marry a black man. Can you go forward without a transitional period? I am concerned about your feelings regarding this transformation. Mom, please talk to me."

Sylvia looked at Laura with tears in her eyes. Laura knew her mom so well.

"Laura, you are so right. However, being his wife, there are special considerations for me. His personality change has been astonishing and welcomed by everyone. With that changed, I have concerns because he is no longer the man I married. He is much kinder, but his abusive behaviors damaged our marriage. He is also a unique race. I love him, as I always did, but we will all need to see a therapist. I love you for considering my feelings and asking about me."

Laura hugged Sylvia and answered, "Mom, thank you for sharing all of that with me. I appreciate your honesty. I almost walked away from Dad over his treatment of Ellen and his years of nastiness toward people he did not consider his equals. However, I am not his wife. There are issues you face that no one else does. If you need me, please never hesitate to call me."

The girls drove back to the house without another word about Greg. They discussed what they wanted for dinner, expecting Greg to be working late. Since it was a beautiful sunny day, and they weren't in a hurry to get home, they drove the long, scenic route they both enjoyed.

Sylvia said, "Since your father will be late for dinner and there is plenty of food in the house for him to eat, how about you and I go to Hot Chocolate for pancakes for dinner? We always enjoy doing that."

Laura smiled and said, "Mom, you always know how to celebrate after a dull day. I would love it."

They had talked so much they arrived home before they even realized it. Sylvia and Laura would freshen up, change, and go to Hot Chocolate. It had been a glorious day. They loved spending time together to relax. Before they could climb out of the car, the radio, which had been playing music in the background, was interrupted with an announcement.

"Tune in at six for a once in a lifetime statement. The United States Attorney General's DNA has changed; he has gone from white to black. Details at six."

They both laughed hysterically. Word was already out there. They could not help but wonder, what would happen next?

Chapter Five

Fallout

"Okay, girl, we are going to our favorite place for dinner. I am so glad we are together today and not facing this alone. That would have been a lot harder. It should be interesting to see how many people approach us while we are out and just how many phone calls we get today and tonight."

They entered the house and flopped on the couch. Laura's phone rang. Professor Williams called to ask if they were okay. He heard the news on his car radio.

Laura told him, "I am so sorry, I intended to call you. My mom and I just got home from the Whitehouse. We are planning to go to a small nearby restaurant we both enjoy for pancakes. What did they say on the radio?"

"No need to apologize, they just reported what had happened. Greg had gone through a DNA change and is now a member of the black race. They will give more details on the hourly news. I just wanted to check on you and your family."

"Thank you so much, Professor, for checking on us; we all appreciate it. We are fine right now. I will return tomorrow for classes. I will call you then."

They heard voices outside. Television vans and media cars lined the entire length of the street, beginning just beyond their driveway. It didn't take them long to converge on their home. Were they followed since leaving the Whitehouse?

Sylvia and Laura freshened up, changed their clothes, and left to speak to the reporters on their way out. Sylvia would take the lead in addressing their questions, but keep her answers vague.

They got into Sylvia's car and headed down the driveway, as the group of reporters ran toward her car. She stopped and opened the window to address them. Questions came from everywhere at once, so Sylvia said, "I can only answer one of you at a time, so please decide who will ask the questions. I will reply to the best of my ability."

A junior reporter from a local TV station asked, "So, how has the Attorney General now being black affected you and your daughter?"

Sylvia told him, "Our family has been through a lot these last couple of months, thinking we might lose Greg. It was weeks before we knew anything. When the doctors told us what they had determined, it relieved us. He is not ill and will live an average lifespan as a black man. He has always been an excellent Attorney General. We think he will be even better now as he gains a greater understanding of racial issues, being a black man himself. You will see him do remarkable things for the people of our country through his gained insight and help from ethnic organizations, who will lend their knowledge to guide him. Now, if you will excuse us, we have a date. Thank you all."

Laura remained speechless. After regaining her voice, she asked Sylvia, "Now, when did you get that savvy? I am amazed and was proud to hear what you said to them. The way you conducted yourself—it was pure perfection. Now let's hope they do not show up at Hot Chocolate."

They both laughed.

"I guess we better get used to being followed, but not being abused."

As they walked through the door, the waitresses all stared, knowing them from many previous visits. Sylvia and Laura just smiled at everyone and waited to sit down.

Sylvia told the hostess they would prefer a booth if she had one available.

They sensed the girl seemed nervous around them. Sylvia stopped her along the way and said, "Please relax, we do not want any special attention. We came because we love the pancakes, and you serve them all day."

The girl smiled and apologized, telling them she saw the press conference on TV before her shift began. "I imagine just about everyone here tonight saw the press conference and knows who you are. I will attempt to prevent the press from disturbing you during dinner."

"Thank you so much; we would appreciate that."

They sat in a booth on the side of the restaurant, with the waitress stating, "I hope this will give you more privacy while you enjoy our delicious pancakes."

They all laughed, then Sylvia and Laura thanked her for her thoughtfulness.

From out of nowhere, a stream of reporters headed toward them.

Sylvia spoke up, "We will not speak to any of you while we are having dinner. We insist you all leave. We will speak to one of you in the parking lot when we finish our dinner."

Laura told her mother, "You were incredible, Mom, I applaud your tenacity. Surprise encounters with the media are becoming a learning experience for both of us. I am already learning so much from you. You nailed it, Mom."

"There is no excuse for such behavior. I just spoke to the reporters at the house. Then they follow us into a restaurant and approach our booth for comments. If members of the media expect to conduct impromptu interviews with us, they darn well better be more considerate of our feelings, or we will never cooperate. See, this gives reporters a terrible name."

Laura and Sylvia broke into laughter. They had to cut the sour mood.

The girl who seated them made her way to their booth and apologized. She was sorry she had not prevented the media from contacting the women.

"My mother handled it. I don't imagine they will come back to your restaurant. She told them she would speak to them outside when we leave."

The hostess thanked them for their understanding and patience with the situation and disappeared.

Their order arrived, which helped to break the mood. The pancakes smelled delicious and were the best around!

"I am so glad Dad isn't with us. It may have been more uncomfortable, but I realize it will happen somewhere soon. We should prepare for it."

The women stalled as long as they were able. Eventually, however, it was time to face the reporters, as promised. Sylvia thanked them all for honoring her wishes by not interfering any further with their dinner.

Several of them spoke at once, so Sylvia spoke up. "I can only answer one of you at a time, and we will answer about five questions then we are leaving, it has been an endless day for us."

An adolescent male reporter asked, "How are you and Laura weathering these changes in your lives?"

"Well, we feared we might lose him. When the doctors presented us with their diagnosis, we were relieved. We have been most concerned with how Greg would adjust. He seems to be doing very well.

"Greg is excited to spend the second part of his life as part of a unique race; we will all learn together. We do not know why this happened, but we realize there is a reason he is living this experience. He will make incredible contributions now that he can understand racial issues from a fresh perspective. To read about it is one thing, but to live the experience is something else."

"That is incredible. Aren't you the least bit upset or concerned with how this massive change will affect your life and your daughter's? You just told us about Greg and how he will handle his DNA changing, but this is happening to both of you, too. You married a white man, and he is now black. Laura, your father has been white your entire life. He is now a black man. How will that affect you and your mom?"

Laura responded first, saying, "It was shocking, but relief set in. I also believed my dad might die and learned he is very healthy, but now a very healthy black man. There will be new challenges. Do I wish this had never happened? He seems more appreciative of everything in his life. I love the man he has become, and I hope and pray he remains this way for the rest of his life."

Sylvia added to what Laura had said with, "I agree with everything Laura has just said. As you realize, I married a white man, and he fathered my beautiful daughter Laura. I am still married to Greg, with many differences. I will embrace the opportunity to learn much more about being married to someone of color. Then how it affects all of us, and how we can take steps to bring about positive changes for people from all countries and all ethnic groups. We are ready to retire for the evening.

"Try not to concentrate on always digging up the negatives in every situation. Greg's transition may end up being a positive change for many people. Thank you all very much for your thoughtfulness and patience. Please approach no one in a restaurant while they are having dinner. It is inexcusable behavior. Thank you again."

The reporters all thanked them in unison for their comments and their honesty. They promised it would never happen again.

Sylvia told them, "I hope not!"

Alan brought Greg home late, so they postponed any further discussion for another time.

Alan had a new skip in his step as he walked to his car. He could not contain the smile that had taken over his face. He was proud of everyone involved, including himself.

Greg delivered the news to the world; no need to hide any longer for fear someone would see him and call the media.

Sylvia asked, "How about some coffee? I made a cake to celebrate if either of you is in the mood."

Laura followed her to the kitchen to give her mom a hand while Greg retrieved his slippers. Now they could relax for the next two days. He would putter in the yard to get ready for spring. What a lucky man he was!

Coffee and cake topped off their fantastic day.

"I am grateful you both came to the Whitehouse to be with me this morning. What a tremendous surprise. Thank you."

They retired to the family room to watch the news together.

The television screen showed the headline, which read, "Shocking news, the man turns black, we've got the facts!"

Greg, Sylvia, and Laura laughed until they cried.

Bill Winter was broadcasting the evening news. They had total confidence he would present the story factually.

Bill began his piece with, "It has been quite a day for the news world. Over the last couple of months, the United States Attorney General has experienced some health issues which may have been life-threatening. Thankfully, Greg is in excellent health. Doctors determined he has gone through a complete DNA transformation and is now a black man. It has been total and is permanent. Now we will show an excerpt from this morning's press conference held at the Whitehouse. But first, our staff would like to extend our very best wishes to Attorney General Gregory Hastings and his entire family. Now, here is the excerpt I promised you."

Bill's reporting of their story was complete.

* * *

Laura woke up early, not understanding what had awakened her. Her mind drifted to Ellen. Did she hear the news? She dozed and woke up again at six thirty, a more decent time to start the coffee. She grabbed her robe and slippers as she headed down the stairs. After starting the coffee, she got the paper, eager to see the morning headlines.

The front page of their morning newspaper read, "United States Attorney General Transitioned from White to Black." Included were several brief stories of people wishing him well and opinions regarding what had happened to him. Laura realized people would say many things, attempting to understand a complicated issue.

Sylvia and Greg smiled when they saw the coffee and paper. Both were impatient to see the stories carried by the morning newspaper.

"What shall we do today?"

Sylvia asked, "Greg, since you've been out of circulation, how would you like to return?"

Greg remained silent for a few minutes considering his options, responding with, "It does not matter where we eat, what I want most is to attend Mass. I've missed it so much. We received a call from our pastor a few days ago since he had not seen us for a few weeks. I explained I had been dealing with some health issues which had ended, and we should return soon. So, tonight is the night."

Laura and Sylvia both nodded in agreement. It would please them all to get back to their routine.

Sylvia laughed as she stated, "Boy, we are something, imagining we will attend Mass, and everyone will smile as though nothing has changed."

He had a sense of excitement welling up inside, almost like a small child waiting for Christmas morning.

About half past three, Greg announced, "Well ladies, it is time for us to prepare for Mass. I will go and take a shower right now."

It was a relief to see Greg smiling and looking forward to attending church together, then out to dinner as they used to do so long ago.

Laura realized they had come so far from where they were a few short months ago. They had the family they all dreamed of, at a price.

Sylvia stared at Laura then asked, "Are you okay, honey? You seem so far away."

"I am perfect, Mom. It has been such a long time."

Sylvia understood. "I can relate to where you are coming from, I had similar thoughts. I have missed this so much too. I have a great understanding of why you stayed away. I am so grateful for the time we've just had together. It scares me, worrying it may not last. For now, let's enjoy every minute we are together."

* * *

They became a little anxious as they approached their church, not knowing how people would respond to them. Greg pulled into the lot and parked in his usual area.

He announced, "Let's go in."

As they approached the main door to the church, the people gathered outside walked toward them. Everyone extended a hand to Greg. They were telling him how happy it made them seeing him and his family back where they belonged.

Roy Williams said, "Greg, we are so proud of you and what you stand for, and that you will continue as our United States Attorney General. You will start some incredible changes in our country. Welcome back."

Greg smiled and thanked them. "We have been apprehensive about this afternoon. We weren't sure how people would react to us, considering what I just experienced. Thank you again."

As Greg and his family walked down the aisle to a pew, everyone that noticed them smiled or waved. Laura had tears in her eyes since everyone welcomed them. She was thrilled for her father.

Before the Mass began, Pastor Muir walked up to the pulpit and made a brief announcement, saying, "I would like to say a few words before we start this afternoon. We would all like to welcome home Greg, Sylvia, and Laura Hastings. We are grateful God has seen fit to bring you through this experience. We are confident He will guide you from now on to find the answers you seek. If any of us can ever assist you, please ask. We are pleased to have you back. Now let us pray."

After Mass, Greg approached Pastor Muir to thank him, saying, "I am sorry I could not tell you when you called me the other day. I needed to wait for the official announcement from the president. I hope you understand. We also want to thank you for what you said this afternoon; it touched our hearts and eased our minds."

Pastor Muir understood, and everyone else did too.

* * *

Greg suggested, "Let's go to the Oceanic for dinner tonight, to celebrate the start of our new lives together."

Sylvia asked, "Greg, how do you expect us to get into the Oceanic without a reservation?"

"I made one yesterday just in case we wanted to celebrate tonight. Also, I wanted to surprise both of you. It will be wonderful having a superb dinner with my two beautiful ladies."

Everyone agreed!

Chapter Six

Phone Call

The valet stared at Greg and said, "Aren't you the guy on TV, the Attorney General?" Then his voice trailed off. "I am sorry. I just meant you are famous."

Greg said, "Yes, I guess some people saw me on TV. Don't worry, I understand."

They approached the desk and the maître d' asked Greg for his name, to which he responded, Greg Hastings.

The maître d' said, "Welcome to the Oceanic. It delights us to have you and your family with us this evening. Please follow me to your table, sir."

They made their way to a lovely table overlooking the ocean. Greg held the chairs for Sylvia and Laura.

"This is the start of our new lives. Things will be different."

Everyone in the restaurant smiled at them. Greg ordered a bottle of wine to toast their discovered happiness and the significant changes in their lives.

When Laura's phone rang, she checked the name. She would not even consider answering while they were having dinner. But this call was different.

So she said, "Hello."

The voice on the other end responded, "Hi Laura, it's Ellen. I saw the press conference today, so I had to call you. I am sorry for what happened to your father. Laura, I experienced an impressive amount of therapy and came out of it stronger than ever. My previous terrible experience, coupled with your father's treatment of me, magnified his actions."

"Ellen, I am thrilled you called. Just knowing you are doing well makes my heart lighter. We are all hoping to see you soon if you are ready to do so."

"There are many reasons for my call, first because I love you like a sister and missed you. I want you in my life forever. Second, your father will need some help, and I hope I can help him. I understand he has experienced many changes. I expect he is now a kinder, gentler man than months ago, or so I understand. Are you by any chance with your parents right now?"

"Yes, we are just finishing dinner."

Ellen asked, "May I talk to your father for a minute?"

"Yes."

She turned to her father and told him someone wanted to speak to him and handed him the phone.

Greg took the phone and said, "Hello."

"Hello Mr. Hastings, this is Ellen. I watched the press conference today, and I am aware of what you all experienced for the last few weeks. Laura told me several times how much you regretted what you said and what it did to me. I know you meant it. I had already been going through a lot, so what you did made me crash. Since then, I've engaged in lots of therapy."

"I'm thrilled to be talking to you and hearing what you just told me. I would be grateful for your help. The sooner the better. How are you doing now?"

Ellen was ready to move forward, which included Laura and her family. She told him she would talk to Laura and schedule something for as soon as they could. Greg agreed and thanked her again for calling. He returned the phone to Laura to conclude their call.

Ellen told Laura, "We will talk tomorrow; I am returning to school to arrange for summer classes. Goodnight."

Laura looked at her parents and exclaimed, "What great news! I am thrilled. Ellen is coming back. So, Dad, what did you get from your conversation?"

Greg choked up and had to take a breath before answering Laura. "I am thrilled, I will have the opportunity to make amends to Ellen. It will be wonderful to see you and Ellen as best friends again. She wants to help me with becoming a black man. This news is so welcome right now."

Greg poured three glasses of wine and said to his girls, "This is to our happiness, new life, and having Ellen back with us."

The food was delicious, and the service superb. The staff was amazing! The family experienced a wonderful sense of relief and fatigue, but the next day they would relax. Laura had already planned to return to school to prepare for classes on Monday.

They talked for a while over coffee before retiring for the evening. The feeling of relief, happiness, and love was felt by all three of them. It had been a long time since they had known such peace in their lives, and they would never let go of it again.

* * *

Laura woke up first and hustled down to the kitchen, eager to see the morning paper. There on the second page, a brief story about them having dinner at the Oceanic and how it pleased the staff and owners. Laura didn't see any reporters. Perhaps they remembered what her mother told them about never approaching them again while they were dining.

Greg smelled the coffee. Laura no sooner finished the article than he walked into the kitchen, still looking sleepy. He smiled and told her it pleased him to come down for coffee and find her in the kitchen. She reminded him she had to return to school in a few hours.

She looked forward to meeting with Professor Williams to begin her project.

Greg was so proud of the work she had started besides preparing for medical school. His little girl had grown up and become an amazing young woman. He was yet to discover what she might accomplish in her lifetime, but it would be newsworthy for sure. Laura handed Greg the newspaper and showed him the article; he smiled as he read it.

Sylvia told Laura, "I am normally the one making the coffee. Whenever you are here, you make it, and it is excellent!"

Greg and Sylvia lounged in the family room, reading the paper and taking their time. Laura kissed and hugged them both, then told them, "This was the best weekend we've had together in a very long time."

Sylvia and Greg agreed it had been pleasant to be together again.

Her parents asked her to call them when she got back to school to inform them she had arrived.

* * *

Laura was excited knowing Ellen would be in her life again. She had missed her, the two not having seen each other for months.

She wondered what people would say when she asked them the question: Did you ever experience discrimination? She couldn't imagine what it would be like for a minority.

It should be more about the person, their morals and scruples, their habits and behaviors, not something they cannot change. We are who we are; it should be enough. Laura judged people by how they treated her, not by anyone else's ideas or hearsay. Imagine trying to sway someone's opinion of another person based on your view of the person. Not because of any fact about them, but because you dislike their race, their age, or their sex.

Millions have suffered because of prejudice. People must learn to look deeper into a person's heart and soul and not judge them by what we see on the surface. It shouldn't be about a person's race. Try judging people for who they are, not who you perceive them to be.

Laura called Professor Williams, who answered on the first ring.

He told Laura, "I've held onto this phone all day, hoping you would call. I have been anxious since the press conference. How are you all doing?"

"I am fantastic! The press conference proved to be incredible. The people welcomed us at church, the restaurant, and everywhere else. I heard from Ellen last night. She wants to get together and help my dad learn how to live his life as a black man. Need I say more? We are all ecstatic! We must meet."

"Can you make it after dinner tonight, around six thirty? Let's meet for about an hour to go over the highlights of your project. I cannot wait to bring you up to date on what I discovered."

"Yes, I will be there; I am eager to begin the project and share the rest of my news with you. See you then."

Laura found herself at Professor Williams's office in deep thought, getting there on automatic pilot. She laughed at herself, then knocked on the door.

Laura told the professor, "I believed I no longer wanted to be part of my family due to my father's behavior, and now we are all closer than ever. We are experiencing the relationship I had always longed for but never dreamed possible to get. It is like a miracle, but the cost has been high for my father."

"So, let's talk about your project for a bit. I talked to many of my friends across the country, most of whom are professors. The people I spoke to love your project. You have already gotten several volunteers for interviews. They were all intrigued when I explained what you are seeking. Several of them are minorities, who, without a doubt, experienced discrimination throughout their lives. Many know other people that might also be willing to submit their stories to you."

"Did you explain our form of payment to them?"

"Yes, I explained, payment for their stories would be a copy of the report and the knowledge they will contribute, educating people as to the damage prejudice can do to the lives of its victims. They are all satisfied with the form of payment and are all willing to sign a release form to attest to the fact."

Laura had a hard time believing Professor Williams had made so many contacts for interviews already.

"Well, Laura, when you trust in a person, and they present you with what you believe is the best project you could imagine then ask you to be a part of it, you do not waste time! Besides, it will add such an incredible extra excitement to my otherwise very routine life here at the university."

She wanted to hear from the laborers, supermarket clerks, and nannies, as much as the doctor and the lawyer. Laura wanted to understand whether the effects might be temporary, permanent, or sometimes nonexistent. Did they still carry the scars of those experiences? Those were the answers she sought. She needed to understand how it affected their hearts and souls to live through such a painful time. Would it ever be possible to ease the pain they carried because of what had happened to them?

The professor remained speechless as he listened to Laura explain what she needed to learn from the volunteers by writing their own stories. If they could do so. He continued being impressed by this incredible young woman who had so much kindness and caring in her heart for others.

He believed she could change the thoughts of some people who had been racists themselves. "You may plant many seeds that will continue to grow within their hearts."

Laura smiled and told him she hoped so. With his help, they might at least encourage people to use their rational judgment.

* * *

It was the first full weekday Laura, her dad, and her mom would live with the entire world knowing their secret! Laura opened her eyes and listened, waiting for something to happen like a drumroll or noisemakers, but it sounded like any other morning in her dorm.

It seemed to be a typical morning; only their lives had changed. Laura got up and started the coffee. She picked up her clothes for the day and headed for the shower. Laura had a seven thirty class with two hours off in between. She couldn't imagine what to expect. What a day this would be!

Coffee, what would she ever do without her morning coffee? Her class would be about five minutes away; she had time to review her notes and gather her thoughts.

Was it irrational to think no one would have questions?

Realizing the other students and faculty deserved some inside information, Laura changed her plan to dodge the questions and decided on the direct approach.

A group of students came running up to her as Laura approached the building which housed her first class. She knew most of them well. They all spoke at once and asked her how she had accepted the experience.

Laura laughed and said, "One at a time, please."

Lisa asked, "Laura, how are you bearing up on your first day back to school, considering everything you and your family experienced over the last few weeks?"

Laura responded, "Thank you, Lisa, for the brilliant question. You just summed it all up in a few words. We are apprehensive, not knowing what everyone's response will be. My father will make significant strides to improve conditions, programs, and information for ethnic groups everywhere. Everyone is beyond relieved he is not ill, but we will all need some time to adjust to his changing DNA. If anyone has questions, please ask me. Thank you, Lisa."

Laura had not found it as difficult for her as she had expected it to be. At least she had gotten through her first response. Laura noticed a lot of the kids waving and smiling at her.

Once inside, Professor Jamison approached her, shook her hand, then hugged her. She asked Laura, "Are you doing okay?"

Laura told her it would take some adjusting for all of them. She thanked her for her kindness and offered to answer questions either before or after class.

Mrs. Jamison suggested, "Since your father's transformation interests so many people, would you consider dedicating a class to the subject?"

Laura loved the idea! They planned to meet that Wednesday at two in her classroom to discuss the details.

As Laura prepared to leave the building, she smiled to herself, knowing she was privileged to be an attending student with the opportunity to explain the situation firsthand. A fleeting thought entered her mind, but Laura dismissed it, then followed through. What if they turned this into a school-wide teaching experience? How about if they built it up and invited her father to come as their guest speaker? How would that work?

"Excuse me, Mrs. Jamison, can you spare a minute? I have an idea to run past you."

"Laura, what did you want to discuss with me?"

"You asked me about doing a class project regarding my father's transformation, which sounds great. Would you like to address it on a larger scale and make it a school project and invite my father as your guest speaker? Would you need to discuss it with whoever makes those decisions? I've said nothing to my father, but I think he would attend."

Mrs. Jamison appeared to be considering one idea after another.

When she answered, she gushed, "I love the idea—what an incredible opportunity for the university and our class! Yes, I will consult with the president. We would also get a lot of media attention, which would be great for the school. Thank you so much, Laura, for the suggestion. Let's not say anything to anyone until I can discuss it with everyone involved first."

Laura agreed they would still meet on Wednesday at two. Laura walked to the coffee shop; she had four hours before her next class. Today she needed another cup of coffee before deciding what to do next.

As she approached the student coffee shop, she saw a group of students huddled outside. As she got closer, it became clear the group was composed of minorities, waiting to speak with her.

"Hi Laura, I am Stan Wilder. We are here to ask for your help. We want to file a grievance. Your father is the United States Attorney General, so we wondered if you might help us with our problem here on campus."

"Yes, my father is the United States Attorney General, but he does not have any authority over university matters. You must discuss grievance procedures with the school office. Have you contacted anyone with your concerns yet?"

Stan said they had not done so. They wanted to discuss it with her first. Laura told them it would be their first step. They must present it to administration and find out how to file a grievance. Stan and his group thanked her and proceeded to the administration office.

Laura hoped it would not be the first of many complaints she would receive from students, since she was also a student.

Chapter Seven

Not So Fast

Greg was meeting with the president before going over to his office at the DOJ. It would not be a typical day. He had several messages waiting for him. Many minority and ethnic organizations from all over the United States had called in. He would assign someone to assist him, freeing him to attend to other matters of immediate urgency.

President Mitchell asked, "So Greg, how are you doing on this beautiful morning?"

Greg's response caught the president by surprise. He said, "I am great! We had a wonderful weekend."

President Mitchell answered, "I am thrilled, Greg. Sorry, but I must rush off to address some issues of national importance regarding immigration. The situation has now reached critical proportions. I am meeting with the committee this morning. We must reach some resolution before going home tonight; this cannot continue to fester without a decision. It is vital to national security that we come up with a plan and enforce it."

"It is great to be back. I am going over to my office. I wish you the very best with your meeting this morning. If there is anything I can do to assist you, please ask. I will respond to the lengthy list of ethnic groups that called in. It is of the utmost importance for me to do so as soon as I can. I will schedule them according to the relevance of their actual immediate need."

Greg asked Alan to meet at their office to discuss their plans as they advanced. Alan complied.

The two men discussed the review of minority and ethnic groups and developing a needs analysis.

Alan believed Janice Carter, the new intern, should be able to handle the assignment. He told Greg he had seen her work, and she was thorough. So, Greg agreed with Alan's recommendation and would give it to Janice. He thanked Alan for his suggestion and told him it would free him to review the rest of his pending items.

"Anytime I can help, please ask. I am always willing to assist you in any way I can."

Before leaving Greg's office, Alan turned around and asked, "Greg, do you feel like a black man?"

"Unless I look into a mirror, I function as though I am still white."

Alan worried it sounded like denial. "I am not a professional by far, but shouldn't you work on attempting to become black? I am sure your therapist will help you. But maybe you could do much of the work yourself. Perhaps we should speed up those meetings with the ethnic groups. They may be more helpful to you than either of us realize, since you announced you would appreciate any help to assist you in learning how to be a black man in today's society. Greg, I am not trying to pressure you. I'd like to help you embrace your new race. You are now just talking about it."

"You may be right, Alan. I cannot allow myself to slip into denial. Thank you so much for bringing this to my attention. I agree with you. I will ask Janice to speed things up with the 'needs' analysis, then I can call the first group and schedule a meeting. What would I do without you assisting me through these troubled and challenging waters?"

Alan appeared relieved and reassured Greg would proceed. There would be an impressive amount to do not only on the minority end but also in overseeing the United States Justice Department. Greg had become a master at it. Their department might be a slight bit behind, but not much. They should be able to catch up, which would allow Greg to concentrate on the national concerns the country faced.

Many of the citizens of the United States hoped Greg's becoming a new race would create a positive effect on many fronts. He would, however, need to learn an impressive amount. He had worked on racial issues for years but could never see them to the present degree.

Developing empathy for others is one thing, but becoming a black man yourself and discovering how to address it is quite another issue. It would take time. However, Greg did not think he had time to waste. Since he lived the first half of his life white, Greg might come to understand and be able to empathize with their feelings, but they would be their feelings. Greg had so much to learn.

Alan brought up some excellent points. Those thoughts encouraged Greg to call for an appointment to meet with Dr. Redding. The doctor was aware of Greg's situation and believed he was more than capable of the challenge of treating him.

As the phone rang, Greg noted a chill of anxiety, just for a moment. Dr. Redding answered the phone himself.

"Yes, Greg, I was told to expect your call. I believe I have gained enough experience over the years to work with you and your family. Your situation is unique, but many of the issues you will deal with are common. We should not experience any difficulties."

"What does your schedule look like for the next couple of weeks? I believe it is critical we meet and begin. Would we be meeting alone at first?"

Dr. Redding told him he preferred to meet with him alone and become comfortable before they had his wife and daughter join them. Greg agreed it would be the best way to approach it. They would meet next Saturday at 10:00 a.m. Greg thanked him for working on getting him in, and they hung up.

Greg was nervous, but also relieved. It would be a relief to start and process all the feelings surrounding his DNA change. Wow, when he said it, it seemed so simple, but it was a tremendous change in his life.

Greg hoped he had not been living in denial the last couple of weeks, for it appeared he was talking about someone else. Wasn't he still white? Was he now a black man? It wasn't possible since no one else in the world ever experienced anything like this. There must be some mistake.

Greg realized he was in denial! It penetrated, then he cried; the tears flowed from his eyes and would not stop. How would he handle this? Would any therapist anywhere ever be able to help him digest all of this and remain sane? He became scared, terrified! He realized there was no place he could hide and continue to be Greg, Caucasian US Attorney General. His life, as he had known it, was over, forever. At that point, he passed out.

Janice Carter came in to ask him a few questions and found him on the floor of his office, unconscious. She called Alan, who rushed in and called for a rescue crew, not understanding what had happened to Greg.

All he saw was Greg unconscious on the floor. It did not occur to him that things were catching up with him.

When the rescue workers arrived, the crew checked his blood pressure and gave him some oxygen. They did not know Greg had an emotional breakdown.

Alan called Sylvia to inform her they were rushing Greg to the county hospital for treatment.

Greg remained unconscious. He had been since right after he called Janice into his office. Sylvia would go to the county hospital and wait for them in the ER since she was closer to the hospital than them. Alan would follow the rescue vehicle and see her there. Inside, he panicked.

They could not remove Greg from the Department of Justice building without attracting lots of attention. Alan claimed Greg fell and was unconscious. His explanation would suffice since he was not sure of the actual cause. It would keep the curious onlookers from speculating for a brief time.

Alan wondered if whatever had happened to Greg had anything to do with what he said to him earlier. Had he been too hard on Greg? He asked himself if he might have been a contributing factor. They would need to wait for the doctors to determine the cause. Alan walked with them to the vehicle. He told the driver he would follow at a distance. He then called Sylvia, enabling her to speak to the rescue crew to answer critical medical questions, allowing them to treat Greg.

Sylvia answered all of their questions, then directed them to contact Greg's primary care physician for more information.

It occurred to Sylvia everything may have caught up with Greg, and he wasn't able to handle it. If he had an emotional breakdown, it would not be an easy recovery, considering everything Greg had experienced in the last few months.

Sylvia rushed into the hospital. As she walked toward the treatment area, Sylvia shook, not knowing what to expect when Greg reached the hospital. Would he be conscious by then? Was there something more serious going on? The human body resembled a complex machine. If one area responded to stress, it might affect other sites. What would they find?

As the rescue crew wheeled Greg into the treatment area, he seemed dazed but conscious. He was just not aware of where he was or what had happened to him. Sylvia panicked. It looked more severe than she imagined it might be. Doctors were terrible when it was their family members; all reasoning sometimes flew right out the window.

She scolded herself. "Stop it, Sylvia, everything will be okay, don't panic yet."

The ER staff took Greg to a private exam area, eager to rule out a stroke. They did not waste time. The doctor did not know who Greg was until he saw Sylvia. He looked at Sylvia and asked, "Is this your husband?"

Sylvia said, yes, they found him unconscious in his office.

"Sylvia, you are aware we must complete some tests before determining the cause of this. Let's not speculate."

Sylvia feared something would happen to Greg, considering all that transpired. Dr. Wilson, the ER doctor, asked her many questions in his effort to gain an idea of what had occurred to cause Greg to pass out in his office. Sylvia referred Dr. Wilson to Dr. Berkin. He was Greg's lead doctor in diagnosing his DNA change. Dr. Wilson rushed out of the room to contact him, knowing time might be of the essence in his case.

As soon as Dr. Berkin received Dr. Wilson's call, he told him, "I will be right there, five minutes at the most. I would prefer to work with you on this case."

Dr. Wilson thanked Dr. Berkin for offering to help. He rushed back to the exam room to inform Sylvia that Dr. Berkin would be there within five minutes.

Sylvia relaxed somewhat. She respected Dr. Wilson for having worked with him for many years, but they could not waste time bringing him up to speed on Greg's history. With Greg's doctor assisting, that would not be necessary.

Greg rallied but still seemed somewhat confused by being in the hospital. He did not remember what had happened before he passed out.

His doctor appeared, out of breath. Sylvia knew he would figure out what happened to Greg or bring in someone who could. Dr. Wilson brought Dr. Berkin up to date on what had transpired with Greg.

Sylvia watched his expressions; he appeared concerned. Sylvia recognized the doctor's looks very well over the time they cared for Greg. His doctor read off a list of tests they needed to run and asked Dr. Wilson if he had any others he would like to add. Dr. Wilson suggested additional tests. Both doctors agreed. Speed became vital, not being sure whether there could be a neurological cause for Greg's unconsciousness and confusion.

Sylvia grew more concerned by the minute and wondered whether she should call Laura. She shared her concerns to which the doctor agreed. If they were correct, everything would be okay, but Greg would need treatment.

The doctor did not elaborate on his suspicions without receiving concrete results first. "We'll rule out a neurological cause first; then we can discuss what else might be going on. I believe you can wait a bit before you notify Laura."

He seemed to read her mind. Sylvia agreed to wait to call her daughter. She had the utmost respect for him. She found him to be forthright—a quality which meant an impressive amount to her in the doctor treating her husband.

Sylvia told him, "I want you to understand just how much we all appreciate you dropping everything to be here for Greg and me today. I trust you. It comforts me, knowing they included you in his diagnosis and any treatment Greg may need."

"Greg is my star patient; I will always be here for him. I see Dr. Wilson coming down the hall; he may have some news for us."

Dr. Wilson smiled as he entered the room to report, "Well, the excellent news is we do not see any neurological issues. I did not note any signs of a stroke, embolism, or any changes in his MRI. The radiologist compared it to his last MRI. His blood work all looks good—again, no changes since his previous testing. It stumps us as to what is going on with Greg. Dr. Berkin and I will compare notes and continue searching until we find the answer. I want to keep him here overnight, just as a precaution. He seems to have come out of his confusion. We want to monitor him for at least twenty-four hours. What are your thoughts Dr. Berkin?"

"It would relieve me if you would continue monitoring him. Greg's emotional status has been a concern for me since I first met him. I thought something might trigger a meltdown. How many people, men or women, receive a diagnosis like the one we gave him? I would wonder about him if this did not happen."

Dr. Wilson nodded along sagely. "He needs time to accept everything that happened to him. He has been attempting to tackle everything with record speed; it may not be in his best interest. He may need to take a break, then reenter his profession. We all need to do what is best for him, or he may have a complete mental breakdown."

Sylvia screamed inside; she too thought it could be an emotional issue. She shared her thoughts and feelings with both of the doctors.

Greg's condition required hospitalization, which would enable his doctors to run some diagnostic tests to determine his status. They would meet again before they released Greg.

Sylvia couldn't imagine what the outcome would be. She did think everything would eventually be okay. Since it would be two hours before Greg could receive visitors, Sylvia went home to call Laura. She had a little more information to share with her now since she had met with both doctors.

Driving home was a blur. It seemed every time they achieved a brief relief, something else happened. She called Alan to inform him what had happened since they last spoke. Alan felt responsible, but Sylvia did not think he had anything to do with Greg's condition. It appeared it all caught up with him. He would need therapy and lots of rest.

Sylvia told Alan, "The doctors do not understand what they will find. It appears to be an emotional meltdown. Concerned about a complete mental breakdown, they want to cover all bases before releasing him. I promise I will keep you informed every step of the way."

"Sylvia, I will need to report something to everyone regarding Greg's condition. I said Greg had fallen. Should I continue along that line?"

"Why don't you tell them Greg got dizzy and passed out hitting his head? They will run some tests to make sure he is okay and observe him for two days. That is just about the absolute truth. We appreciate all you've done; you are a genuine friend to all of us. I will stay in touch and inform you when the doctors believe it is safe for Greg to receive visitors."

Alan agreed to do as Sylvia suggested, and they hung up. Sylvia pulled into her driveway, broke down, and cried. She needed to talk to Laura.

Laura answered the phone and asked Sylvia, "Is everything all right?"

Sylvia told her, "Honey, your dad had a minor problem at work today, and they took him to the hospital. They are keeping him for observation for two days. Dr. Berkin will continue to monitor his condition as they run some tests to determine what is happening. He was found unconscious on the floor in his office. The doctors agree it is an emotional response to all he has been through, a meltdown. Dr. Berkin expected something like this might happen. He also thinks your dad may have gone back to work too soon."

Laura cried and asked, "Did we miss something?"

"He is more fragile than they realized. Greg always showed his more powerful side and tried to take things in stride. Your dad has seemed so strong. I cannot even imagine what I would experience if I were him. It must be difficult to take it all in stride. Answering the questions and attempting to schedule meetings, while not acknowledging even to yourself you've gone through a total transformation. It is staggering if you let yourself consider it. How do you give up who and what you've been your entire life, then embrace this unfamiliar person, almost without missing a beat?"

Laura agreed. Then she asked the dreaded question, "Mom, did you inform the media?"

"I told Alan to say Greg got dizzy and passed out hitting his head; they will run some tests to make sure he is okay and observe him for two days. It will satisfy their hunger for information. Please try not to worry. All of his preliminary tests are negative, along with the MRI and the blood work. They think it is emotional and not physical. Let's try to take this one day at a time and wait for the doctors to inform us of their diagnosis. You need not come back home; I will inform you every step of the way."

"I trust your judgment, Mom; I will wait for word from you. If anyone asks me questions, I will repeat your message to Alan. Try to get some rest yourself; it sounds like you will need it. I love you, Mom."

* * *

Dr. Berkin called Sylvia at seven to inform her that Dr. Redding spent two hours with Greg the night before. When he received the call, he proceeded to the hospital to see Greg. Both doctors agreed Greg had suffered an emotional meltdown, but not a mental breakdown.

"He is confident he can help Greg and believes they have already begun therapy. It will take a while. He said the man is overwhelmed! Who would not be? Anyone else would have crumbled on the day of his diagnosis. Greg did well to hold it together until now. It just got the better of him.

"Dr. Redding further explained that Greg had a significant panic attack regarding his situation and found no way to win or get out of it. He found himself unable to accept he was no longer the Caucasian United States Attorney General, which had been the case for years. He crashed and passed out. It became his brain's way of protecting itself—it just shut off. He is now aware of everything that happened, including his thoughts, right before he passed out.

"Greg told Dr. Redding he acted and lived as a white man. Unless he saw his image in a mirror, he functioned as though he remained white. The image in the mirror caused a significant battle to develop within himself. Wreaking havoc within his consciousness, and he could not accept it. He began coming apart! He had to become one person or the other, not continue being both races and survive, but in his mind, he could not choose. When pressured to make a painful choice, people sometimes just blackout. The options were too painful to face, as they became for Greg.

"Sylvia, do you agree that Dr. Redding may be right?"

Sylvia continued holding her breath. She exhaled before she spoke, then said, "Incredible, he got that much meeting with Greg for a few hours on one occasion? Yes, I agree, he is correct. We've said it before. He did not accept this without difficulty. It would not be normal; it goes against human nature. We are all going to need help. We need to acknowledge it before we can even accept it. Do you agree with Dr. Redding?"

Dr. Berkin did not even have to consider his response. "Yes, I agree with him. I spoke with Dr. Wilson, and he concurs with us. Greg appeared to be far too matter-of-fact about his situation. It signaled he might not be facing the intensity of what had happened to him. I commend him for his strength. So now, we can be comfortable with Greg going through his therapy with Dr. Redding. He seems to possess an extreme sense of the situation. Dr. Redding is a very kind person, which is just what Greg needs right now. He will be a very positive influence for all of you as counsel to your family. Did I answer your question? I am sorry I got carried away with my response."

Sylvia responded, "I appreciate everything you said. You expressed yourself without saying more than necessary. I trust your judgment and opinions, which comfort me. I know you have our interests in mind at all times, which makes this situation so much easier. Yes, I agree with you. Greg has incredible strength; now, we will help him get through this healthy and happy."

"Dr. Redding would like to transfer Greg to the Hope Gardens Facility, which is two miles from the hospital. He will meet with Dr. Redding daily and work with a group. It will give Greg a chance to return to reality in his own time at his own pace. They will allow visitors based on his wishes; no one he disapproves of will see or speak with him. They maintain total anonymity, which is what Greg needs right now. I wish I knew how long it might take Greg to return home, but it depends on his progress. We all want him to return to a healthy life. Dr. Redding has discussed this with Greg. They are both in agreement; he will talk with you before any changes take place. I asked him to call you tonight at eight; I hope the time is agreeable. How does this all sound to you?"

Sylvia's response surprised even herself when she blurted out, "Frightening, it sounds terrifying!" She continued as she regained her composure. "It is frightening to realize something like this will be necessary to rescue Greg from the brink of where he has gone. I wanted to think with lots of love, understanding, and excellent food he would come back to us as healthy as ever. He needs professional help and guidance. I also agree that an environment such as you described will be what is best for him.

"He needs trained professionals to guide him through this if he is to be healthy once again. So, as much as I find it upsetting, I am also embracing it. We want Greg back as soon as possible, but we want him to be as healthy as possible, for himself and those who love and count on him. Most of all, we want him to accept his new race and find comfort and peace within himself. It sounds like this is where he will find it. I cannot help but wonder if passing out at work has become a blessing. I applaud your decision. We will do whatever we can to support his full recovery."

"I am so glad you see the benefits of Greg going to the Hope Gardens Facility; it will not disappoint you. Dr. Redding would like to move him tomorrow, but he will discuss all of it with you when you speak with him tonight. It is Greg's best chance. We lack a comparison; no one else has ever experienced this. We can refer to our training, our healthy minds, and our powerful sense of what has helped others through a devastating experience. Together, we can and will help Greg regain his sense of self, to be happy and healthy once again. I will talk to you after you speak with Dr. Redding. Please call me when you conclude your conversation."

Sylvia agreed. She sat for a few minutes, going over their lives together. The good, the bad, and the ugly, up through the present. It had been quite a ride with all of its trials, but she loved Greg. She wanted him to be healthy and for them to go forward with their lives. Greg must spend whatever time they deemed necessary at Hope Gardens to be one hundred percent healthy. It sounded beautiful. Dr. Berkin would not be recommending it if he didn't believe it was the absolute best thing for Greg.

Her senses told her it would be a lengthy stay. Greg had a lot to work through, to merge his two selves. Sylvia was sure they could not shortcut his recovery. They had to allow him whatever time he needed to become whole once again.

She realized now it had been a dream for any of them to imagine Greg would get through this with weekly therapy. He needed in-house treatment, which the facility would provide. His job went through her mind, but it should not be the top priority. The priority would always be Greg's health.

"Laura, I am so glad you are available. I want to discuss some news on your dad with you right away. Are you able to do so now?"

"Yes, Mom, I have a three hour break."

"I just got off the phone with Dr. Berkin; he told me Dr. Redding visited your dad last night as soon as Dr. Berkin called to inform him your father had passed out in his office. They spent about two hours together. Dr. Redding seems to have a firm handle on the issues and believes he can help him. He has recommended they transfer Greg to the Hope Gardens Facility for intensive therapy. It will give him a chance to accept his new identity and merge his two selves into one yet unknown person, his present self.

"We did not realize it, but he has been having a terrible time accepting that he is now black; he still sees himself as white. When he tried to force himself to assume the change, it overwhelmed his mind, and he passed out. He attempted to move forward too fast. He experienced such an incredible transition; his brain would not accept it.

"This step will allow him whatever time he needs to make the change and become his new self. I will speak with Dr. Redding at eight o'clock tonight, so there will be an opportunity for me to ask him more questions. I am not looking forward to this, but I agree it is best for your father. The facility is about two miles from the hospital in a lovely, quiet, very peaceful, rural area. Any job decisions will wait until he is ready to return, which may never happen."

Laura answered through tears, "Mom, I also agree, this is the best thing for Dad. It is so hard to accept and wrap my head around. I guess he seemed to do too well, but I hoped he was doing as well, and he appeared to be. Not realistic for sure. We all want what is best for him, and it sounds like this is what he needs. I am on board with whatever is in his best interest, and will abide by their recommendations regarding visits and everything else."

"I sense it will be a longer stay. Greg has a lot to deal with, and acceptance may take time. We must be open to that fact."

"Mom, you are so right. Whatever you or Dad need, I am here; just let me know."

Sylvia would be lonely in their big old house without Greg around. She would stay busy until Greg returned home, ready to go forward with his new life. She kept working with some chores around the house until she spoke to Dr. Redding.

The phone rang. Dr. Redding apologized for calling earlier than planned. He had an unexpected appointment and wanted to talk to her before he left.

Chapter Eight

Healing

Dr. Redding informed Sylvia, "I believe Dr. Berkin discussed our final recommendations with you. We would like to transfer Greg to the Hope Gardens Facility. Sylvia, I wish there was a faster and easier way for Greg to reach a level of peace transitioning from one race to another without him having to be away from home. He needs the peace and tranquility the facility will offer him and the guidance we can provide with therapy seven days a week.

"You realize Greg's situation is unique. He needs special care to ensure a positive outcome. We will be successful, but I cannot even venture into how long his treatment will take. Sorry for going on like that. I am sure you have questions for me.

"My head is still whirling with thoughts and questions," Sylvia confirmed. "I understand you cannot even guess how long Greg will need to remain at Hope Gardens. Laura and I would love to have him home soon, but neither of us wants you to cut his recovery short. Our desire is for him to receive treatment until you are sure he is well and has an excellent prognosis of living a full and happy life. With him in control, and having complete acceptance of his transition. Laura and I are on board with you for whatever you recommend and however long it takes. We will both abide by your wishes for the duration."

"That is excellent news," replied Dr. Redding. "It will make our work and Greg's recovery much more comfortable. I will provide you with a schedule as to visiting hours for you and Laura and inform you when the time comes that Alan can visit with him.

"Sylvia, we must not burden Greg with anything within his office or the Whitehouse. He cannot handle it at this point. He is not sound enough. I wish it were possible to give you some time frame for him to return. But I will not know until we can work with him for at least a month. You may wish to share that time frame with the president.

"Between you and me, it will be several months as far as I can see now, but we cannot say until we begin. We are talking about a man who has been white his entire life suddenly becoming black. We must allow him the time he needs to accept his new self."

"Dr. Redding, how should we go about informing the public what has happened to Greg?"

Dr. Redding replied, "I realize how sensitive handling this will be. You have informed the president, and the public, of everything that has happened so far.

"It should be understandable to anyone with a heart and any empathy to understand. Greg needs time for his mind and body to catch up and reach a full understanding and acceptance. I would be more than happy to indulge in a lengthy conversation with the president either on the phone or in person to inform him of all the medical facts involved. Just inform me which method he chooses; I will abide by his wishes."

Sylvia thanked Dr. Redding and added, "We appreciate you agreeing to take on Greg's treatment. I imagine you realize what a tough situation this is for everyone. We are grateful for your kindness and compassion. I am sure we will talk many times over the coming months. Please, text me a list of what to bring for Greg tomorrow? Also, please add a copy of the rules and regulations. Along with everything else, we should know to enable us to comply with the facility's regulations."

Dr. Redding assured Sylvia that Greg was in full agreement with spending time at the Hope Gardens Facility.

"Greg acknowledged he needs to be there for as long as it takes to be himself, or should I say, his new self. When he is ready, it will be helpful for him to meet with some ethnic group leaders to educate him regarding what it is like to grow up black. I do not want it to happen before he is ready. If we discuss it before then, it may put him in jeopardy. We will weigh every step he takes to ensure it is timely and not harmful.

"We must proceed with caution, and remember, Greg may always relate to being white within himself. He may never connect to the thoughts minorities display. He spent the first half of his life white. It is complex. We will talk again tomorrow. Oh, before I forget, Greg is leaving for Hope Gardens at about 10:00 a.m. tomorrow. You are more than welcome to visit him, then follow us over.

"It may be very comforting for Greg if you're with him so that he can see firsthand you are accepting his decision to transfer there. Rachel Larsen, your contact person, will send you a list of what you can bring to him. You will receive the information within the hour. Thank you for your understanding and cooperation. We will talk soon. Goodnight."

Realizing Hope Gardens was what Greg needed most for a complete recovery, Sylvia and Laura would do everything in their power to enable Greg's transition. Sylvia knew Laura would still be up waiting for her call, so she dialed her number.

"It is as we expected; Dr. Redding thinks they can help your dad, but it will take some time. He agrees with us, Greg must stay there as long as he needs to reach full healing and to merge both of his races. The doctor said your dad may always relate to being white within himself. His assistant Rachel Larsen will contact me by email tonight to inform me what your dad will need me to bring to him tomorrow morning.

"I told Dr. Redding you and I are both amenable to whatever we can do to help your dad, and we will follow their guidelines. He could not even offer us a rough estimate of how long Greg will remain there. Dr. Redding will speak with the president to explain what his treatment will involve. I'll keep you up to date as more results are available, and I will share with you how tomorrow goes."

"So sorry not to be there with you, Mom."

"Stop, we will all be okay. I have enough work to keep me busy. Please don't worry about me; we will get through this together, I assure you. You should be busy with school, and there is your project with Professor Williams. It will be so valuable; it may also contribute to helping your father. As soon as I get the information regarding the visiting days and times for your dad, I will send it to you. Now you must promise me you will continue with your work and let the doctors help your dad."

Laura promised not to worry, as long as Sylvia kept her informed about her dad's progress.

Sylvia climbed the stairs to their bedroom; she had become so weary it made her weak. She lacked the strength to gather Greg's clothing; it could wait until morning. Sylvia sat on the edge of the bed and stared into space, remembering all the years they had lived in their home.

She did not remember one night in the past, other than when she gave birth to Laura, when they did not sleep together. Until the present situation occurred. It would be difficult for her to adjust to living and sleeping alone. It would not be as easy as she would pretend.

Sylvia awoke to the sound of the birds right outside the bedroom window. She smiled as they chirped their morning ritual. She loved their home and everything about living where they did.

There was a lot to do; stalling would not prevent it from happening. Sylvia had a sense of hope, knowing this would be the first step on Greg's road to wellness and recovery. She checked her computer. She had received a lovely email from her contact. Rachel Larsen listed all the items of clothing Greg would need, visiting hours, and offered additional information for reference. Sylvia looked forward to meeting her. They would communicate an impressive amount while Greg remained at Hope Gardens.

Sylvia put together everything on Greg's list, made her bed, showered, and dressed for the day. She even found time to pack some treats Greg always enjoyed. Sylvia had tears in her eyes as she closed the door to the garage. Everything hinged on his progress!

Sylvia arrived at the hospital in about ten minutes. She mustered up a smile as she approached Greg's room.

He looked at her with the smile she loved so much and said, "Honey, everything will be all right. I need their help to go on with our lives. Please try to be patient with me."

"I understand! I am glad you agreed to go to Hope Gardens. We want you to come home healthy. We love you, Greg. Please do not worry about Laura or me; we are on board for the duration. We will always be here for you."

Greg smiled with tear-filled eyes; he felt gratitude for Sylvia and Laura's love for him, and their patience and understanding. With them by his side, he could take whatever time he needed to accomplish his goals.

Since Sylvia had never been to the facility, she met the transport vehicle to follow them. She circled the parking lot and pulled up behind them. Sylvia had mixed feelings while driving; it became difficult for her to discern one from the other.

It always surprised her how the area thinned out and resembled the country. Greg would love the rural area, making it more enjoyable for him to be there. Before she realized it, they entered a very long driveway lined with beautiful cherry blossoms. Sylvia liked it already. She noticed the loveliest gardens straight ahead of her, with benches throughout to sit and read or relax. She drove on to the main building. Parking was on either side. Greg's driver told her to pull up to the main door, and someone would unload Greg's belongings and park the car for her. The woman at the registration desk was aware that her husband would be checking in.

The receptionist responded, "Hello, Mrs. Hastings, we have been expecting you. Please rest here. I will request someone to come out with a cart to retrieve Mr. Hastings's luggage. It should only be a few minutes."

Sylvia thanked her and found a seat. The friendliness and kindness displayed by the receptionist were indeed refreshing. She noticed a man coming toward her with what looked very much like an elegant hotel luggage cart.

He smiled at her and said, "Good morning, Mrs. Hastings. I am Fred Mulley. Please direct me to your car, and I will bring Mr. Hastings's belongings to his room."

Sylvia walked back out the entrance to her car. Fred removed all the items Sylvia brought for Greg and took them to his room. The valet parked her car and returned the key along with the parking space number. Then directed her to Greg's quarters.

Greg smiled as he told her, "It's very peaceful and seems like an excellent environment to relax and get some serious work done. Rachel Larsen is coming soon to take us on tour, which we are both looking forward to."

"Yes, I am eager to see the areas where you will stay and work. Just having a picture in my mind will make it easier for me to imagine where you are. I am also eager to meet Rachel since she will be our contact person during your stay."

They no sooner finished discussing Rachel than she walked in and introduced herself.

"Hi, I am Rachel Larsen. I will be your contact person while Greg is here, and your tour guide."

The cafeteria resembled an elegant restaurant with everyone ordering from a menu, though Rachel explained most people preferred to eat alone. They cooked all food daily onsite; nothing was precooked or made elsewhere. Greg liked that feature.

The gym offered a trainer on duty at all times to enable everyone to stay fit, which aided the mind in many healthy ways.

They continued to the conference rooms and private counseling areas, then out to the spectacular gardens. Birds chirped and butterflies circled. There were small ponds surrounded by flowers, and benches to sit on and relax while watching the goldfish. Sylvia watched Greg's face as he attempted to drink it all in. It made her heart glow to realize he would be at peace there and able to address all the issues he needed to confront.

Greg announced, "I know I will enjoy staying here in this peaceful and beautiful environment for however long is necessary. It appears to be conducive to one's recovery. Thank you, Rachel, for this lovely tour and your kindness. It will be a pleasure to work with you as our contact person while I am here."

Rachel blushed then responded, "Thank you for your kind words; it will be my pleasure. Sylvia, it is wonderful to meet you. I look forward to being in touch with you during Greg's stay with us. Please call me anytime with questions. There is no counseling today since this is Greg's first day. You will find a full menu in your room. Sylvia, you are welcome to accompany Greg to dinner if you like."

Sylvia and Greg stayed out in the gardens, just sitting and watching the birds and the butterflies, holding hands on a bench. They exuded a newly found peace sitting there in the gardens. Greg asked Sylvia if she would like to accompany him to dinner; she said she would love to.

He chose a lovely table with a view of the gardens, pulled out the chair for Sylvia, and slid it in as she sat. A young woman brought them their menus and told them she would be right back to take their orders. They looked at each other and smiled, then enjoyed a quiet evening.

Greg spoke up first, saying, "We are having such a splendid time at the facility where I will stay to retrieve my new self. Sylvia, I love you with all of my heart. Please try to be patient with me."

Sylvia smiled and told him, "We will be patient. Do not rush your recovery."

After dinner, Greg and Sylvia walked back out to the gardens to enjoy the evening air before Sylvia left to drive home. When she got into her car, she had tears in her eyes. They were tears of joy, knowing they would come through more durable than ever before. She wondered why it had to take such an extreme event to change her husband. She would never have an answer. She had to acknowledge it even just to herself.

Sylvia and Laura spoke on her drive home. Laura delighted in hearing Greg liked his beautiful room and the facility's peace. Sylvia assured her she'd receive the email regarding hours for visits by immediate family members as soon as she got home. She would also contact the president the following day to inform him as to Greg's current status. They concluded their discussion and hung up. Sylvia had already reached home. The facility was close, yet it appeared to be in a distant place.

* * *

Sylvia reached President Mitchell by phone. He answered in his usual cheerful tone, "Good morning, Sylvia, how are you doing today?"

"I am well, Mr. President; I hope you are too. I'd like to bring you up to date on Greg's condition. You are aware he passed out in his office two days ago. He has been through extensive testing, including a long meeting with a top psychiatrist, Dr. Redding. They had already scheduled an appointment before the incident in Greg's office. Dr. Redding met with him for two hours the first night he arrived at the hospital.

"He concluded that Greg collapsed due to the emotional stress of acceptance. Although he lives and acts as if he is still white, he is now a black man. He's had a grueling time adjusting to the DNA transformation. Greg attempted to rush the process and became overwhelmed. His mind shut down and caused him to pass out. Dr. Redding believes Greg returned to work much too soon, not knowing how things should conclude, and has lost some ground. He has transferred him to the Hope Gardens Facility for rehabilitation. It will take a month to analyze Greg's condition. He would welcome the opportunity to discuss this with you in more detail, either by phone or in person; the choice is yours."

The president took a deep breath and stated, "I am so sorry to learn this, Sylvia, I too have worried about him. I cannot even imagine what kinds of thoughts go through his mind minute to minute. I understand his need for rehabilitation, for as long as he needs. We will work with Alan and fill in where necessary. Greg's health is my prime concern. I will speak with Dr. Redding. I am sure a telephone conversation would be adequate, but it is good to learn he is open to meeting with me in person. Please give him my contact number and ask him to call me at his earliest convenience. I will inform the staff to be expecting his call."

"We both realize he needs whatever time it takes for him to be healthy again. I will adjust. I followed them over from the hospital, and we toured the facility together. After which I stayed for dinner, which was delicious.

"The gardens are beautiful and peaceful. I am sure the environment will aid in Greg's recovery. Laura is busy at school while I will continue to see patients. We will stay busy without putting pressure on Greg, which is most important at this point. Thank you so much, Mr. President, for being understanding of this issue; we all appreciate it very much. I am sure it will provide Greg a sense of peace to take whatever time is necessary to recover and not stress his job security."

The president responded, "Please don't you worry about it either, we are all here for you. If you need anything at all, ask. Please ask Dr. Redding to call me. Thank you for sharing this information with me. Take care."

Sylvia replied, "Thank you, sir."

Sylvia was much calmer after speaking with the president. Even if Greg decided not to return, he could decide for himself. She dialed the phone and reached Dr. Redding.

"I just spoke with the president. He would like you to call him as soon as you can to discuss Greg's condition. He said they are there for us for whatever we need. His position is not in jeopardy. Let me give you his number so you can call him when it is convenient." Sylvia gave Dr. Redding the number, and they hung up.

* * *

When Greg awoke, he was more rested than he had been in quite a while; it seemed like forever. He focused and looked around his suite—very impressive! He got up to go to the bathroom and noticed someone had left him a pot of coffee and the morning paper. What a lovely touch, and so appreciated. Breakfast was at eight, and it was only six thirty. He had time for coffee and to read the paper and shower before making his way to the dining room. He sighed with relief. Greg enjoyed being at Hope Gardens, working on making himself whole once again. He was full of gratitude for the peace which engulfed him and the kindness of the staff. It would aid in his recovery, somewhere down the road, but not today! Today he would begin his actual healing. To merge his two selves, to become a more resilient, robust, healthier, kinder, and more compassionate person than ever before. Something had changed!

With everything cooked to perfection, it was the most relaxing meal since, well, since dinner last evening with Sylvia. Greg's first appointment would be at ten o'clock in Dr. Redding's office. He watched the birds and butterflies for what seemed like an hour. It brought him back to Laura's childhood when they took her to the park to see the birds.

Greg walked down the hall to Dr. Redding's office and knocked on the door. Dr. Redding greeted him like an old friend. He invited Greg to sit down and join him. "Let's talk about whatever you would like. What thoughts are occupying your mind since you arrived? We are all here to help you, so please enlighten me."

Greg found it easy to talk to Dr. Redding, which brought him a glorious sense of relief. "I must tell you I woke up more rested this morning than I can remember for a very long time. The kindness of the staff and this peaceful environment is refreshing for me. I guess I needed to be here from the day of my diagnosis, but I did not realize it. I must thank you for agreeing to take my case and working with my family and me; we are all so grateful to you."

"I was selected as your doctor. You might have chosen another. I am eager to assist you in getting to the bottom of your issues. You will accomplish bringing both of yourselves together with help from our entire staff."

Greg told him, "Yes, I realize what I must accomplish to be whole, and no longer divided by whether or not I am looking into a mirror. I will accept this as a new page in the photo album."

"Wow," Dr. Redding responded. "Descriptive, Greg."

"Now, I realize it is so much more complicated. Before I passed out in my office, I struggled with my DNA transformation. I realized I could not accept becoming black since I had been white my entire life. I felt like I was white and lived and acted as though I was still a white man. Unless I looked into a mirror, I believed, in my mind, I must still be white. Attempting to force me to admit I no longer was my race caused me such stress. There must have been a mistake. I cried, and I could not stop. How would I handle all of it? And I panicked, wondering whether any therapist anywhere could help me. There was no place to hide and continue to be Greg, white US Attorney General. Believing my life, as I had known it, had ended…I just…well…at that point, I guess I passed out."

Dr. Redding explained, "What you experienced is common. When your mind deals with a stressful situation, you can pass out. Your mind was protecting you."

"It makes sense when you explain it that way. As I told you when we met at the hospital, for years now, I haven't been a kind man. I was cruel to people unlike myself. Whether their financial status was less than mine, their race differed, or their level of education wasn't up to mine, I did not accept or respect them. Who did I believe I had become? I am so sorry for all of it today. Where do I start?"

"Please try to be patient with yourself. It will take time. I must tell you I advised Sylvia it would be a month before we even know how long your recovery will take, or how long you will need to remain here at Hope Gardens. So, try to relax. Talk to me about Greg from childhood until today or anything in between. Can you describe your childhood for me?"

"I grew up in a middle-class neighborhood with terrific parents. I have a younger brother and an older sister. They are nothing like me. I wasn't born to be a bigot; it just seemed to develop within me as I aged, excelling at everything I attempted. I hid it in the earlier years.

"None of my friends were minorities. Deep within myself, I felt they did not belong in my neighborhood, my school, or my life. Back then, we did not discuss racial issues. All of my friends were white. Today I am ashamed of my behavior.

"My daughter tried to educate me, but I would not listen. I just continued saying whatever I chose to, no matter whether I hurt people's feelings. It did not matter to me. When I became the United States

Attorney General, I got even worse. My sense of superiority became incredible. I could not seem to stop my behavior. I also offended my family.

"Laura begged me to listen to her, but I ignored her pleas. I hurt her best friend from college who is from Nigeria. I saw it as joking. My sick joking amounted to cruelty. Please help me forgive myself and rid me of the pain I now carry for how I abused so many people. Help me apologize to as many as I can remember because they deserve it.

"Isn't it amazing I became good at my job despite my racism? It confuses me. Along with the change in my DNA, I have also become a kinder, gentler, and more empathetic human being, for which I will forever be grateful. It is not, however, effortless for me to forget all the harm I caused as a white man. I must repent. So, Dr. Redding, can you help me?"

"Yes, Greg, I believe I can," Dr. Redding replied. "I am pleased you already recognize so much of what has happened in your life and why. We need to concentrate our efforts on your DNA transformation. To help you adjust and accept who you are now and forgive yourself for who you had become. Making amends will then help an impressive amount. I believe most people did not realize how prejudiced you became, am I right?"

"As painful as it is for me to admit, you are right."

Dr. Redding understood the pressure Greg had been under before and after his transformation. He realized the intensity of the work they needed to do.

"Greg, you covered a tremendous amount today and shared a lot of what you kept hidden for many years. Let's stop for now and continue in the morning."

Greg needed to walk through the gardens, and told Dr. Redding, "I agree with you. I will see you tomorrow at ten. Thank you so very much."

Chapter Nine

Laura's Project

Professor Williams's door opened; he rushed out as Laura attempted to go in. She seemed to interrupt his thought process; he looked surprised to see her there.

"Oh Laura, I am sorry I am running late, walk with me to the coffee shop. I need a cup right about now before we start our meeting. How about you?"

They walked and talked along the way. Professor Williams asked about her dad. She brought him up to date regarding his transfer to the Hope Gardens Facility.

Professor Williams stated, "Your dad accepted the monumental changes in his life too easily; it did not seem natural. What has happened since seems more like typical human response and behavior."

"I agree with you. My mother and I expected something more to develop. It confuses us how he will come to deal with these important and unique changes. We wonder whether Dad will ever behave like a black man, or just pretend to, and inside, nothing will change. Will he ever be able to accept himself as he is now?"

Professor Williams was pleased that Greg received treatment at Hope Gardens and would continue for as long as he needed to be there.

"I have news for you. My professor friends contacted me. They, too, believe your project will be an incredible learning experience for everyone, causing people to reflect on their feelings regarding racism and discrimination. For some, it may be enough to reevaluate their behaviors, which would be fantastic!"

"Thank you so much. I am amazed you had such good luck so soon. I am eager to speak to every single volunteer and listen to their stories. Imagine what they will say! It should be a unique learning experience."

"What a fabulous idea! Even those people who've done studies on the subject will learn a lot from this project."

They sat at a table outside in the shade and talked for a while. In a short amount of time, Laura and the professor developed a plan of action for the next step of the project, titled "Racism and its Long-Reaching Effects."

Professor Williams said, "I've never found it so easy to work on a project as we are with this one. We just sat and talked over a cup of coffee and already planned our next step and titled the project. Our ability to work well together will lend a positive effect on the outcome of this project."

"I think I've matured about ten years in the last few months if it is possible!"

"Experiencing what you and your family have may cause a person to mature. I can see firsthand you've done so. The changes are positive. I will be in touch with you the minute I get more information for you."

* * *

Laura slowed down her pace on the way back to her dorm, wondering about Ellen, and when she might talk to her again. They both enjoyed their time together so much. She had missed her for the last few months and wondered whether they would ever recapture the depth of their previous relationship. The conversation Ellen had with her father had encouraged her. She would forgive him, considering the circumstances.

Coming around the bend in the walkway, she heard someone say, "Hey, where are you rushing to?"

Ellen was smiling down at her from the top of the steps. Laura ran up the stairs. They hugged, each of them crying with relief, to put the nightmare behind them. They walked up to Laura's dorm room and talked. Laura had no classes all afternoon. They spoke for about two hours then went to dinner. Ellen asked about Greg. Laura filled her in on his condition.

"I was in shock when I heard the broadcast on TV. It was unimaginable to hear your dad had experienced a total DNA transformation to black and will remain so for the rest of his life. All the anger and resentment drained from my body. It should not have happened to him or anyone else. I meant every word I said to him; please let me help him in any way I can. Laura, I am well and very stable. To forgive and learn is incredible. I am thrilled about your project! I would love to work with you on it; it should be fantastic. Teaching people to communicate on racial issues will be amazing."

Laura's relief overwhelmed her, just to hear Ellen say what she had hoped and prayed for since she disappeared.

The girls drove to their favorite restaurant for the very best pizza around. They were laughing, as usual, when they walked through the door. Their favorite waitress stood there, holding two menus as she always did. She asked where they had been.

They had an impressive amount to catch up on, but they had the rest of their lives to do so. They were ready to go forward. As soon as they sat down, Greg called.

Laura answered, "Hi, Dad, how are you doing?"

"Very well, my first therapy session was quite successful. We covered a vast amount of ground."

"Dad, I am sitting here with Ellen at our favorite pizza restaurant."

Greg asked to speak with her. Laura motioned to Ellen; would you like to talk with my dad?

Ellen took the phone. "How are you doing?"

"Thank you for asking Ellen. I have already made an impressive amount of progress. You understand these things take time. I am eager to see you and am so very sorry for the way I spoke to you. It will never happen again."

"I am no longer in a fragile state, I've recovered too. When your doctor says it is okay for me to visit you, I would love to come by to see you with Laura. Then we can talk about how I might assist in your recovery. I am not sure whether you noticed, but I am black too." At that, they all laughed.

"We can learn from each other. Take care of yourself and be patient; it will all come together. Please do not rush your recovery. We all want it to be permanent. Now I will let you talk to Laura."

Laura took the phone. She heard her dad crying, but he sounded good. She sensed relief in his voice, not noted before.

"How is your day, dad?"

"It was good, but after speaking with Ellen, and now you, I am fantastic. I am hopeful, Laura, we will work things out. I do not know what the future holds, but I am no longer worried about it. It will take care of itself. I resigned myself to deal with my therapy and complete recovery now while I am here. I want to return home healed and ready to go on with my life and our lives. With that, I will say goodnight. We have a full day tomorrow, and I want to say goodnight to your mom too. I love you, Laura."

"I love you too, Dad."

Laura told Ellen, "I am so happy you and my father spoke and gained a better understanding, and you and I are here together. You are my dearest friend, a sister to me. Now perhaps we should order our pizza!"

Ellen kept the best for last. When Laura asked where she would stay, Ellen responded, "In my dorm room, where else?"

"I stopped there this morning, visited my counselor, and signed up for my classes. They put together a program for me to catch up on anything I am missing. We will graduate together! I continued my assignments at the hospital and have stayed on top of my grades. I have dropped a little. Studying kept me sane, which sounds like a contradiction, but true. It is great to be back."

Before she left Ellen's dorm, Laura hugged Ellen and said, "Welcome home. See you tomorrow!"

On the drive back to her dorm, Laura reflected on what a fantastic afternoon it had been. Ellen had returned, her dad had begun treatment, and her mom was catching up with her patients. It would all take work. At least they were back on the right track.

Would her dad ever go back to working as the US Attorney General? In time he would decide. Laura wanted the best for him.

Laura called her mother before going to bed to ask how she was. Sylvia picked up and stated, "Your dad told me you spent the day with

Ellen, and the two of them spoke. What wonderful news; I am so happy for you."

"It has been a spectacular day. I got my best friend back, and she will graduate with me! Ellen and Dad had a great conversation, and I met with Professor Williams this morning regarding our project."

"That is fantastic news! I hope you realize your dad will be okay. It will take time, considering he is experiencing the pain he has caused so many people. This change will be permanent!"

"I believe you are right. Dad will remain this kinder, more thoughtful person he is now and never regress to the monster he was before his transformation. I, like you, have been afraid to believe it for fear of being disappointed. I also wanted to tell you a little more about Ellen. She is one of the kindest and most thoughtful and considerate people I have ever had the pleasure of meeting. She is a joy to be around. I consider myself extremely fortunate to have her as a best friend. Mom, she reminds me very much of you. That is probably a large part of how she has come to mean so much to me. You two are very much alike, and she too is beautiful."

"Well, thank you, Laura, what a wonderful thing to say about me. I am so pleased to know you girls are so much alike."

"I love you, Mom, talk to you soon, goodnight."

Laura and her mother had just hung up when her phone rang again. Professor Williams was calling to tell her they had located her first volunteer. She was an African American woman who worked at a local hospital in Laura's hometown. She was from Kenya. They could meet in person. He said the volunteer was very excited to take part after hearing about Laura's project. He gave Laura her phone number with the best time to call her.

Over the next couple of weeks, Laura interviewed several people by phone. She met with three of them in person and determined all of her volunteers had been victims of racism. She wanted to learn why perpetrators appeared to unleash their anger on minorities just because they could. Laura wondered what caused them to hurt others in such a tragic manner for no genuine reason. None of these people had done anything to cause their dislike; they had never met them. Could it have been what they observed in their homes? Maybe peer pressure, or were they evil?

She then realized her father could never wholly relate to people born black. He had the first half of his life to connect to, and it differed from theirs. He would never feel what they did, even though he had become black himself. The more she learned, the more apparent the complications became.

They would never be equals. Her dad could only sympathize with people who had lived through racial discrimination themselves. Although, he would most likely experience discrimination himself during his lifetime, now that he was black. Would people accept him for what he had become? He was now a part of their race as an adult through a process, not through birth.

Chapter Ten

Progress

Greg had been meeting with Dr. Redding for three weeks, daily, for therapy. They made progress, although not as quickly as Greg had hoped. He wanted all the answers to appear immediately, then to embrace his transformation. However, it was not how therapy worked. It's a tedious process a person must go through to make lasting changes within themselves. To gain a better understanding of how they came to the present point in their life that led them to need therapy. Now patience became the operative word! Greg understood, but he wanted to be ready to go home. Dr. Redding reminded him almost daily that he must travel a long hard road first.

Greg had reached an additional level of gratitude, one he never experienced until arriving at Hope Gardens. He knew the staff wanted nothing but the absolute best for their patients. They gave everything they had to assist every patient in regaining their health and finding peace. It enabled him to move forward and fight to restore the Greg he had within himself.

After a month, Dr. Redding thought Greg could handle a visit with Alan, but with no discussions regarding their work. No talk about the White House. It must be general and light. Greg contacted Alan to ask him to come by for a visit. Alan agreed; he had been waiting for Greg's call.

"Dr. Redding instructed me to keep our conversation light with no discussion about work. However, we can visit and conduct some light conversation. I miss seeing and talking to you."

Greg told Alan about the times available for visits, and Alan chose one.

"I pray you are making constant progress. We all love you, Greg, and want only the best for you. I will see you tomorrow, is there anything I can bring you when I come?"

"No, I am all set, but I would love it if you'd join me for lunch at noon if you can."

Alan agreed.

Greg smiled; it would be nice to see his old friend, share a pleasant, relaxed conversation, then have a delicious lunch together. He called the cafeteria to inform them he would bring a friend to lunch.

Greg arrived for his therapy session and reported to Dr. Redding that he had invited Alan to join him for lunch.

"I told Alan we must keep the conversation light with no discussions about work at all. Dr. Redding, I am not interested in discussing work with Alan. My interest lies in my recovery. Everything else will wait until I am strong enough to handle more than I can now. Even if the day should come when I realize it is not healthy for me to continue as the US Attorney General. I will adjust my life. I never realized I could even consider the possibility, but now I can. You've helped me to see what is most important, and I will always be grateful."

"Greg, I am delighted you got to this point. I imagined your primary goal would always be your work and how quickly you could get out of here to return to it."

"It was my thinking at first, but having had the time to work with you, I am coming to realize what my priorities are by using my experience. I can help others find peace in their lives, as I see in mine. I've never known such an incredible level of peace of mind and heart existed before now. When I look back at my life, I lived it as a bigoted racist, so not very much touched my heart before now. If I cannot do my work as the person, I am today. I will find another way."

Dr. Redding knew they still had a lot to do, but they had broken through to Greg's heart and soul, which was monumental!

Over the next few weeks, Greg grew more robust and could schedule a visit with Ellen, one of his primary goals.

"Remember Greg; if spending time with Ellen is overwhelming, you need to conclude the conversation and end the visit. It will mean you are not quite ready for that level of conversation or such an emotional visit. I believe you are ready, and everything will be okay. Will Laura be coming with her?"

Greg told him Laura would accompany Ellen to Hope Gardens for their visit. Greg had spent no actual time with Ellen, so other than the telephone conversations, it was all yet to come.

"Greg, you've made incredible progress since coming to Hope Gardens. You will be ready to return home and to your life soon. Let's see how today goes and how strong you are. Since your experience with Ellen has been one of the leading forces beneath your illness, I am delighted you are ready for this visit. Many of your answers lie with her. She will help you. Perhaps you will help each other more than any of us realize."

Greg could not wait to meet Ellen. She and Laura would arrive at eleven and accompany Greg to lunch about noon. It would give them time before lunch to talk a bit. Then lunch would allow them a diversion before walking in the gardens, which would be a peaceful experience. Greg was showered and dressed by 6:00 a.m. He couldn't sleep.

Greg had made enough progress in confronting his torture of Ellen. The experience had put both of them into psychiatric facilities, which contributed to each of them making incredible progress. They could now experience the opportunity to work together and become friends.

As Greg watched the butterflies in the garden flit from one flower to another, he thought how similar his life had been, flitting from one victim to another. All the racism Greg had unleashed, on one poor soul after another. It was a bizarre analogy since he had been nothing like a beautiful butterfly, far from anything attractive at all.

Greg no longer had the desire to hurt anyone, quite the opposite. He hoped to contribute to healing others. He realized he could now look at himself in a mirror without having his mind go into overdrive and spin-out, trying to deal with what he saw. Greg saw a youthful black man with memories of days gone by as a Caucasian. He could also say those words without thinking his world could end. Greg wanted to go home but knew he would miss the beautiful gardens and kind people so instrumental to his recovery. He realized many things about himself just sitting there, watching the butterflies and remembering the past.

He wondered if they could duplicate a significant part of the gardens at their home for everyone to enjoy.

Greg looked up and saw Dr. Redding walking toward him with an enormous smile. Greg stood to greet him.

"So, Greg, how is your morning going? Are you ready for this most important visit?"

"I am beyond excited. It is so important to me. I have reached the point where I am ready to greet and become acquainted with Ellen on a new and healthy level. It is all thanks to you. I hope you realize that."

"I am so proud of your progress. I can almost feel what you must be experiencing. I realize what it means to you to make things right and begin a new relationship with Ellen. Greg, I wish you all the very best with your visit today and with the rest of your life. You are an exceptional person, and I believe you will accomplish amazing things. Now I must go to another appointment; I will leave you with your thoughts. We will talk later."

Greg walked over to the entrance to greet Laura and Ellen when they arrived. As he approached the main entrance, he could see Laura and Ellen coming up to the door. Everyone smiled as they met.

Laura led the way and greeted Greg with a hug, then turned and said, "Dad, this is my dear friend Ellen."

Both Greg and Ellen reached out and hugged each other, wearing the most amazing smiles.

"Ellen, it's such a pleasure to meet you. I cannot wait to discuss everything we need to talk about."

"I am pleased to meet you too. Yes, we have a lot to discuss. If you get the least bit stressed, please tell me, and we can change the subject of our conversation."

Laura stood, watching her dad and Ellen. Finally, they had come together. Everything would be okay now between her dad and her dearest friend. They had just begun a whole new chapter.

Greg told the ladies they would have lunch at noon; until then, they would visit the gardens. Laura chimed in, noting there was something extraordinary about the gardens, almost magical. They walked out to the rear garden amongst the beautiful butterflies and found a small set of table and chairs set off by itself, perfect for them to begin their conversation.

"Ellen, we want you to understand you will always be welcome in our home. Hopefully, you will enjoy it enough to come and stay for extended periods, and it will seem like your home. Our house has a lovely guest room. Laura, Sylvia, and I discussed having you stay with us, which we would all love you to do."

Ellen smiled and told Greg and Laura how much she appreciated their offer, then asked Greg many questions about adjusting to being black.

"I accept it, but I must be honest with myself. I was white for the first half of my life. It is as important to me as it is to anyone that is black, African American, or anyone of another race. But I've come to a level of acceptance with my transformation.

"Please tell me, Ellen, what did you experience growing up in Nigeria? I would like to know everything you can share with me, or should I say with us. Did you associate with white families, or did you grow up with African neighbors and friends? How did you prepare for coming to the United States? Were you anxious or frightened, since you came here alone to attend school?"

"Wow," Ellen said. "It will take a bit of time to respond to your questions. Africa is different. I lived in the country with African friends. Just the thought of coming to America alone terrified me, but my desire to get an education and become a doctor in America outweighed my fear. I am here on an educational visa. Other than two unpleasant experiences since coming to the US, I must admit I love it here. I miss my parents and my little brother. So, we Skype, which helps. How have you dealt with becoming another race?"

"It has been humbling to a degree I would never have imagined. I have such gratitude for the personality changes I experienced. It is no surprise to you, but I have not always been a likable person. Something came over me years ago, causing me to develop an extreme sense of privilege.

"Please help me understand what racism does to the heart and soul, how it changes people! How can we communicate with people who discriminate against minorities? We must encourage communication to educate perpetrators as to how they are hurting the people on the receiving end of their anger and viciousness."

Ellen had tears running down her cheeks as Greg spoke. Laura cried too. It was incredible to realize he heard her.

Ellen told Greg, "I am so pleased with what you just said. We can be friends and work together to help you gain a better understanding of racism and its severe effects. I cannot even imagine how I would have adjusted if it happened to me. It must have been overwhelming as you attempted to accept it as a permanent situation. Thank you for allowing me into your life, mind, and heart, with an issue as sensitive as this one. I've prayed for you and your family as you went through this transformation and will continue to do so."

Greg thanked Ellen for her kindness and welcomed her into their family, then it was already time for lunch.

They chose a lovely table overlooking a garden area. Ellen asked Greg how much longer he would remain at Hope Gardens.

"It is funny you should ask me that today. I spoke with Dr. Redding before you both arrived. He said I would go home soon, but did not mention what 'soon' meant. I am unsure whether I want to return to my position as US Attorney General. I am not saying the job of the United States Attorney General is easy or unimportant; it is not the case. There will be decisions to make. I never asked you why you asked, Ellen."

"You should not rush such an important decision to make it before you go home. You've earned lots of time off, haven't you?"

Laura laughed at the statement. Her dad never took time off, so the last time they discussed the issue, he had accrued about six months of comp time.

While looking at her father and best friend Ellen, Laura said, "I am so happy to be here with both of you. I cannot find the words. I hope we are all close forever."

At that moment, their waiter arrived with their lunches, which all looked and smelled delicious.

They ventured back out to the gardens after their excellent lunch. Ellen loved being there with Laura and Greg. She stated, "I am so in love with these gardens. I see why you enjoy spending so much time here."

Greg and Laura hoped the garden would work as well at their house.

Greg told the girls what he had been considering. Could they encourage communication between all races? Sincere dialogue between people might reveal their actual feelings. It might bring about a new understanding. They could begin with a group of people willing to talk, start an honest conversation, and bare their souls. Honesty is vital.

Greg asked the girls, "What are your initial thoughts? I do not expect it to be an easy fix. I would be kidding myself if I did, but over time I am hoping it will be accepted. We may learn why people are so bitter. Sorry, I asked you both for your thoughts, but I did not allow you to respond. I am so excited we may find an answer to improve relations between races. So, what do you both think?"

Ellen spoke first, saying, "Your simple idea sounds amazing; the answer is communication, mutual respect, and a desire to understand and learn. I can picture people gathered at an informal get-together, talking about the differences between races, coming to know what they've all been through in their lives. Imagine doing that without violence or arguing—it would be beyond amazing! Mr. Hastings, I believe you have a fabulous idea, something that could be huge, and I would like to help in any way I can."

Laura added, "I am already interviewing minorities. We will learn together."

Greg thanked them both. He appreciated their honesty and willingness to help. Now how would he fit this into his job as US Attorney General?

"Ellen, you must call me Greg. Mr. Hastings is much too formal after what we have all been through."

Laura was thrilled to witness the comfortable exchange between them.

Greg announced, "I will try to find out who designed these beautiful gardens and ask whether they would create one for us at home."

It was time for Greg's afternoon meeting. Ellen and Greg said their goodbyes with a hug and kiss. They were both eager to begin their work.

Chapter Eleven

Renewed

Greg sat for a short while before joining the rest of the group, wondering whether he might be ready to return home. Greg joined the group and shared his feelings of apprehension and gained a lot of very positive feedback. Dr. Redding asked him to remain for two minutes at the end of the group. He told Greg the time had come for him to meet with a few ethnic group leaders and indulge in an in-depth discussion with them.

"Greg, you are so much stronger now than when you first arrived. You seem able to accept that you are now black, whether or not you are looking into a mirror. Trouble is understandable since you grew up as a white man.

"You lived the first half of your life white. No one can take it away from you, nor should anyone try. Your memories are an enormous part of what makes you the person you are today. Greg, it will be complex for you. I wish I had a better answer which would fit into a compartment known as life. Can you rise to the occasion and be the stronger person?"

Greg looked Dr. Redding in the eyes and told him, "I never considered my situation the way you just explained it to me, until now. You are right. I need not let go of my past to embrace the present and the future. It is my marriage to Sylvia and the birth of our beautiful daughter, Laura. My family, my childhood, and my many friends, relationships, and my career as the US Attorney General. I love all of my memories and would not want to sacrifice even one of them. Thank you so much, Dr. Redding. With your help, I made such a revelation tonight. I am ready to meet with the group leaders now. Shall we make those appointments?"

Dr. Redding realized there would be issues, as everyone deals with, but Greg could now cope with whatever came along. He would handle it.

* * *

Both the excitement and his nerves kept Greg awake. His first meeting with a minority group would be that afternoon. Dr. Redding would sit in with them to observe. He hoped this meeting might set the tone for the future with minority leaders from around the country. Everyone needed to see the sincerity in his desire to encourage actual communication between races and an additional level of understanding.

Dr. Redding; Kenneth Landstrom, the director of the Group for Equalities from Washington, DC; and two of his supervisors had been seated when Greg arrived. They appeared excited to be present.

Greg asked them, "Please relax, and we can get started. I imagine you all met Dr. Redding, the man who has brought me through all the confusion that accompanied my transformation. I must tell you, going through a complete DNA change does not come without its issues. It has been a process and an incredible learning experience. I imagine you all know as much about me as I do about myself at this point. I believe in total honesty, which is what you will always get from me. When I learned of my DNA transformation, I thought I could handle my life changing a little without too much trouble. It proved not to be so, as you may well imagine. I could not have realized the intensity of the changes it would bring about in my life. I must say this out loud. I went from being white to becoming black in just a few short weeks. No one does that, and I could not do so without professional help.

"After coming to this fantastic facility, I am back to some semblance of normalcy. They helped me to understand how all of this has affected me. It changed me for the better. I realize now, with Dr. Redding's help, I will never know what it would have been like to be born black. I was born white and lived the first part of my life as a white man.

"I am now a black man. I need all of you to help me understand what you experienced being born black or African American. Have you experienced racism; if so, how did it affect your heart and soul? Did it change you? I have a powerful desire to develop what I consider a communication program. We would meet at different facilities throughout the country, similar to an evening with the US Attorney General. We would invite people to come and discuss racial differences and how we might improve conditions. I want to know your thoughts."

Kenneth spoke up, saying, "Greg, I am intrigued. I attended the press conference. I imagined you would be livid at the mere thought of becoming a minority, but you are not, even now. How do you feel about becoming a black man?"

"I accepted it and carried on as though nothing much had changed. Until I tried to let go of my white self and become black. It confused my mind so much it closed down, and I passed out. I couldn't seem to process the fact of a total and permanent change. When I wasn't looking into a mirror, I still thought I was white. Only when I saw myself did I realize I was now black. Dr. Redding and his staff helped me to merge my two selves into one and accept my transition. I owe them a debt of gratitude like no other ever known to man for all the help and guidance they gave me. But I am two hundred percent better. I am not now, nor will I ever be able to relate to growing up black. I can only connect through your stories from your childhood.

"Trying to force myself to let go of my white roots was where I had the problem. Now I realize it is unnecessary to let go of my earlier memories to embrace the rest of my life as a black man. I will always have a white past and a black future, which has become comfortable for me. Does that answer your question?"

Greg more than explained his feelings regarding his transition. His incredible progress moved everyone.

Kenneth told Greg, "We will all be able to work together. What are your thoughts about how you can get through to minorities to encourage them to listen to you?"

"I intend to be honest and explain how I see it. It seems, in most cases, people who discriminate against minorities are responding to what they thought to be real or how their friends treated minorities. They are holding something against them that they have no control over. People do not choose a race or whom they are born to; it is out of their control. The color of a person's skin does not dictate what they feel. It makes them look different from one another. Through honest communication, we can educate people about how racism hurts the recipient. They have been the targets of anger and hatred, which often is unfounded. I believe we must communicate without arguing, name-calling, and bitterness if we ever hope to learn about one another and develop a genuine and lasting connection with mutual respect.

"Through research, I have discovered that racism can cause significant mental and physical health consequences for its victims. Minorities often seek additional education to secure employment which non-minorities would not find necessary. People are sometimes overqualified before they even begin.

"Honest communication is the place to start. I would love to see all ethnic groups sit down together and face one another while sharing how they feel in their hearts and souls. Then discuss how it affected them short and long-term. Ask them what can lessen the original pain and improve conditions between them today. Then ask them to discuss their genuine hopes for a better future working together."

"Greg, you are onto something," Kenneth declared. "Once minorities come to realize you are serious and non-minorities want to understand what they are experiencing, people may talk about their personal feelings."

"So, Kenneth, have you suffered from discrimination during your lifetime?"

"Yes, when I was very young. I attended a mixed-race school; the kids were brutal, and their parents backed them up. I loved baseball but couldn't play because I was black. They did not want a black kid on their team. Then again, during college, also when I began working after college. I was a minority! I suffered from panic attacks, depression, and high blood pressure beginning in my early twenties. These experiences are an enormous part of why minorities stay with their race and do not even attempt to meet non-minorities to begin a friendship.

"It sounds as though I may be sorry for myself, but it is so much more. If there is anything we can do to assist you with your neighborhood meetings, we are interested in participating!"

Everyone seemed comfortable by the end of their meeting. Greg couldn't wait for the next session. Before leaving, everyone exchanged contact information and promised to be in touch soon.

Dr. Redding greeted Greg on his way back down the hall and asked, "If you have a few minutes, I would like to talk to you."

"I do. I am eager to speak with you, too, to get your thoughts on how you think the meeting concluded."

Dr. Redding smiled the biggest smile Greg had ever seen on his face. It resembled pride as he told him, "Greg, I am so proud of the progress you've made. I am thrilled to be a part of your recovery. What I observed in that room today convinced me you had made your way back through the most painful experience anyone has ever had. You've transitioned from your birth race to your present and future race. Coming out of it with more grace and heart than most people I've ever known. I feel honored to know you, Greg Hastings!"

Greg was at A Loss for Words. Tears filled his eyes and ran down his cheeks. He said, "Thank you so much, Dr. Redding. My gratitude is immense for your patience, guidance, and care from the moment I collapsed. After working with me, you can handle anyone that comes along. Together, we met the challenge and conquered it!"

"Thank you, Greg, for the trust and confidence you've shown in me. We can now prepare for your departure; I would imagine you would like to go home and be with your wife and daughter. We advise you, though, to take a week or even two weeks to unwind and settle into your life before you make any big decisions regarding your work. You are now a changed man. I would like to continue with our appointments for a while. Beyond that, I will always and forever be here for you whenever you need me. I am only a phone call away."

"When can I go home?"

"How about unwinding tonight and being released tomorrow morning? Would that be too soon?"

"Fabulous," Greg answered, "I cannot wait to call Sylvia, but, before I do, I must ask you an earnest question. Is there any way the person who built the gardens here could build one for us at our home? We've never enjoyed a sense of peace as we feel out there. It would be wonderful to have a bit of it right outside our door. Is it possible?"

Dr. Redding laughed and nodded to Greg. "Yes, we can arrange it for you."

* * *

A very soft-spoken elderly man entered his room and said, "You must be Greg Hastings."

"Yes, I am, can I help you?"

"I believe it is I who can be of help to you. Dr. Redding just stopped me in the hall to tell me you would like a garden constructed at your home, similar to the one here."

"Yes, that is correct. What is the secret to the sense of peace we find when we go out there? Can you duplicate it for us? I am sorry I did not even ask your name."

"My name is Henry; I can duplicate the sense of peace you find here in the garden at your home. The secret is faith and love, and I sense you possess both."

"Thank you, Henry, you are correct. We have both the faith and lots of love. How soon can you come by to help us plan the garden?"

"Will Saturday work?" Henry inquired. "You will go home tomorrow, correct?"

"Yes, I will," Greg said to him.

The men exchanged contact information, and Henry left to go home himself. Greg thought he seemed very sweet and kind. Sylvia answered her phone on the second ring; she had been waiting to learn all about the minority group meeting.

Greg told her, "Honey, so much has happened this afternoon, where do I start? The meeting was fabulous! Dr. Redding sat in with us to be sure I did well. He was so impressed with how I conducted myself he said I could come home tomorrow. He suggests I take two weeks off to settle back into life before deciding anything regarding work.

"I saved one minor surprise for last. I just met with Henry, the sweetest senior man. He is the person responsible for the beautiful gardens here. He has agreed to come to our house and help us plan our very own gardens! I asked him what the secret to the peace we all feel here in the gardens is, he said it is faith and love. He sensed that we have plenty of both. So what do you say about that?"

96

Sylvia laughed aloud and cried at the same time.

"Greg, I am beyond thrilled to hear you will be home tomorrow. What time can I pick you up? Did you call Laura?"

"No, I wanted to call you first, now I can call Laura. I want you to know how good I feel. I am not saying there won't be the usual aggravations that life presents us with. But it will not be because of my past behaviors, that I can promise you. Oh, I did not answer your question; please pick me up about ten, or eight for breakfast."

Sylvia loved the idea and told Greg, "I will be there at eight for breakfast. I cannot wait to see you, pack up our car, and bring you home with me for good! I've missed you so much."

"Me too. I'm eager to come home. My appointments with Dr. Redding will continue for a while and as needed after that. He will continue to be available to you and Laura if you need him. I am grateful to him and his staff."

"Greg, there is such relief in my heart. There are no words to explain it to you right this minute."

He called Laura to tell her the news.

"Hi Dad, how are you doing today? Today was your big meeting day, so how did it go?"

"Great!" Greg told her he had some other news to share with her. He whispered, "Honey, I am coming home! We are getting our garden!"

Laura was crying.

Greg broke into her thoughts with, "Laura, are you okay?"

"Sorry, Dad, yes I am fantastic, my dad is coming home. It will thrill Ellen, too. She asks me every day if there has been any news regarding your release. It has been a long haul, hasn't it, Dad? You sound great, though. Did your meeting go well today?"

"Yes, Laura, it was phenomenal, and I am grateful and stronger than ever. I am going home to get on with our lives. We can discuss today's meeting when I see you. I love you. I will see you soon! Goodnight, honey."

"Goodnight, Dad."

Chapter Twelve

Trip Home

Greg was going home to plan moving forward with his life after receiving a tremendous amount of therapy and guidance from one of the world's most prominent psychiatrists. He would leave Hope Gardens with most of the tools he needed to go forward.

Greg awoke at five, showered and dressed, then poured himself a cup of coffee while he read the newspaper and waited for Sylvia to join him for breakfast. What a lucky man he was. Sure, he had been through a lot during the last few months, but his family was still intact, and their love for him secure.

It would be nice if some positive news made it into the paper. It seemed worse than ever, with lots of negative racial issues. Greg sensed a stirring inside of himself, almost an excitement. However, he was not sure how to approach it but would give it his best effort, accepting the fact he would like to stay on as the US Attorney General. He would have more of an impact in his present position than by leaving his job.

As he walked down the hall, he reminisced about all the time he had spent in the gardens. How enjoyable and peaceful it had been for him and his family. Now they would construct their own for all of them to enjoy whenever they would like.

Sylvia walked out to the gardens, knowing she would find Greg waiting for her there. They went to the dining room together for breakfast.

Greg chatted on like an excited child, like old times, when they would talk together for hours. She had enjoyed it immensely and missed it.

Greg reiterated, "Sylvia, we will plan our garden right outside our door."

Sylvia knew they would all enjoy it, including Ellen, the newest member of their family.

"You seem ready to come home. Do you agree?"

Greg told her he did. It seemed like a fresh start, and a unique chance to get it right and live the carefree lives they should have always lived.

Dr. Redding appeared and summoned them into his office for Greg's discharge meeting. He also discussed Greg's sessions for the near future, with an open completion date.

"It has been enjoyable working with all of you. I am thrilled Greg has made enough progress to be ready to return home with you, Sylvia. Never would I have imagined when we first began your therapy, you would improve the way you have. I am thrilled for you. We Americans will prosper in racial relations with you as our US Attorney General. Now I realize you have not decided on your job for the future. I am just speaking of the status at present. My sense is you will end up staying on and accomplishing incredible things. Best of luck to all of you."

Dr. Redding hugged them both goodbye. Greg and Sylvia walked back to his room to pick up Greg's belongings; an assistant was waiting to take his bags to their car.

Sylvia asked Greg if he would like to drive home, but he declined. She smiled and told him she would love to escort him back to their home; she radiated happiness.

* * *

He breathed an enormous sigh of relief and looked around. Nothing had changed, but somehow it all seemed renewed. Greg saw his life and his world through fresh eyes. Greg and Sylvia sat together on the sofa, planning their future. The newfound peace was so apparent.

"I have never known this level of happiness and contentment with myself. I am stronger and more determined to tackle whatever is necessary to go forward and bring about changes in the world. I will always be grateful we agreed on Hope Gardens and chose Dr. Redding to work with me and us. We have regained our lives, we're stronger than before. Bless you for your patience with me."

"It was never easy," Sylvia responded, "but I always loved you and wanted the best for Laura, so I continued. As you learned through our sessions with Dr. Redding, there were many times when I came close to calling it quits. You were an evil human being. Please, never return to the man you used to be. There is no way I would remain married to him. I must make that clear to you."

"Believe me, I understand and do not blame you."

"How about some lunch? I picked up all of your favorites. You should call Laura and let the girls know you arrived home."

Greg picked up the phone while Sylvia left to make lunch.

They had two free weeks ahead of them. Greg booked two weeks in Barbados to surprise Sylvia. They had earned a unique getaway. Sylvia loved it there, and was still on leave. Greg made all the arrangements and left her bathing suit on her pillow and the new travel brochures, which he had delivered to Hope Gardens when he made the reservations.

After lunch, she disappeared upstairs to change and came running down the stairs screaming, "Greg, what did you do? It's incredible!" It thrilled her!

"Honey, we deserve some time away, and you earned this trip!"

"We will have a marvelous time! I am looking forward to spending time alone with my husband and enjoying some actual conversations once again. Thank you, Greg!"

"You are so welcome. I want you to remember how very much I love you and always will. So, can you pack and be ready to leave in two days?"

Sylvia would be ready; she had already organized all of their closets and laundered everything they owned. Her primary goals were to call Laura, then notify her office staff and the covering doctors. Everyone would be ecstatic to cover for her a little longer, knowing their situation.

Greg called Dr. Redding to inform him they would be away for two weeks. They needed to reschedule his next appointment. Dr. Redding reminded Greg he would be there if they needed him. Greg thanked him for everything and told him he would see him when they got back.

Chapter Thirteen

Getaway

Greg and Sylvia held hands and smiled as they gazed out the window during takeoff.

Landing in Barbados was smooth and without incident. They disembarked from the plane and picked up their luggage. Both had terrific memories of their previous stay in Barbados, many years ago. It was a gorgeous sunny day, warm for ten in the morning, just the way they remembered it.

Greg booked them into the same hotel as their last visit. The service had been fabulous. They occupied a beautiful spacious suite with a king-size bed, two bathrooms, a lovely sauna, a kitchenette, and a balcony overlooking the ocean. What a lovely sight, pure white sand as far as one could see, with dark blue beach umbrellas lined up in the sand. They were eager to check into their hotel and head to the beach. The smiles had not left their faces since they landed.

"Two weeks on this gorgeous island, can you imagine it, Sylvia?"

"It is as beautiful as I remembered. We will enjoy a fabulous time. And no one knows us, which means no media! We can relax and breathe without thinking about being followed or being the subject of their next photo opportunity."

"I never considered that for a second. I am still the US Attorney General, and we are the biggest news to come along. We should watch out for the media. I am not concerned about what we might do because we are mild-mannered people. I just don't want to see us on the cover of a newspaper or magazine."

Sylvia agreed; she was joking, but Greg made an excellent point. As long as they remained in the public eye, they should always be aware. It would not deter them or ruin their vacation, just make them aware.

"So, Sylvia," Greg gushed, "let's go to the beach for the afternoon, then we can eat dinner wherever we like."

Sylvia loved the idea. She changed into her swimsuit.

"Am I going to the beach alone, or are you coming with me? I am already changed, but you are still in your traveling clothes."

Greg smiled, undressed, and waited for Sylvia by the door. She joined him with the sunscreen in hand. They picked up towels for the day, found two lounge chairs and an umbrella, and reclined. The water sparkled as the sun glinted off the turquoise blue sea with a slight hint of darker bluish-green hues. The waves crashed against the rocks with the incoming tide, producing white foam that spread the entire length of the beach. What a magnificent sight! There were no clouds to hamper their day of sun. The hotel provided lunch for their guests on the beach.

Sylvia and Greg had a relaxing day sunning on the beach and playing in the water. It reminded them of another time, long ago. The couple both enjoyed the day and looked forward to many more like it during their two-week stay.

Greg and Sylvia planned to eat at their hotel. They were eager to partake in the fantastic pig roast, prepared by the chef on the beach. The dress was beachwear. Before they returned to their room to shower and dress for the evening, Sylvia and Greg took a long walk down the beach. They talked about their day and what they hoped to do there during the coming two weeks.

They had walked past the next three hotels to the submarine launching area before they went back to their hotel to shower and dress for dinner. As they walked, Greg and Sylvia continued to talk about everything they had bottled up for so long.

"Sylvia, what do you think about asking Ellen to spend summer break at our home with Laura if she is not going home? Providing Laura agrees. They will graduate in two months, then start medical school together in September. It would be fantastic for all of us to enjoy the opportunity to become better acquainted, and for Ellen to feel at home since she is so far away from hers. Perhaps her parents and her brother could join her over the summer. We have enough room. So what do you think?"

"Greg, I am at a loss. I've never heard you suggest anything like this. We will need to check with Laura to see what her thoughts are. We are her parents, but it is her home too. If Laura would like Ellen to stay at our house for the summer, then I agree. It is an excellent idea, right down to inviting her parents to visit for a while. However, we should not get our hopes up too high. Laura has said nothing about wanting Ellen to stay. She may prefer to be with us alone. Greg, it would be fun to have another daughter around, and it would be a good home away from home for Ellen. Perhaps we should do a trial run when we get home. We will say nothing to Laura until they return to school, but she may mention it before we have the opportunity."

"Sylvia, I hope it all works out. Now let's go take a shower; we have plenty of time before dinner!"

They ran down the beach. Sylvia and Greg were starting over.

They could see the fire burning below as the cooks prepared the pig roast for dinner on the beach.

Sylvia still loved Greg; he was once again the person he was when they fell in love. His race did not matter, he was the man she loved. She enjoyed their time together and was eager to see how things developed. Greg felt such gratitude for reestablishing a relationship with his beautiful wife as they possessed long ago. He knew of no reason it would not continue for the rest of their lives.

They both dressed for the evening, looking casual. Mr. and Mrs. Hastings made quite a handsome couple walking down the hall, holding onto each other's hands. They walked down the stairs and out into the fragrant night air. The gentle breeze carried the aroma of the beautiful flowers surrounding the hotel—a magical evening and long overdue.

"It looks like dinner is ready."

They each ordered wine and sat at a table for two to enjoy their first dinner together in Barbados.

Greg held up his glass and said, "This is to us, Mrs. Hastings, you are the Love of My Life. May our happiness this evening continue for the rest of our lives."

"Mr. Hastings, you too, are the Love of My Life. I hope what we discovered this evening will be a permanent state of mind and heart for both of us."

As they clinked their glasses together, Greg reached over and gave Sylvia a gentle kiss on her cheek.

Greg had taken the activity information sheet with him to dinner and shared it with Sylvia. They planned to snorkel the following day, after which they would get lunch at an old favorite restaurant they had enjoyed in the past. They served the best lobster salad they had ever had.

Dinner smelled delicious! They both realized they had not attended a pig roast since their last trip there. Nothing could even compare with the way the chefs cooked this meal, prepared Hawaiian style. Which gave it an excellent smoky flavor you could not achieve in an oven—just delicious.

After dinner, Greg and Sylvia strolled down the beach, reminiscing about their first day in Barbados. One could only describe it as a romantic rediscovery of the love that brought the two of them together. They had both feared that Greg's DNA transformation would endanger their marriage. The outcome was the exact opposite. Their feelings for each other surpassed even their most significant memories.

They swam for what seemed like hours, enjoying the breathtaking underwater views. The vibrant colors of sea life within the Caribbean ocean were some of the most incredible on earth, and they couldn't get enough of it. Both of them became so entranced with the beauty the sea offered, they could snorkel every day and never tire of it. They discussed taking an evening cruise on a sailboat within the next few nights, then added it to their list.

The following evening they boarded a beautiful sailboat for an evening cruise. It was a wonderfully romantic time, dancing and relaxing while gazing at the moon and the stars. They discussed their future and what they hoped and prayed was ahead for all of them. They felt reborn and were enjoying every moment they had together.

Time flew by for the lucky couple; they snorkeled, swam, cruised, and relaxed, as the time to return home closed in. Sylvia had texted Laura a few times to share: We're having a glorious time.

They bid farewell to Barbados, knowing they would leave some of themselves behind. However, they were taking so much more home with them.

As the aircraft touched down, Sylvia and Greg both sighed. As much as they loved their lives and Laura, their vacation had ended. The actual world awaited. They had to disembark.

After collecting their luggage, they found a taxi to take them home. Sylvia noticed Greg was whistling, which he had not done in years; it sounded good.

The driver unloaded their luggage and brought it into the foyer. Greg paid the fare and closed the door.

Sylvia suggested, "How would you like to go to Hot Chocolate for pancakes for dinner, then we can relax for the rest of the evening. Do you agree?"

"I do. It is a terrific idea! We are still on vacation."

They walked into Hot Chocolate to the smiles and waves of the staff and the customers. Greg and Sylvia both smiled and waved back. While they enjoyed their pancakes, they discussed Greg's ultimate decision to return to work, after doing lots of soul-searching. He loved what he did and knew it would be very beneficial for him to continue his present position as the US Attorney General. Sylvia agreed.

"I want you to be happy with whatever you do. You will contribute to racial issues worldwide, as long as you are ready to begin the task. I am with you all the way. But remember, we must never lose ourselves or our relationship again."

Greg assured Sylvia it would never again be an issue. He realized second chances did not occur often, and he wanted to protect theirs with his life.

They waved to everyone as they left the restaurant and walked out to their car.

After spending a lovely quiet evening together, they went to bed early.

Chapter Fourteen

Moving On

Sylvia awoke to the alarm ringing in her ear at 5:30 a.m. Where was Laura when she needed her to make the coffee?

Greg called Alan on the way to the office to discuss clearing an hour to catch up. Alan agreed to meet.

"It has been tough not to discuss all the details with you, but I understood why I couldn't. I can meet with you as soon as you get to the office and grab a cup of coffee."

Greg's thoughts drifted to how his job evolved over the years. Now he would add a novel concept: more empathy, and open communication! Greg wondered how his first meeting would go; there was so much at stake. He would open the doors of contact for all ethnic groups. There must be communication on both sides. He hoped everyone would soon come to see he wanted to connect.

Greg pulled into his assigned parking space; he had to admit to himself, it felt fabulous to be back. He walked through the massive double doors leading to their private office space within the building, then stopped to look around. The architecture of the Department of Justice building was beautiful. Greg had always been proud to have an office within such a magnificent building. This time the feelings were genuine, with no false sense of grandeur.

Greg took a deep breath and reached to open the door to his office area. The staff greeted Greg as soon as he arrived.

Alan approached the area, knowing Greg had arrived, and invited him into his office to catch up on the latest happenings.

"Greg, it is wonderful to have you back."

"Alan, it is wonderful to be back," Greg responded. "I did not realize just how much I missed being here until I pulled into my parking space, then walked through those massive double doors. It has been a long time, but I am now ready to tackle whatever comes our way."

Alan brought him up to date on daily business issues and everything they had pending.

Greg smiled and responded, "Wow, it has been busy while I was away, but I am sure you handled everything without a problem."

Alan told Greg, "Do not get the wrong idea. We managed. You keep this office running. We put some things off, not wanting to disturb you while you recovered. Welcome back, Greg!"

Greg's gratitude overflowed. He touched on his vacation with Sylvia and expressed how thankful he was. She hung in with him and she still loved him.

"We recaptured the love we always had for each other. After discussing the issues, we left the negatives behind. We will return to Barbados.

"I must call the president this morning to inform him I've returned, and I am ready to tackle anything he needs me to do. I met with the director of the Group for Equalities from Washington, DC, Kenneth Landstrom, and two of his supervisors, Matt and Charles. We met for two hours just before my discharge from Hope Gardens. They offered to join us at the first group meeting we schedule."

"I've received many calls requesting they meet with you to discuss how you plan to move forward, to bring about improvements in minority relations. We told everyone we would be in touch with them as soon as you return from your leave. Greg, I got a very positive response from everyone. They all hope you will make progress. It's a tall order, but they sound confident, they believe in you."

"Well, Alan, it seems rather simple to me. I believe letting people know I care and want to hear firsthand about their experiences will touch them. I think the actual answer is honesty and empathy. People realize when those feelings are genuine and when they aren't. We need to sit down and talk about racism and how it has affected their lives, without arguing threats or violence. We must come together. I can relate to their present and future while they educate the rest of us on their past. So what do you think?"

As Alan digested what Greg said, he took a deep breath and answered, "I believe it is an excellent idea, brilliant, yet simple. It is honest and real; I think it will be successful. I am sure everyone, no matter what their issue, needs complete and total honesty. So when do we start?"

"I will meet with Janice Carter this morning to determine how far she has gotten on the needs analysis. We can schedule meetings with them as soon as they are available."

"I worried about you and everything that has happened. It is a pure pleasure to sit here with you now and listen to you speak with so much kindness, concern, and humility."

Janice informed Greg, "I identified one hundred fifty separate groups within the US. Sixty-five were active and taking part under the guidelines for ethnic groups. Many had questions that Alan responded to, leaving you with forty teams who want to meet or speak with you."

"You have been busy, Janice. I am impressed with your thoroughness with this assignment. I realize you understand the essential nature of this issue. I would like you to continue working with Alan and me on this project."

Janice thanked Greg and returned to her office.

Greg informed the president he was about to begin his minority group contacts. He promised to keep him informed as they moved forward.

His first call was to the Minorites For Progress group. He spoke to their director, Martin Chase, who stated, "We are all looking forward to meeting you. I must tell you; I am amazed you were able, in such a brief time, to return to work. I cannot imagine myself having gone through such a life-changing ordeal. Then wanting to rush back to help others deal with their racial issues; you have earned my total respect!"

"I appreciate it Martin, I thought people might judge me for needing to deal with the emotional side of my transformation. You have provided me with a sense of relief concerning the issue."

"Greg, it is one thing to be born black. You lived your entire life as a white man who has become black. It is a life-changing event to digest.

Please go easy on yourself. I could not have handled it as you have. Let me say, we applaud you for working on our behalf."

"Martin, we are all going to do our best to make improvements. Honesty and empathy will make an incredible difference. We would like to see people of all races sit together to talk without arguing or raising their voices in an informal environment. People have blamed blacks for being a unique race, which they have no control over. They did nothing to offend their perpetrators. It seems to be widespread discrimination against the entire race, not the person. I may be crazy, but I believe we can educate people to open their minds and hearts."

Martin answered, "Well, I expected nothing like this. I am almost speechless. I agree with you. I always thought if we communicated, we might break through some of this hostility built up over generations. I would love to see you put your mission in writing, it would be most helpful for all of our groups. Would you be willing to do so and share it with us?"

Greg agreed to work on it and forward it to Martin when he finished.

He continued making calls throughout the morning. Two organizations asked for meetings as soon as possible, planning to invite a group of people to meet with Greg and his staff.

Greg was excited but apprehensive. Could they be wrong? He dismissed the idea, knowing an enormous effort was made to improve race relations.

Janice would go along to help with administrative duties on their trip. They would leave on Tuesday morning for Alabama, then on to Louisiana on Wednesday evening. It would enable them to arrive back in Washington on Friday afternoon. Their journey across America was about to begin.

Greg called Martin Chase to inform him of their itinerary for their first meeting.

"Well, this is it. We will soon find out what the residents of Alabama are thinking about my transition. I am excited yet guarded."

"If you are as honest with the people you meet as you've been with me, you will not fail. Ask your questions and tell them how you feel. They will listen to you and be grateful for what you say. I will see you at the airport on Tuesday morning. Enjoy a great weekend."

* * *

"Laura and Ellen are coming for the weekend. I told her we would love it. We had already discussed it, hoping they would spend a weekend with us."

"It is the best news I've received all day. It will be fun to have them around the house. So, did you tell her yes?"

"I did, it is what we were hoping. Now tell me more about your day."

Greg told her they would talk more about it over dinner.

"Ok, I need to see a patient. Enjoy the rest of your day. I love you!"

He wondered about Sylvia and her little patients; she always enjoyed working with the children. Greg wondered if it might make up for the fact they only had one child.

* * *

Greg and Alan met to discuss their trip: what to bring, times and how they planned to handle them. Alan was becoming as excited as Greg and pleased to be going along on this groundbreaking experience. They accomplished an incredible amount in just one day—imagine what a few months would bring!

Sylvia left the office a little early and started dinner before Greg arrived. They concentrated most of their interest on the girls' visit. Sylvia filled Greg in on their conversation. They would come on Friday afternoon to be home for two nights together, then leave on Sunday afternoon to go back to school. Sylvia planned to freshen up the guest room and add some of Ellen's favorite things. Laura shared her favorite flowers, scents, and colors. Ellen might feel more welcome if she found a few special touches in the bedroom and bathroom for her. Everyone wanted Ellen to feel it was her home away from home.

"I wish I could convey how blessed I feel right now. My beautiful wife is by my side, and our wonderful daughter and her best friend will spend the weekend here at home with us. We never even dared to dream we would get to this point, with everyone coming together and an additional level of trust and caring developing between us."

"I love you, Greg. I'll be forever grateful for everything we all share. While I was busy working today with some of my little patients, I remembered when Laura was their age. We've endured so much since then. An incredible rush came over me, realizing how wonderful our life together is today. We may consider Ellen like an adopted daughter. We can share her with her parents and look after her when she is with us—no harm, is there? I hope we can meet her parents and her brother over the summer. If not, at some point, maybe we could all travel to Africa to meet them."

"What a fantastic idea! I never gave it a thought; it would be doable. Let's see what happens over the coming months."

Sylvia called to see if Ellen had any dietary restrictions. "We are studying, so I will ask her right now." Laura came back and told her, "Ellen does not have any dietary restrictions and likes everything I do. She does, however, like plain oatmeal for breakfast. Otherwise, she is flexible. So how are you and Dad doing?"

Sylvia filled her in on her dad's progress, which Laura relayed to Ellen. It pleased them to get excellent news. Laura told her she and Ellen were looking forward to spending the weekend with her and Greg. Sylvia told her they were too.

The next couple of days flew by, with both Sylvia and Greg busy in their respective occupations. Greg prepared for his trip and caught up on details of current projects, signed agreements, and discussed assignments with Alan. Sylvia was planning a thank-you dinner for all the fantastic people and friends on staff that worked so hard for her while she was on leave. They were a very busy family.

Before they realized it, Friday had arrived. The girls would be home that afternoon. Sylvia put out beautiful, new, fluffy towels for Ellen in her favorite shade of yellow, along with yellow sweetheart roses and lilac drawer liners. She hoped it would please her, and she would feel welcome.

Laura called to request homemade macaroni and cheese with cornbread for dinner. Sylvia would happily oblige, along with a fantastic special dessert.

It would be close, but Sylvia had every intention of arriving home before the girls to be there to greet them. She was sure they would excuse her if she didn't make it, knowing how busy she was.

Sylvia and Greg had breakfast together, discussed the weekend, then headed off in different directions for their workday.

Sylvia's schedule had become crammed with patient exams all morning and a staff meeting after lunch. Somehow the session ended early enough for her to arrive home and put all the ingredients together for dinner before the girls came. She even had time to make her famous iced tea, and chilled it before Laura drove into the driveway.

Laura yelled out, "We are home, is anyone here?"

Sylvia walked to the door and responded, "Yes, I am here, welcome home, ladies!" She hugged and kissed the girls, saying, "I am so glad you are both here, Greg and I were looking forward to this weekend."

"Thank you, Mrs. Hastings, I have been looking forward to it too, very much."

"Now, Ellen, you must call me Sylvia or something other than Mrs. Hastings. You are part of our family now. I made some tea, so when you are ready, it is waiting for you. There are other beverages in the refrigerator and a little snack I put together to hold you over until dinner. Your rooms are ready, too, so please do whatever you like. Ellen, please make yourself at home!"

Ellen smiled as she said, "I am so pleased to be here with all of you for the weekend. It is my dream coming true."

"It has been ours too!" They were ecstatic to welcome her. "What are you ladies planning to do this afternoon?"

"We are planning to drive around a bit so I can show Ellen where I grew up, attended school, and hung out over the years. We will come back and help you with dinner."

"Thank you, honey, I am all set. Please be back at six o'clock for dinner. There are no formalities here. Enjoy yourself. I will see you for dinner."

Laura and Ellen enjoyed the iced tea and homemade cookies while Sylvia ran off to change her clothes to work in the garden.

Sylvia yelled back to them, "Enjoy, you two. I will see you later; got to change."

Laura showed Ellen her room and answered all of her questions before returning to her room to freshen up before their town tour.

When Ellen walked into her room, she was at a loss for words. The drapes filtered the sun, causing the rays to dance on the wall and creating an almost magical effect. She saw the fresh flowers in her favorite color, which she stopped to smell on her way to the bathroom. When she entered, she noticed the fluffy, pale yellow towels, realizing that Sylvia had exerted extra effort. It was like being home. She felt thankful to be at the home of her dearest friend and feel so welcome.

Ellen unpacked. As she began putting her things in the drawer, she noticed the beautiful drawer liners in her favorite lilac fragrance. She freshened up and changed her clothes to be ready for her drive with Laura.

She went to Laura's room to share how thoughtful her mom had been with the flowers, towels, and drawer liners in her favorite fragrance.

"Mom is very thoughtful, but she also wants you to know you are now a welcome part of our family. She has always been my rock. If you are ready, let's go for a ride before dinner."

Laura drove toward the center of town, enabling Ellen to see all the points of interest. They went by a lot of small shops which interested both of the girls.

"This town appears so sweet and welcoming. I understand why you love shopping here. I can imagine poking around the stores, stopping for ice cream, and watching the people passing by."

"Let's come tomorrow. Check out the shops, then stop for lunch. Then we can go by the Emporium, it's a superb place to shop. They sell everything!"

They drove by the high school, the library, the primary hospital, and Sylvia's office. The buildings were beautiful. Ellen had pictured the town being much smaller. The enormity of it all surprised her.

Laura asked Ellen about attending church with them on Saturday night. Ellen told her she would love to go to church; she had often gone by herself.

"I did not realize that we can go together. I, too, have attended alone, because I miss going, but I do go when I am here. So, we can all attend church together tomorrow night!"

When Greg came in, he bellowed, "Hello, everyone, I am home."

"Dad, we are all in the kitchen."

Greg walked in, smiling, and said, "Hello, ladies, it is great to see all of you." Then walked over and kissed Sylvia, Laura, and then Ellen, and said, "Welcome home, Ellen, we are all so happy you are here."

Ellen told Greg she too was glad to be there.

"We drove around a bit this afternoon. I wanted to show Ellen some points of interest around town and Mom's office. We talked about church, and Ellen would like to go with us tomorrow evening."

Greg and Sylvia loved the idea and said, "Then we will all attend church together, then go out for a lovely dinner."

Ellen thanked Sylvia for the beautiful flowers, fluffy bath towels, and the wonderful aroma of the drawer liners she put out for her.

Sylvia told her, "You deserve surprises with unique touches of things you like. It is a way for us to say welcome to your second home."

Tears filled Ellen's eyes, and she appeared to glow with happiness.

They discussed many things and ended up playing some fun board games, which had them all laughing until they cried.

Sylvia announced, "We have a fabulous dessert and coffee, milk, juice, or whatever else you would like. I will go out to the kitchen and get it ready while you three relax."

Laura joined her and let Ellen and Greg talk for a few minutes. She said, "Mom, I think Ellen is enjoying being here with us, don't you?"

Sylvia agreed and responded, "Honey, it is terrific just seeing the two of you together. Ellen is a joy to be around. I understand why you get along so well. The next couple of days will be fun for all of us."

Sylvia poked her head into the family room to announce, "The dessert is ready."

Ellen told Sylvia, "You cannot spoil me like this. The chef there does not cook as you do, and he has no desire to spoil us."

"Well, let me enjoy spoiling the two of you whenever you are here. At school, you are on your own."

Ellen knew she belonged after attending church with Laura and her parents, then enjoying a lovely dinner at an excellent restaurant.

The girls chipped in and cooked breakfast for everyone before they had to leave to return to school.

Ellen told Sylvia, Greg, and Laura, "This makes me feel like I have come home after a long time away. It truly is wonderful. Thank you all for the most enjoyable weekend I can remember. It is a fresh start."

They all hugged and kissed goodbye. Ellen felt like she had known all of them her entire life.

As they were driving, Laura spoke up first, saying, "Ellen, I am so glad you enjoyed the weekend as much as the rest of us did. It was wonderful having you at home with us; I hope we can do it again soon."

"I would love that, being with you and your parents came to seem like home to me. You are right, they are amazing, and I did say that to them. It is clear your dad is genuine, and his changes are permanent. He has become an incredible person. Becoming acquainted with him has made the memories of our first experience fade away as though it never happened."

Laura pulled into a parking lot, parked the car, and turned toward Ellen and asked, "We are graduating soon. Are you going home for summer break?"

"I haven't had a job this school year, so I am not in a position to go. Why do you ask?"

"Well, I wondered, if you will be here, would you consider staying with us for the summer? My parents would love for you to stay."

"I love you all for asking, but having another person around the house for the entire summer would be a huge imposition."

Laura told her it would not be an imposition, and it would be a fantastic experience for everyone. Laura agreed to ask them about it and promised she would tell her the truth. Ellen vowed to abide by their decision.

"Okay, I will call them when we get back. Mom packed lunch for us, so tell me when you get hungry."

"Well, since we have it with us," Ellen stated, "perhaps we should stop if we find some picnic tables. We would not want such a lovely lunch to spoil, would we?"

They stopped at the first picnic area they came to and enjoyed a fantastic homemade lunch, just like mom would make! Chatting nonstop made the time go by; they had both done their homework and were up to date on their assignments, so they had the evening to themselves.

"Laura, I am sorry, I have some laundry to do tonight, or I will have to do it during the week."

"Do not be sorry, we spent the entire weekend together; we both have things to do and we will talk tomorrow. Do you need to pick up anything before I drop you off at your dorm?"

Ellen was all set, so Laura dropped her off and drove to her dorm to get settled. It was incredible spending time together with Ellen and her parents. Everyone enjoyed themselves.

Laura called her mom as soon as she got into her room, to tell her about the conversation she had with Ellen, and ask, "Mom, what would you and Dad say about having Ellen stay with us for summer vacation? Would it be an imposition for either of you?"

Sylvia almost screamed to Greg, "Laura asked if we would mind having Ellen spend summer vacation here with us!"

Turning back to the phone, Sylvia said, "Laura, I must tell you, your father and I already discussed how much we would love to have her stay here for the summer. We did not want to get ahead of ourselves considering something which might never materialize. So, my dear daughter, the answer is a definite yes, from both of us. Hold on a minute; your dad wants to say a few words."

"Hi honey," Greg chimed in. "Your mom and I would love for Ellen to stay here. We already discussed the possibility of inviting her parents and brother to come for a while."

Laura responded, "I am so thrilled, Dad, I cannot get over what you just said. Ellen already told me she would abide by your decision when I asked her if she would like to stay with us. It would be so fabulous. But let's invite Ellen first. Then try to determine what her family can afford to do, and how proud they are. I would not want us to hurt their feelings, and I am sure you wouldn't either."

"We will be very cautious about asking her family to come for a visit. It will be so much fun having all of us together before the two of you start medical school in the fall. We must give some serious consideration to graduation for you and Ellen. Well, I will let you talk to your mom before you hang up. I love you, Laura, have a wonderful week. I'll call you when I return on Friday."

"Thank you, Dad, the weekend was wonderful. I loved every minute, and I am looking forward to much more."

"Your mom and I enjoyed it too."

"I am thrilled to hear the great news. You and Ellen will both be home for the summer! It will be such a perfect time."

"Thank you, Mom, for the incredible weekend and the picnic lunch. We enjoyed every bite, I assure you."

Sylvia assured her she would be in touch, expressed her love back, then hung up.

Chapter Fifteen

United

They were about to begin their first two-day trip! Jim Stacy had been working with his team for about fifteen years. He would be a tremendous help to reach the members on a personal level. They invited people of several ethnic groups, wanting to understand the effects of racism. Greg and his staff arrived in Alabama at 10:00 a.m. Jim Stacy greeted them as soon as they walked through his door for the first meeting.

"Greg, it is a pleasure to meet you and be a part of a significant step in addressing the racial tensions plaguing our nation for centuries."

"Thank you, Jim, for requesting this meeting and gathering the people to take part in this first discussion. It is a huge step forward in defining and understanding discrimination on a much deeper level. We will contribute today and set the stage for further discussions throughout the country."

"We've prepared a continental breakfast. Let's join our staff, and I'll introduce all of you."

Jim's staff consisted of white, black, Hispanic, and Asian individuals, both men and women.

"Jim, I am pleased you have quite a few people of various races; it is great to see."

"At present, we have an excellent mix of employees of many races and ethnic groups. We learn from each other about recipes, family beliefs, and then, racism and discrimination."

Everyone wanted to begin their meeting with the US Attorney General, so Jim proceeded with the introductions. "Welcome, everyone; we are all here today to meet our US Attorney General. Greg has a plan he thinks may be a significant help in bringing together people of all races, and he is eager to discuss it with us. So without further ado, I am pleased to present to you Greg Hastings, our US Attorney General."

"Thank you so much, Jim, for your introduction. My transformation proved to be such a shock to my system. I required some intensive therapy and got some much-needed rest at Hope Gardens. I believed I could change races and go on like nothing ever happened. Boy, was I wrong! It required a change and educational period for myself and my family. Can you imagine living the first half of your life white and the second half black? I came to meet with you today to enlist your help. I need some of you to enlighten me by sharing your experiences.

"Ask questions of the person sitting across from you about each other's lives, jobs, families, hopes, and dreams for the future. Please show respect for one another, be honest, and exercise empathy. Before we break into twos, are there any questions?"

Ruby asked, "So, Mr. US Attorney General, you've been a black man for about five minutes. What makes you an expert on racism? From what I understand, you grew up in a beautiful middle-class neighborhood with very loving parents. Now you come here and act like the Messiah, hell-bent on saving the world. What gives you that right?"

"I've never claimed to be the Messiah. However, what has happened to me is a privilege, to be fortunate enough to live the rest of my life as a black man. Together we can improve race relations, and I would like to try. Education could benefit us all. Now shall we try sitting down in pairs and talking to each other? Let's see what might happen."

They matched everyone in twos, making sure each was a different race, but the same sex. Jim had secured many small tables, which they arranged with two chairs to allow for private conversations.

Greg announced, "There is a list available on each table as a guideline, an icebreaker, nothing more. Please discuss your choices with each other as long as you show respect, honesty, and empathy. Let's take fifteen minutes for this first round."

The first session went well. People were laughing and talking about their work, families, their hopes and dreams for the future.

The majority responded, asking for another half hour. Greg granted their request. The staff was aware they had the entire day if they needed it. Everyone had cleared their calendars. Lunch would arrive at twelve thirty.

The meeting progressed as Greg had hoped. His matched partner, Akira, experienced discrimination since arriving from Japan. When he obtained a job, his fellow employees shunned him for years. It was an excruciating time for him. He was the only Asian employee and it made others uncomfortable.

As they neared the thirty-minute mark, Greg asked him, "So what did you gain from speaking with me today?"

"I realize you and I are more similar than we are different. We both have families, hopes, and dreams, and we could be exceptional friends. The only difference I see is our race. Thank you so much for sharing your life with me. Now tell me, what did you learn?"

"I've learned an impressive amount about you, and as you said, it had nothing to do with our racial differences. I have an excellent feeling about you that makes me wish to get to know you. Good luck with all of your hopes and dreams for the future. Thank you for sharing a small portion of your life with me."

The buzzer rang to signal the thirty-minute mark, and an echo of "Oh no," sounded throughout the room. Greg announced a ten minute break for coffee, restrooms, or to stretch their legs. There was a lot more to come.

"There will be ample opportunity for everyone to continue their conversations with their present partner and others. Jim and his staff have ordered lunch. We will break from twelve thirty to one thirty. Before we break, I have one question for all of you. Did you enjoy this exercise?"

A roar sounded, a definite YES!

"Ok, let's take a break."

After the break, people seemed more comfortable from the start. Conversations flowed. The results continued to amaze the staff.

During lunch, most people chose someone different to sit with, not with their original groups.

Both Greg and Jim took several pictures of the attendees for their progress scrapbooks and notes of essential details. Greg wondered if it would go as well in Louisiana. Perhaps it might continue across the country.

Greg announced, "Let's have an informal group discussion to get a sense of how we are doing. You can all remain where you are sitting. We would love you to share your feelings about your experience to this point, one person at a time, please. Participation is voluntary, so please do not feel pressured to speak. Let me start by asking, has today been anything like you expected it to be?"

Ruby spoke first, saying, "I would like to apologize to you, Greg, I was wrong in my assumption you came here to control the situation. I see now you have all of our best interests at heart. Today has been a fantastic experience for me. After meeting some lovely people, I found out once you get beyond our skin color, we are very similar. What a thrill it has been to have the chance to attend. I expected a day of preaching. A dear friend of mine convinced me to come. I am so glad I listened to her."

Greg thanked Ruby for her apology and her honesty regarding her experience, then asked, "Would someone else like to share their feelings about the day?"

A youthful man at a corner table raised his hand and began speaking when acknowledged.

"Hello, my name is Andrew. I thought white people all believed they were better than black people, so it was difficult for me to attend today. I always wanted to ask questions of a white person, today has given me the opportunity. I harbored so many preconceived ideas of what they were like; this experience has shown me they are just like me. They are no more responsible for their race than I am for mine.

"The people I spoke with today were all amiable and seemed honest. They have children, and work, and struggle, as my wife and I do. They may also be in about the same income bracket as we are. At this moment, I am not sure why I ever had a doubt, except for it being drilled into me since I was a child. This experience will stay with me for the rest of my life. It will encourage me to reach out and befriend people of unique races, to expand my horizons and those of my family. Thank you for this opportunity."

Both Greg and Jim spoke in response to Andrew's comments.

Jim spoke first. "Andrew, I am so happy taking part in this group has had such a positive effect on you. It is marvelous to know you see it as a motivator for you and your family. I hope you attempt to befriend people of races different from your own. You may develop some lifelong friendships. Thank you so much for sharing your feelings with us."

Greg responded with, "I am humbled by what you and others have said. We came together today to share our opinions and learn from each other. By discussing our lives, likes, and dislikes, with empathy and openness, but without judgment, violence, or arguing, this gathering has produced a fantastic outcome. I hope you are all as pleased as I am."

Amanda responded, "I enjoyed spending time with the first woman I met. It has been wonderful. Each of us sharing our photos, talking about our children and grandchildren; they are all beautiful. We even shared some cooking tips. I would love to stay in touch with her, our conversation was so enjoyable. We just might become friends."

Neil chimed in, "I learned a lot about farming from William, and shared my work in the law field. I am black, and he is white. Once we started talking, it did not matter. He is a respectful guy I could relate to, and we had a pleasant conversation."

Tonya added, "I enjoyed talking with Ursula. I am white, and she is Indian. We shared a particular recipe and talked about families and women's rights in the United States versus India. She found wonderful opportunities available to her here. It left me wanting to fight for the rights of others having less than we do. It's been a fantastic learning experience for both of us."

Frank spoke through sobs, saying, "Years ago I was the victim of racial discrimination. I am a black man. I've never gotten over it. I was carrying the pain and anguish all these years until today. I spoke with a white man named Edward, who is very kind. We discussed many things this morning, and I shared my memories with him. He apologized to me for what those men did to me so long ago and hugged me. There are no words to describe how much he helped me. The pain drained out of me, and I felt a sense of peace. I will forever be grateful to Edward and all of you for arranging this incredible meeting."

Jim said, "Frank, I am so happy you found the peace you so deserve. It took many years for you to find it. And having our US Attorney General and his staff come here today to bring us together. He told us he feels blessed to have the opportunity. I believe we are all blessed to know him and have the chance to share his miracle. Do you all agree?"

Everyone stood and clapped in agreement.

Jim continued, "I propose we meet here every month to continue getting acquainted with each other on a new, more direct, and honest level. Imagine what may develop as time goes on! We might change the way we look at and value one another. New relationships may develop, and life-long friendships may begin. Today is just the start. I will keep you all posted on dates and times, please make sure we have everyone's contact information. The day has come to a close."

Jim made the last announcement saying, "It has been our pleasure to spend this incredible day with all of you. We've learned and gained so much by being here today. We hope this will not be your only visit to our conference center. We are looking forward to having you join us for many other meetings. I will be in touch with everyone to keep you informed of our progress with future meeting dates and times. I hope you will carry memories of this day and the fantastic people you met here. Have an enjoyable evening."

It exhilarated Greg and the staff. Together, they had accomplished something no one believed possible, other than Greg. Even he could not be one hundred percent sure. He just thought it would work. It was already late afternoon when everyone shook hands, and Greg and his staff left for their hotel.

They proceeded to their rooms to freshen up and relax a bit before dinner. Greg called Sylvia to share the news.

"Hi honey, how are you doing?"

Sylvia had been waiting for Greg's call. She responded, "I want to hear about your day, how did it go?"

"Sylvia, it was incredible! I wish you had been here. It worked! Everyone cooperated, got along well, and are looking forward to the next meeting. I am sure some people exchanged contact information and are now open to learning more about each other's traditions, cultures, and even recipes. It is so heartwarming to witness all of this unfold. It was a dream come true for a lot of guests today. They are planning to meet regularly and continue their dialogue with each other. I would imagine when word gets out, more people will attend."

Sylvia cried as she told Greg, "I am so happy for you and all the people who took part in today's exercise. I hope and pray it goes as well tomorrow in Louisiana."

"Please call Laura for me? I want to talk to her, but I won't have time now, and she will be impatient to hear."

Sylvia happily agreed to call Laura to share what Greg had just told her. Greg thanked her, and they hung up. Greg was thrilled with the outcome; even Ruby came around.

There was a lovely quiet restaurant close to their hotel, which enabled them to walk to dinner. They discussed their feelings about the day. Everyone agreed: you had to experience it.

Janice spoke up. "Even a video would not portray the events as they unfolded today. It was indescribable. Thank you for inviting me to attend. I've never experienced the total sense of accomplishment of today. Can I continue working with all of you on this amazing project?"

Greg agreed they should all remain involved from now on and see it through together.

Martin added, "Greg, I enjoyed being with all of you today. The results are beyond my wildest dreams. I am eager to get back to my staff to schedule our group meeting. You gave me an incredible form to follow, and I cannot wait to get going. With that said, I'll fly back home in the morning. My staff will be excited as soon as I share the news with them. Thank you so much for allowing me to accompany you today. I learned an impressive amount from all of you."

Martin thanked everyone and continued to enjoy his meal.

Greg requested a taxi to drive everyone back to their hotel; they had an early wake-up call for their flight to Louisiana in the morning. Martin changed his reservation but would ride with them in the morning, giving everyone a chance to say goodbye before boarding their respective planes.

* * *

They arrived in Louisiana, hoping the next meeting would proceed as the one in Alabama had. The limo driver met them at the baggage claim area, holding up a sign which read, "Racism is so yesterday!" They all loved it and laughed as they approached him. He explained that Bob Richards asked him to make up a catchy slogan for his sign, so he did.

Approaching the conference center, Greg noticed some items requiring attention. Especially the siding and windows. Greg would discuss the maintenance items with Bob Richards. It would be nice to have them repaired before their membership increased.

Bob and his staff greeted them with smiles and very grateful attitudes. Jim briefed Bob and shared the delightful news regarding the success of the previous meeting. Bob hoped theirs would be as successful as Jim and his team's.

They would follow Jim's schedule for the day, beginning with a continental breakfast.

The guests arrived at ten o'clock as specified, which gave them two hours before lunch. They began with coffee, pastry, and a brief conversation.

Bob opened the meeting introducing Greg, who explained why they were there and what they all hoped to accomplish. He further discussed their meeting the day before in Alabama and how enlightening it had been. Somehow it seemed to bring a sense of comfort to the listeners, knowing they were not the first group.

The staff quickly matched all of the attendees. Greg sat with Henry, who was Navajo. Since he had fallen in love with Louisiana, remaining there had become a serious consideration. Although he had become an attorney, he faced racism during his college years because of his American Indian heritage. Henry still bore the scars of the limitations it put on his career choices. He told Greg he could not even begin to compete with his story of changing races. The two men got along exceptionally well and promised to stay in touch.

Alan paired with an older black man named Claude, who, until then, had been a bitter man. Alan asked him a lot of questions about his life, occupation, children, and his likes and dislikes. He softened a bit. Claude answered Alan's inquiries, then addressed Alan with his own, asking about Alan's life. Alan replied, then Claude came up with more, and they were having a discussion. He told Alan he had no white friends; he had derived his opinions from others' experiences. It may not have been fair at all, according to Claude, who was realizing Alan might be an okay guy. Alan smiled and told him he was an excellent person. Claude laughed, which Alan loved to see.

As soon as the break ended, Greg announced, "It is time for us to change partners and get acquainted with someone new."

A young white woman named Lucille responded, "I just had the most fantastic experience speaking with Tonya. She is from Syria; she speaks in broken English but clear enough for me to understand every word she said. Tonya cried as she described how happy they were the day they arrived here in America. We shared pictures of our kids and talked about our childhoods, which, even though they were worlds apart, were not so different. We discussed the schools we attended. As we spoke, the differences between us seemed to disappear, and we were two mothers examining our lives and families. Tonya is a lovely lady; I hope I can get to know her. Thank you for this opportunity."

Bob thanked her for sharing and asked if anyone else would like to speak.

A young black man named John stood up and offered this: "A Latino gentleman named Jose and I shared details of our lives this afternoon and learned about each other. Imagine, he and his wife met the same way my wife and I did, at the library studying for final exams in our senior year of high school. How is that for a coincidence? Now add the fact he and I both became dentists, and our wives are lawyers. It has been an enjoyable experience for all of us to attend your program. Thank you for opening our eyes and our hearts; you've enriched our lives so much more than you can imagine."

Next, a middle-aged black man named James stood up and asked to share his incredible experience with a white man known as Steven. "After discussing many commonalities between us, I shared my experience with him. My earlier years were harrowing due to my parents being extremely unforgiving. They carried the stories of their ancestors to an extreme degree. They stated they hated all white people because of what they heard their ancestors had experienced. Yet they had never gotten to know anyone that was white. They forbade me to form friendships with anyone that was white while I was growing up. For fear of being repeatedly punished as a child, I agreed not to associate with anyone that wasn't black. I tried to be loyal to them, despite the fact I met a lot of nice white kids when I was in school.

"Steven told me he was sorry that I was forbidden to associate with white people. It was regrettable that my parents were so unyielding in their beliefs. Steven understood what can happen when we are told stories from the past and not allowed to judge for ourselves and make our own decisions. Perhaps it is not too late for us to become friends. We got along so well and seemed to have so much in common. We are going to stay in touch and introduce our families to one another. He also told me he is very sorry that my parents have already passed away. We might have been able to enlighten them today."

Greg stood up with tearful eyes, said, "I would like to thank you, John and James, for sharing your stories with all of us today. We hoped this program would be successful in opening the eyes and hearts of many people here today, and you just confirmed it for us. Since my transformation, I had a dream that we would improve racial relations through honesty and empathy. We possess the opportunity to accomplish our goal and enrich the lives of people everywhere. I hope you and Jose, along with your wives, become friends; you already have so much in common. Let's take a break and stretch our legs for fifteen minutes before we move on."

Bob told Greg, "I am in shock with all the remarkable things we've heard here today. What a great outcome! I, like Jim, will schedule these meetings once a month to keep the communication going. It should not be difficult; we will follow the script we used today and see what happens. It will not be for everyone, but attendance may be excellent. These people will tell their friends and families about their experience here today, and others may also want to join."

Greg asked, "Bob, from what you have seen today, do you think we can be successful in organizing this program in ethnic groups across the country? Would you be interested in supervising half of the locations if Jim will do the same with the other half? I am asking for the sake of time constraints. It will take at least two years to attend and organize every startup meeting necessary across the country. I want to see this program up and running a lot sooner. We must get it moving as fast as possible. Please talk to Jim. I will also speak to him to get his thoughts. Then we will talk again.

"By the way, I observed the need for some exterior work on your building. Were you able to put the figures into your budget for approval?"

"I wasn't able to add exterior repairs to our operating budget; I had to put it off."

"Please get me three reliable quotes for all the work needed. I will see what I can do to assist you in obtaining approval."

Bob thanked Greg. He did not realize he could request additional funding for their location. It would be a shot in the arm for the area for them to make the necessary repairs to update their conference center.

After the break, Bob announced, "We are coming to the end of our day. Before that time comes, we would like to conduct an informal group discussion. Before we begin, I have another announcement. We want to offer these meetings once a month to everyone interested in attending. Let's keep the momentum going and not regress. All we ask is that you confirm you are attending to give us a total count for each meeting. Please provide us with your contact information if you are interested in returning. We will contact you regarding dates and times. Please arrange your chairs in a large circle so you can see everyone."

As the meeting drew to a close, Bob announced, "We would all like to thank Greg, Alan, and Janice for coming here to be with us today to improve racial relations in Louisiana. We are all forever grateful to you for coming."

Everyone clapped and cheered.

They had completed a fantastic first meeting. Everyone was ecstatic considering the many future conferences they expected to hold there in the conference center. Bob wondered what would develop once the press became aware of their program.

They talked for a while before Greg's team left for the airport. Bob and his staff felt assured they could establish programs with Bob and Jim conducting their training, then continuing to oversee their progress.

Greg told them, "We are pleased with the way everything concluded today; it exceeded our hopes as I think it did yours. Thank you for the work you and your staff did to bring this together. Please send me those quotes as soon as you receive them. I will submit them and get back to you with an answer."

They all shook hands as Bob and his staff walked out to their taxi.

Chapter Sixteen

Meetings

The outcome was the best Greg could have imagined, and it was only two states; there were so many more to contact. Janice, too, would be a fantastic asset from now on with all of their future programs.

Greg wondered how much time Jim and Bob would need to contact the directors of all the remaining ethnic groups. Then schedule dates for each group to hold their meetings. Within a few short months, all the groups might have their meetings scheduled or already concluded.

Greg and Alan entered the conference room to report their progress to the staff. Janice joined them before anyone else arrived.

She announced, "I hope you don't mind Greg, but I recorded both of the sessions in Alabama and Louisiana. I thought you might need them. I meant to tell you, but we got busy. I want to give you these tapes."

Greg and Alan stared at Janice, then Greg responded, "Janice, I cannot believe you did this. What a brilliant idea! They will be helpful as we put together the training for the remaining groups. I never gave recordings a thought; this is a win-win situation. Now we will not need to rely on memory. Thank you, Janice, for thinking ahead."

Janice thought Greg would be furious with her. Instead, Greg and Alan were both most appreciative.

They reported the success of both programs to the staff, stated some essential details, then summed it up with, "We are ecstatic with the progress we made in the last few days."

Greg said, "I spoke to Bob Richards after their meeting in Louisiana. I asked him if he would be willing to be a supervisor and trainer for one half of the remaining locations if Jim agreed to do the same with the other half. If they agree, Bob and Jim will both come to our offices for training. After which, they'll hire additional staff to travel with them and assist as we have all done together. We are awaiting their response. It would enable us to have designated locations up and operating within a few months rather than two years to organize all of them ourselves."

Everyone loved the idea! It would save time, bringing Bob Richards and Jim Stacy to the office to train for two days. It would ensure their readiness to guide the other directors as they prepared to hold their first meetings.

Greg, Alan, and Janice were ready to sit with Cindy, the clerical director, to review every step they took for each meeting to enable her and her staff to write all of it into the program directions. Greg used the recordings as a guideline.

"Cindy, do you have any idea how long it will take you to dissect our information and produce the guidelines for every group in the US to follow?"

Cindy considered it for a minute and answered, "I believe I can do it in about two weeks, a maximum of three weeks. If you can give me your undivided attention for two days, we may do it sooner. We must be sure our finished product is easy enough for everyone to follow."

"That sounds terrific, Cindy; we can be ready to meet with you on Monday morning. Can you be ready that soon?"

Cindy told them she could and suggested ten on Monday. Everyone agreed.

Before their Monday morning meeting, Greg, Alan, and Janice met to discuss their strategy for organizing the information to share with Cindy. They had Janice's tapes to follow, which would allow them to fill in the blanks. They would meet on Monday at eight to review the recordings before Cindy joined them.

* * *

129

Greg pulled into the garage and saw Sylvia's car; it made his heart smile, knowing she was already home.

Sylvia asked how he was doing.

"I am fine now. Let's go out for dinner; we can go casual if you like."

"I thought of saying no, but it sounds good not having to shower or get changed. If you are ready, we can go. Then come home and relax. Maybe watch a movie and have popcorn."

They drove to Hot Chocolate. Only Laura was missing; they had an idea she and Ellen might be eating at their favorite pizza restaurant.

After dinner, they relaxed and watched a movie while enjoying homemade popcorn. It had been a crazy, busy week. It was nice to be home with no place else to go.

* * *

"I hope you all realize how amazing this is for the entire country. If this progress continues throughout the other groups, we will be on our way to making some lasting changes in racial disparity. It was thrilling to hear the remarks made by the attendees regarding their experiences. Their discoveries about one another were terrific. We are all quite the same other than our skin color.

"Speaking with empathy while removing anger and resentment from the equation made a tremendous difference. There was an impressive amount of talking, laughing, and sharing of family pictures while discussing their hopes and dreams for the future. We are hoping the directors from Alabama and Louisiana will oversee this project. We will all go to some areas to assist, but we are hoping they will be successful on their own."

Greg added, "We will adjourn the meeting at this point to allow us time to design the guidelines with Cindy. We will keep you all informed regarding our progress."

After the staff meeting, Greg, Alan, and Janice remained in the conference room to review the tapes. Janice did a brilliant job capturing vocal portions of the sessions. The directions given to the groups were audible, which would make them easy to adapt to written instructions. Janice outdid herself this time; even she had not realized how critical the recordings would be in designing the instructions for setting up the group meetings. Greg told her he did not know how much time she had saved them, but it was substantial.

Cindy arrived and asked if they had all reviewed the recordings, and would they be helpful?

"Cindy, we have all reviewed them and concur, everything that transpired regarding directions at those meetings is on these tapes. We have nothing to add. I am not trying to downplay your job in this, but it will be easier than it would have been without the tapes. Alan had five more copies made, just if you want someone else to assist you in putting this together. We will keep two copies in the vault."

"Please play a little from the first one for me so we can all listen and comment."

Alan started the first tape. As the recording played, it brought the three of them back to Alabama. It enabled everyone to picture what happened as they listened to the voices. They did not realize Janice had also added some recordings of herself, asking people what they thought about the day's happenings during the lunch break. She got some lovely comments from attendees. It was great info for them to keep in their files. Cindy would transcribe their conversations and present them to Greg when completed. They listened for about an hour, then Cindy shut off the recorder.

"Enough, I've heard enough; this is fabulous. All of it is crystal clear. I will not have a problem organizing the directions, which will be easy to follow. I want to handle this project myself. If I run into trouble, I will ask one of my staff to assist, but I do not foresee a problem. Thank you, Janice, for doing such a fantastic job with the recordings. You captured everything right down to the mini-interviews you conducted during lunch breaks. Please give me two weeks, but I may finish sooner. I will inform you as to my progress. It will be a pleasure handling this for you, realizing how important it is. Thank you."

Greg and Alan thanked Cindy for accepting the challenge of single-handedly creating their program. They much appreciated her desire to see it through herself. It would make an enormous difference having Cindy be the lone transcriber and designer of the program. She took the information to her office to begin designing their program.

Greg turned to Janice and said, "I do not have the words to thank you for the extra time you spent, and the creativity involved in capturing these recordings. You even recorded conversations during lunch; how did you ever consider doing that?"

"We played around a little with recordings in the past, with music, and audiences. So, I used my experience and what common sense told me you might need, and the tapes are the result. It was enjoyable coming up with what I imagined might help you and Alan to be more creative."

Greg stated, "Well, Janice, there is enough information here to enable Cindy to design the programs with minimal difficulty. Your extra work has saved us all an impressive amount of time. I will not forget your extraordinary performance at your scheduled review. We all appreciate your additional efforts."

Cindy made several trips to Greg's office for clarification for her program design. Then, she got it and she didn't stop. Not only did Cindy put everything together, she enjoyed every minute. She loved working with the minority programs, and it showed. Her excitement became contagious!

Greg called both of the managers to inform them of the progress with the plans. He questioned whether they could travel to DC within the next couple of weeks. It was the most significant thing they had tackled since Greg's DNA transformation.

Within a week, Cindy requested to meet with Greg, Alan, and Janice to review the program plans for all ethnic groups. It astonished them to receive her request. Did they dare hope she had completed them? It seemed too soon to be real; they all showed up early as requested.

Cindy arrived on time, bringing stacks of paper. Without saying a word, she entered the conference room, spread all of her documents in front of her, organized them, and sat down.

She looked at the three anxious faces and addressed Greg, saying, "We are ready to go, as long as you agree with how I organized and designed the program. You all provided me with so much information it almost designed itself."

Cindy passed packets to all three of them, sat, and waited while they looked over their information. She observed their faces, one by one, as they smiled, and the smiles became broader. Then they responded aloud, almost in unison, "Yes!" They loved it!

"This is fantastic," Greg replied. "It is amazing to see this all come together. I, for one, did not expect you to complete it so fast. It is like déjà vu. I cannot wait to get started and experience the feedback; it will be amazing. Thank you so much, Cindy! It's perfect."

"You cannot imagine how thrilled I am to be a part of this great program. It will have a tremendous impact in every area it touches. Thank you for allowing me to do this; it has been a pleasure to design. If I can help, please ask."

Greg announced, "I will call Jim and Bob this morning and schedule their orientations as soon as possible. Cindy, if you agree, it would be appropriate for you and Janice to conduct their training. You can work on it with Janice since you possess extensive training experience. I am sure she will be a tremendous asset to us all."

Cindy loved the idea. "I am sure we can work well together. Janice, why don't we go to my office and start working on our training plan right away?"

Alan and Greg sat shaking their heads. The Minority Program design had come together so fast it took them by surprise. Greg called Jim and Bob to request they come to DC on Wednesday and Thursday of that week. Greg noted the excitement in their voices.

"We are happy you will both be overseeing the groups. It will enable us to move ahead much more quickly. Cindy's design of the programs is impressive. Without a doubt, it should be almost foolproof to institute. We might have several of the locations up and running within a month. As soon as everyone has gotten comfortable with the setups, they should move along quickly. I will hang up now and see you on Wednesday morning. Let me try to switch you over to Cindy. If she is not available, please leave a message, and she will get right back to you."

Greg moved on to several other issues already in progress. He always loved his work, but these days, even more. He knew he was making a difference.

Their day arrived. Bob and Jim were ecstatic to be leading the way by overseeing the entire operation of established minority conference centers. They would divide the minority groups in half, each managing one half of the selected teams and taking them through the new program setup. It would be a tremendous amount of work for both of them, but they were determined to complete their assignment.

Greg called the meeting to order and turned it over to Cindy. She began her explanation of the specific details on how the groups would form and run from the point of inception. It would leave nothing to chance.

Cindy announced, "We are dealing with people's lives here. Racial issues and disagreements have caused enough pain. Now, if you will bear with me, I will go over the plan step by step and explain the reason for everything we do. I would also like to share with you, Janice recorded everything that transpired at both meetings. It provided us with information we needed to design the new program; we all owe her a debt of gratitude."

The next couple of days encompassed a whirlwind for Jim, Bob, Cindy, and Janice. Meetings, directions, sample programs, discussions, and more discussions, until Jim and Bob had memorized every step and became comfortable setting up every appointment required, and organizing the entire program from start to finish. Everyone felt confident about its success. Cindy also designed the notification letter and package for every director in the circuit.

The team enjoyed dinner together before Bob and Jim left to return home. It was the staff's way of saying, "Thank you for everything."

Greg reminded Bob to get the quotes together for the repairs to the conference center as soon as possible.

"It would be nice for all the locations to be looking good as their membership increased," Greg told him.

"I hope everyone is ready. Cindy and Janice will send out packages to all of our directors tomorrow. It will inform them which of you will supervise their training and their first meeting, then supervise their program from then on. Please keep in touch with Cindy every step of the way."

After assurances and handshakes, and two hugs and kisses, Bob and Jim returned to their hotel. They would both be returning home early the next morning.

Cindy and Janice sent all the packets to the program directors on Monday morning. They worked through the weekend to accomplish the incredible feat. Their desire to get them in the mail surpassed any amount of fatigue they experienced. This project was innovative; it drove them to finish.

Within two days, Cindy, Jim, and Bob began receiving calls. The callers were bursting with excitement over what they had read in their packets. It was something they dreamed of but never believed would happen. Cindy included every detail, leaving nothing to chance. Still, the directors wanted to speak to her, Bob, or Jim. They needed to hear it for themselves. Most of them called Bob or Jim, asking that they tell them more about their experiences with their first meetings. What did it feel like to bring people of unique races together for an honest conversation without anger or violence?

They wanted to understand how difficult it was to organize a get-together such as this. Could everyone handle it without Greg? Bob and Jim told them they had spent a tremendous amount of time in Washington, DC, training for this and assured the directors they could do it.

Bob and Jim spent a lot of time on the phone. They had organized a schedule of dates for every meeting. A special request arrived for Greg and his staff to attend one meeting in Kansas City, Kansas, and another in Raleigh, North Carolina.

They were breathless when the last call ended. Everyone raced to finish, wanting to achieve the fantastic results which would reach every state. They visualized it as an enormous wave going from state to state until it covered the entire country.

Greg, Alan, Janice, and Cindy gathered in the conference room to share their thoughts. Things were coming together at a fantastic rate.

"I cannot fathom that our plan has come together and received such a speedy and joyous response. You are all about as excited as I am. Now I can call the president and inform him of our progress to date.

"I want to schedule our trips to Kansas City and Raleigh by the end of the month if everyone is available to do so. I realize Jim and Bob are planning theirs as soon as they can. Our visits will generate even more feedback from the press and instill more hope as other cities await their meetings. Thank you, everyone, for the tremendous efforts you put forth to make this project such an incredible success."

Sylvia arranged for a surprise lunch delivery for the entire office to thank the staff for all their extra work for Greg. Greg smiled. Sylvia showed her thoughtfulness to everyone.

Greg slipped into his office to call the president to share their progress to date. It shocked him. Never did he expect they would have gotten so far this soon.

"Greg, I knew you had a magnificent idea, but I would never have imagined this response. Knowing you already trained two directors to conduct these meetings across the country is just beyond our wildest hopes. Thank you so much for calling me today with this splendid news. Do you have a rough idea when you will conclude the meetings?"

"We are hoping they can accomplish it within the next six months if everything moves along as it has so far. My staff and I will do two more states ourselves at their directors' request. We conducted two from which I chose the directors to oversee this project. Jim Stacy and Bob Richards committed to conducting three meetings each week. It will be a tight schedule for quite a while. They will complete this project as soon as possible to bring the entire country up to speed. We hope once the initial meetings have taken place at all group locations, the attendees will invite their friends. Then more people may want to attend. It will not solve all the racial issues, but it will be a great beginning. Also, I would imagine the press will carry stories in their newspapers, which will help."

"Thank you, Greg, I have the utmost faith in you and your staff, and I trust you will conclude this project with the greatest respect and consideration possible. I appreciate all of your efforts. We will talk soon."

Greg sat for a moment, reflecting on their conversation, then returned to the conference room for lunch.

Everyone present for lunch had contributed to the project's success. The entire staff had a sense of accomplishing something phenomenal. Such a simple idea had a powerful impact. Enlist honesty and empathy while removing anger and violence, enabling genuine conversation, conducted with total respect and consideration.

* * *

A few months later, Greg's phone rang very early one morning. It was Jim Stacy telling him both he and Bob Richards had completed their last group meeting the day before. It delighted him to learn they had finished earlier than expected.

"This is the best news ever. I realize how much effort you both put forth to complete the project."

"Bob and I are grateful you chose us to oversee this training. It was intense and exhausting, but also rewarding, tender, and dear to us both. The memories will always remain deep within my heart. You enabled me to contribute in this area. I could not be happier. You allowed me to help to repair racial relations within the United States. The feedback has been heartfelt. We will schedule activities and field trips to enable everyone to take part together and become acquainted with each other. We videotaped every session; I will send copies to you on Monday."

"Jim, I cannot wait to share your news with the rest of the staff. Everyone has become involved in this project and has been cheering you on from a distance. You deserve a few days off if you can take them. I will speak to you next week. Enjoy the weekend."

Greg asked Cindy, Alan, and Janice to come into his office. They had all been sitting on the edge of their seats awaiting news on the project.

Greg announced, "Jim and Bob concluded their final meetings yesterday. Jim stated it was phenomenal! The groups are planning to meet monthly to keep things going. They will be scheduling events, field trips, etcetera, to allow them to become acquainted on a more personal level. Is that splendid news or what?"

They were so excited it brought them all to tears. They put their hearts and souls into the project to achieve a terrific outcome. Greg could call the president and report on the final meeting to enable him to alert the press.

Chapter Seventeen

Press Conference

"Hello Mr. President, I want to inform you the last of the minority group meetings took place yesterday, with phenomenal results. No negative issues of any kind, with all groups reporting they will meet every month. Many of the attendees will bring friends and family to meetings and on trips to become better acquainted."

"Greg, I am thrilled for everyone concerned, I am sure this approach has already gone far to heal some damage and division. I cannot find the words to express how grateful we all are to you for bringing the project to this point. I will schedule a press conference today. Please ensure the staff who worked with you on this project, along with the two directors and yourself, are present. Thank you, Greg."

"You are welcome, Mr. President; I too am thrilled. Please inform us as soon as you have a date for the press conference."

"You will receive ample notice regarding the date and time of the press conference. It is important for everyone involved to attend."

Greg could hardly speak. As soon as he and the president concluded their call, he informed the staff they would attend a press conference with the president soon. The excitement was incredible.

Greg called Jim Stacy and Bob Richards to inform them there would be a press conference within the next week. They would receive enough notice to book their flights to DC and back. He reminded them once the press conference took place, they might need to hire more staff. They had both gone above and beyond to complete their assigned meetings, besides keeping their centers operating. "Exceptional work, we will not forget it."

He wandered out to the kitchen and found Alan at the coffee pot. Alan smiled when he saw Greg and said, "Greg, I am still shaking my head, unable to absorb everything that happened, just the way you planned. I am so proud to be working with you on this fantastic project. You never underestimated the response of the people, did you?"

"I never expected it to this degree. I am thrilled beyond my wildest dreams. What an excellent response. It proves underneath it all we are so much alike, no matter what our race or nationality."

Alan just stood and smiled at Greg, remarking, "Well, Greg, it just took a simple change to your DNA!"

They both laughed until tears streamed down their faces; they could not stop themselves.

Greg said, "As Sylvia and Laura always say, you just cannot make this stuff up."

That statement caused the men to laugh even harder!

* * *

Everyone in the house needed a break to relax and unwind. They had no schedule to follow, just pure relaxation for the duration of the weekend. The girls would be home at three o'clock on Friday and stay until Sunday afternoon, which would be fun. Ellen felt so comfortable it seemed like she had always stayed with them, and everyone loved having her there.

Sylvia continued to put fresh flowers in the girls' rooms before they arrived, which they both loved.

Ellen suddenly noticed the garden and the butterflies. She ran to Laura's room and asked her, "What do you see?"

Butterflies flitted from flower to flower. The benches were in random spots where they could sit and gaze at the view. Henry had even put in a lovely fishpond with water lilies and butterflies flying around them.

Their reactions were worth so much more as a surprise. Greg and Sylvia were ready for their responses as the girls discovered the gardens.

Sylvia and Greg videotaped the entire experience for the girls with two video cameras. Sylvia hid in the hallway upstairs and Greg outside. So between them, they got it all on video.

Then they both joined Laura and Ellen in the garden. It delighted the girls they loved the garden. Everyone sat and enjoyed the butterflies. What a beautiful sight!

After dinner, Greg and Sylvia showed the girls the videos they made while the girls were discovering the garden. They all laughed; it was endearing.

Another Scrabble night. No one could keep up with Ellen. She won every game, then served the coffee and dessert. They all sat around the kitchen table and talked for two hours.

"I feel so much a part of this family. I have grown to love all of you so much. I cannot imagine any of you not being a part of my life forever."

They all spoke at once, saying, "We all feel the same way about you. We will all be part of each other's lives forever. We are family!"

Everyone laughed at the statement.

Ellen asked everyone, "So tomorrow is Saturday, are we attending church together this week?"

Greg answered, "We are, don't families attend church together?"

Sylvia chimed in, "Ellen, we love having you girls here as much as possible, and we want all of us to attend church together as often as it can happen. Occasionally, you may want to make other plans when you are here at home that may not include us. We would understand, and it would be acceptable. Please, don't either of you feel guilty if you find you would like to do something alone."

Ellen thanked both of them for being so understanding and direct, but wanted them to know she had no desire to set out on her own. She loved being with the family.

Laura woke up very early as usual on Saturday morning and smelled the coffee; she couldn't imagine who was in the kitchen. As she rounded the corner, she saw Ellen getting ready to prepare breakfast for everyone. She smiled and said, "Good morning Ellen, what got you up so early this morning?"

Ellen looked a little embarrassed as she replied, "I just woke up and wanted to surprise all of you since either you or your mom always starts it first. I want to do my part, too; I am no longer a guest."

Laura laughed and told her, "You are family now so you can help. Let me take care of the table. I enjoy doing even simple chores with you; I feel as though you are my sister now. Please don't misunderstand this, it worked out well. You look like our father, and I look like our mother."

The girls laughed until they cried, then hugged each other in agreement.

At that moment, Sylvia and Greg walked into the kitchen, wondering what brought on all the laughter. Ellen had to share with them what Laura just told her, and they loved it. It felt very appropriate.

Greg and the family had another fantastic weekend. It felt as though Ellen had become their second daughter. They were blessed!

Chapter Eighteen

Request

Greg wondered what he would find when he arrived at the office. Perhaps more news from some of the ethnic groups. They were finally moving forward. He hoped they would continue at the present rate and soon change the racial standoff.

When Greg arrived, Alan looked as though he would burst with news about something! Greg waved him into his office and asked if something had happened.

Alan could not stop smiling as he announced, "Greg, I have the most important news to share with you! Jim and Bob each received almost two hundred requests over the weekend from people wanting to come to their next meeting. People hear about meetings from friends, relatives, and coworkers, and will want to experience it for themselves."

Greg sat for a few moments staring at Alan.

"Alan, I am thrilled, I did not expect it to happen this way, or so soon. Let's get a pot of coffee in here, then send for Janice and Cindy, and tell them the excellent news."

The coffee arrived within a few minutes, as Greg picked up the phone and called Janice and Cindy. He requested their presence immediately in his office.

They arrived within two minutes, wondering why the rush. Greg motioned to them to get some coffee and sit down; they had something to share. Since Alan received the call from Jim, he asked him to tell them the news.

"I received a call this morning from Jim Stacy. He and Bob each received about two hundred calls this past weekend with requests from new people to attend their next meeting. The calls came from family members, friends, and coworkers. That number is not including the many requests the other groups received. Jim said he would get back to me when they receive the remaining teams' totals after their offices open."

Cindy added, "Imagine how large the total number could be when all the chapters report! These results are beyond phenomenal! We still have a press conference. Imagine the number of extra members we will gain after that!" Cindy looked over at Greg and said, "Greg, I am speaking for all of us when I say we are so thrilled for you. It was your idea. You believed it would happen, and now it is becoming a reality."

"I am thrilled for all ethnic groups and every citizen. I am also happy we all accomplished this together; every one of us at this table played an intricate part in this wonderful project, and we've just begun."

Greg received a call from the president telling him the press conference would be in two days. He asked him to make sure everyone who played any role in their project would be in attendance. Greg assured him everyone would be there.

He turned to his group and said, "Well, it is now official. The press conference will be an amazing event for everyone! Thank you all sincerely. You had faith in me and our project and gave it everything you had, and it paid off."

It surprised Jim to hear from Greg so soon after speaking with Alan earlier in the morning.

"Good morning Greg, how are you? I spoke to Alan this morning to share the delightful news, but I do not have any further news if that is why you are calling."

"No, I am calling to inform you the president has scheduled a press conference for Thursday at 10:00 a.m. Please call Cindy to make your reservation right away, and if possible, plan to arrive tomorrow evening and stay overnight. You should try to prepare as much as possible for a vast number of new contacts after the press conference. You may want to bring in some extra people to answer the phones and share information regarding your meeting dates, etcetera. Imagine what this will do for racial relations!"

"Greg, you are right. I guess we did not consider it in those terms as we were laying out our plans. Then it was hope. Now it is becoming a reality, and it is tremendous. I could not be happier; everyone I know is talking about it, favorably. It is about time we come together as people no longer divided by our races. It is so heartwarming. Once again, Greg, thank you for including me in training. It's been an incredible labor of love. I can only hope and pray we will live to see the day when racial issues become a thing of the past."

"Don't lose faith, Jim, the day is coming. Hopefully, sooner than we expect," Greg responded.

"We met so many pleasant people who shared their hearts and souls with us during the last few weeks of our training. They've always been there. They just needed to trust others and their feelings, allowing themselves the liberty of showing what they had inside."

Greg and Jim, being busy, concluded their conversation. Greg assured Jim he would call Bob before they hung up.

Greg called Bob and repeated what he had shared with Jim. Bob assured him he would arrive the following night and be ready for the press conference on Thursday morning.

Chapter Nineteen

For Laura

"**D**ad, have you considered coming to my school for the presentation we talked about two months ago? I realize you are in the middle of many other items, but I would love to tell them you will come."

"Yes, please tell your professor we will be there. Let me know as soon as you hear when they would like to schedule their program. Also, what type of slant would enable the students to gain the most. Then I will put something together."

Laura thanked Greg, and they hung up.

Laura's professor was ecstatic knowing the US Attorney General would come to their university to share his story with them. Especially knowing their university would be the only one he planned to visit. Mrs. Jamison would inform her supervisors and get back to her with a date and more precise information on the defined subject for discussion.

Professor Jamison called back almost immediately, saying, "Laura, as soon as I informed the school president, he said he would love to have your dad come to our school. It would be best if he tells his story his way, and plans a program that would be the most beneficial for our students and staff. We can schedule a date for three weeks from now. If we push, everyone can be on board by then. I am thrilled you suggested it."

"Mrs. Jamison, I am happy we could put it together."

Mrs. Jamison thanked her and said she would be in touch.

Greg couldn't say no to taking part in a program at Laura's university. He could share an impressive amount of information with the students, then conduct an actual program demonstration encouraging them to communicate with each other. It would be a fantastic opportunity for Laura and Ellen, too, just before graduation.

* * *

Their press conference drew the highest attendance in history. A tremendous number of people arrived, attempting to fit into the chosen area. Expecting a significant turnout, the president had enormous video screens installed on the exterior of the building to enable everyone to see and hear the entire presentation. It was a beautiful sunny day, which encouraged a more massive crowd than they had anticipated. The mood was elation amongst everyone in attendance. All they knew was the president wanted to speak to them regarding positive progress in racial relations within the United States.

President Mitchell appeared to be happier than anyone had ever seen him.

"Ladies and gentlemen, it gives me the greatest pleasure to announce to you this morning that our US Attorney General, Greg Hastings, came to me with an idea a few months ago. A plan to bring people of all races together to hold informal meetings at ethnic group conference centers across the country. There they would discuss the similarities between people beyond the color of their skin. Knowing if people came together with empathy and honesty while removing violence and arguing, they would discover they had much more in common than they realized. I trusted him and gave my approval. Now I would like to turn this meeting over to Greg Hastings himself."

"Good morning, everyone! My staff and I are pleased to be here with you on this memorable day. We want to share the results of our incredible journey. As most of you know, I experienced a complete transformation from being a white man to becoming a black man. As I progressed through my change, I visualized people of all ethnic backgrounds coming together. I believed if people of various races could become acquainted personally, they would find many similarities. The only contrast was their skin color. It appears many of these people may become friends.

"Many people who admit to having discriminated against another person, also state they did not meet anyone of another race when they were growing up that influenced them. They gained most of their preconceived opinions from others. It wasn't from their firsthand experience. When they began talking to each other, they realized just how similar their lives were with their careers, marriages, and children, and their hopes and dreams for the future, for themselves and their families.

"I would now like to introduce you to our brilliant staff. First is my assistant, Alan Harrington. Alan is my right hand. He has been by my side and supportive of me since the first day we met many years ago. He has helped to get me through my transformation and the changes that followed. I would not be here today had it not been for this man's support, encouragement, love, and help to myself, my wife, and daughter. Alan is incredible! He volunteered to create and develop this ethnic program with me. Thank you, Alan, I will always be grateful for you.

"Next is our assistant Janice Carter. She is a relative newcomer to the Attorney General's office. Alan suggested she do some work for me on this project. She did a fantastic job and has been beside us every step of the way. Janice's initiative aided us in putting this project together.

"Many thanks to Cindy Summers, our clerical manager. Cindy wrote the directions to enable directors across the country to duplicate our efforts from the first two meetings and did so in one week.

"Jim Stacy, our Alabama director, is one of the two men who oversaw this project. Jim accepted his assignment without question and worked right alongside our second director, Bob Richards.

"Bob is our Louisiana director, whom we visited on the second day. He, too, accepted his assignment without question. He and Jim have worked to develop the groups in record time.

"These two men worked above and beyond to improve minority relations in our country, with excitement, anticipation, and dedication. They both traveled, teaching at least three broad groups of people per week across the country. We would not have accomplished anywhere near this much without them. It was because of their total dedication and love for their fellow man. Now I would like them to each tell you their excellent news."

Bob spoke first. "Good morning, everyone, I cannot relay to you enough how thrilled I am to be here today. I want to share some numbers with you. The Monday following our meeting with Greg and his staff, we had received two hundred calls requesting invitations to our next meeting. They were friends and family members of people who attended our first meeting."

Jim added, "Good morning, I would like to add I too am thrilled to be here. I told Greg this had been a labor of love for me. We, too, received about two hundred calls, but since we completed the training across the country, every unit has reported similar results. The fantastic news is the word is spreading faster than anyone dreamed it would. We may see an incredible improvement in race relations, and we are all prepared to keep it going. It is beyond words to describe how we all feel. Thank you, Greg, for including us."

"You are all welcome," Greg responded. "We are so grateful you are here with us. I would now like to introduce you to my assistant, Alan Harrington."

"Thank you, Greg and all the members of our group," Alan said in response. "We all worked very hard, pushed through against some overwhelming odds, and accomplished our goal. I want to ask for everyone's support in keeping this incredible progress of ours moving forward from now on. These meetings will occur across the country at all ethnic group conference centers; they are all listed in your programs. Please contact one and attend a meeting. Become acquainted with a minority. We are all more alike than we are different. Thank you."

Greg stated, "If you have questions, please contact our office. I want to conclude by saying, thank you, Mr. President, for the confidence and trust you displayed in me. I am grateful you allowed us to go forward. Thank you, everyone, for attending today."

President Mitchell stated, "I thank you, Greg, and your group for everyone's efforts. Because of you, we are making progress by leaps and bounds. We've only just begun."

Many attendees and the media thanked Greg and his staff for all they had done and hoped to do to improve race relations. There was an incredible sense of excitement amongst the people!

The staff gathered in the conference room for coffee and a wrap-up discussion. It was exhilarating. No one could even imagine what the numbers would look like since they had concluded the press conference.

* * *

The press conference was over! Now, with luck, the groups could continue to move forward, with less involvement for Greg. He could concentrate on other legal issues pending within the office of the AG. Greg shook his head. So much had happened.

He called Laura to share his news; she answered right away.

"Hi, Dad," she said. "How are you doing? So, how did the press conference go?"

"Honey, without a doubt, terrific. Two thousand people were standing outside. They installed monitors before the conference, expecting a massive turnout. We can only hope the numbers continue to climb. It is encouraging, but we can't let it die down, or the numbers might drop off. How are you and Ellen doing in school?"

"Great," Laura responded. "We are working on last-minute items for graduation, and staying busy. We study together as much as we can. We help each other and understand the pressure each is experiencing. I asked Ellen whether her parents would come for graduation, and she said she believes they will make it. Would you mind if they stay with us?"

Greg answered, "We would love it. We look forward to meeting them and showing them around. I think Ellen would be pleased for them to be here too. Everything would be complete for her, don't you agree?"

"Yes, I agree, and it would be nice for us to get to know them," Laura concluded.

"Laura, please keep us informed when you discuss it further with Ellen. There are plenty of bedrooms. Her brother might like the guest quarters in the basement."

Laura said she would keep in touch.

While Greg watched the butterflies and fish in the pond, his phone rang. He decided not to answer, it but noticed it was from Jim Stacy, so he picked it up.

"Hi, Jim," Greg stated. "How are things going there?"

Jim told him, "Greg, you cannot imagine what is happening here. We received five thousand calls in the last couple of days; the staff cannot keep up. It is beyond amazing! Everyone wants to come in for a meeting, all wanting to experience what their friends and relatives have. Many are calling because of the press conference and the articles in our local newspaper. It will necessitate our adding meetings five days a week and maintaining a waiting list to attend. I spoke to Bob this morning; they are experiencing the same situation there. Once again, Greg, I have no way to thank you."

"No need to thank me, Jim," Greg exclaimed. "We accomplished this together through our belief, hard work, and tenacity. I cannot help but wonder where we will be six months from now. We will ask Cindy to send out a mass email asking for everyone to report their total number of calls received in more detail. We will need the totals for our records, and I am sure President Mitchell would also love to have them."

The national movement had taken a positive direction!

Before ending their call, Jim shared his wishes with Greg, saying, "Sleep well Greg, your idea has changed the world. Talk to you soon."

Greg had been an incredible bigot with a massive sense of entitlement. Today he was making an honest difference for people around the country.

Chapter Twenty

University Presentation

G reg's college visit was the dominant topic of conversation with Laura and Ellen over dinner. It overcame the girls with excitement, knowing he would present there within a week. They shared the opinions of several of the students with him. Just being aware the Attorney General would visit raised their spirits and their expectations. Most of them had known for years Greg was Laura's dad, but now the fact became magnified. He impressed many of the students. They prepared their lists of questions, intending to learn as much as possible. Greg's visit would be a once-in-a-lifetime opportunity for the students and staff. Laura and Ellen would meet Greg and his team and escort them to the conference area.

The next order of business was graduation for Laura and Ellen, being only about six weeks away. They covered all the details. Sylvia visited the Peaceful River Country Club, which was about thirty minutes from their house. She toured the facility and brought back their brochures with all of the dates available right after graduation. It was a beautiful place, located in a country area with a small pond and lots of butterflies and breathtaking flowers. The banquet area was lovely, just the right size to comfortably hold all their family members and Ellen and Laura's friends. The girls were thrilled with the possibility of having their party there, together. By now, everyone knew the girls were as close as sisters, so it was quite fitting. Only one critical question remained, which Greg had not asked.

"So, Ellen, do you know whether your parents and your brother will attend your graduation?"

"I just got a letter from my mom; she said they are coming but are unsure where they will stay."

Sylvia responded to Ellen's statement, "Greg, Laura, and I discussed how much we are looking forward to meeting your family and how fantastic it would be for them to stay here with us. The area downstairs would be perfect for your parents or brother, and there is a private bathroom. We would love to welcome them into our home, show them a bit of the United States, and enable you and your family to spend some time together. So, what do you think?"

Ellen cried. She couldn't believe their generosity. They were offering to welcome her family into their home. She could not immediately respond; she was too overcome with emotion.

After a few moments, Ellen finally said, "I will talk to my parents and extend your kind invitation. They know Laura and I are like sisters and how much I love all of you. I will let you know as soon as I can talk to them. Thank you all!"

The following day Ellen reported to Greg, Sylvia, and Laura; her parents would love to accept their invitation to stay with them for as long as their vacations will allow them. They had cleared three weeks, which included travel time. It thrilled her brother Joe to be coming to America to visit his sister and her newfound family. They could reserve a date they all felt would work, giving her parents a few days after graduation to settle in before the party.

Four years had gone by. Ellen and Laura would soon be off to medical school, a dream come true for both girls.

* * *

The plan was to meet at Greg's house and drive the two hours to the college together. They departed at six o'clock, intending to stop at Laura's favorite restaurant for breakfast around seven. It was a beautiful, sunny day with a gentle breeze, the perfect day for a driving adventure.

It would be the team's only presentation at a university, which would include its own set of challenges. They expected a huge turnout.

At breakfast time, Greg cut off the highway to the restaurant parking lot; hunger won out. Thanks to the restaurant's speedy service, they were back on the road sooner than expected, all geared up for the best presentation to date.

Greg brought copies of reports and statistics for the students, along with a laptop; it thrilled him to see the positive response from the students at this university.

As they approached the doors, a sizeable group of students was visible. It was apparent they were waiting to greet Greg and his staff. It showed how important they considered the issue.

"Good morning everyone, we are pleased to see so many of you here to greet us. Are there any concerns you would like to address before the program begins this morning?"

A young man moved to the front of the group and answered, "Good morning, I am Peter Sampson. I have been chosen as spokesperson for our little group this morning. We are all prepared with many questions to ask you. Will we experience working in the same setting you've worked in with groups around the country? It would enable us to learn more about each other. And will you be addressing discrimination today?"

Greg responded, "I am so pleased you are aware of what we have done around the country, and have the interest and desire to duplicate it here. The answer to your question is yes. You will work in the same setting we have used throughout the country, and we will address discrimination with all of you today. We would all like to freshen up, please excuse us." The group dispersed as Greg and his team walked toward the restrooms.

When the team emerged, Laura and Ellen were waiting. They walked down the long corridor to the main doors of the conference center.

Greg told Laura and Ellen, "I am surprised at the size of this center. You described it to me, but I did not visualize it being quite this large. We should not experience any problems with our setup, no matter how many people take part. They have also provided enough tables, chairs, and microphones."

The university president arranged for several students to come in ready to move chairs or tables to meet Greg's requirements, which worked out well. They were quickly prepared for the students and faculty to arrive.

Greg and his staff designed the table and chair setups so many times they had become experts at what worked for the audience.

The atmosphere was almost magical as the students and faculty filed into the conference area, expecting a wonderful experience.

President McGuinness told Greg he had invited professors from other colleges.

Greg responded, "The more people gaining this knowledge and the lessons from today's exercise, the better. If we provide you with the guidance needed to duplicate today's program, would you be willing to offer this training here at your university, from now on, to future students and faculty?"

It took President McGuinness a moment to respond, then he replied, "That sounds great. Let's talk after the program. I love the idea!"

Greg told him, "It would be wonderful to have discrimination addressed and taught here at the university!"

Greg and his staff directed everyone to seats as they entered. He asked them to please sit to enable them to get the program underway. Everyone found places.

President McGuinness opened the program by announcing their excitement to welcome the US Attorney General, Greg Mitchell, and his staff. "We know their team will present a fantastic program from which we will all benefit and will aid us through the rest of their lives."

He then introduced Greg, saying, "I am thrilled to introduce our incredible US Attorney General Gregory Mitchell, who will direct the program."

Greg took the microphone and began, "Thank you so much, President McGuinness, for your introduction. For those of you who may not be aware, I experienced a complete transformation that involved my race changing from white to black. It included a period of illness and mental confusion as one might expect. It is a process to change your race and requires time for acceptance. I've become a much kinder and more patient person than before the transformation. Now I view racial issues and discrimination more personally than I did in the past, never realizing the depth of pain a person experiences when subjected to discrimination. Someone who does not even know the recipient can create a racist situation based on their skin color.

Mary L. Byrne

"I believe if we were to bring all ethnic groups together, without anger or violence, yet with honesty and empathy, we may learn more about each other and find we are more alike than we are different. We may also find the only actual difference between us is the color of our skin, which we had no control over. The results so far are amazing. Many people forged new friendships through newly found trust. We've received thousands of calls across the country with more and more requests to become part of this unbelievable movement that has begun.

"Before we break into twos, there are many microphones throughout the conference area. We want to take questions from anyone that has one."

A young black male stood up and stated, "Many of the students attending our university come from countries all over the world. Will today's program help guide us to bridge the gap and become acquainted with these students on a more personal level?"

Greg answered, "I am thrilled you asked such a question. It shows your genuine desire to come to know students from other countries. I know we can help you make the introductions and understand each other on a much deeper level.

"There will be time for questions and comments in between our sessions this morning and afternoon. I would like to introduce you to my team. Alan is my assistant. We are fortunate to have him with us here today. Janice is our clerical assistant. She is new to the AG's office. Janice has done a fantastic job on this project; we could not go forward without her. Cindy is in charge of the clerical department for the Attorney General's office; she put this entire program together to enable managers throughout the country to guide their members through the training. Cindy shortened the time of production from many months to two weeks. We are all here to answer your questions and guide you through this process to enable you to get the most out of this program. Now let's begin."

Alan announced, "All attendees will sit with someone of the same sex. Each table will occupy people of two different races. If everyone would please form a line beginning to my left, you will be directed to your seat. All staff members are wearing a yellow T-shirt and will guide you throughout the day. They are here to answer questions."

Staff members directed people to their tables, matching those of the same sex but of an alternate race. Everyone moved to seat the

155

participants while staff members passed out the suggested icebreaker questions. They were ready!

Greg asked everyone to consider each other's feelings and confidentiality. He suggested they ask whether discrimination had ever played a part in their lives if both parties accepted the question. The first session would last thirty minutes. The professors assisted the staff in ensuring international students paired with students of all races to enable a more in-depth introduction between them, which the first student had requested.

Greg asked everyone how they thought their first session concluded. Had they discovered anything they did not already know?

A female student named Presha from India stated she had spoken with a beautiful white student known as Marsha. Presha found her an excellent communicator. She had seen her around the campus, but they had never talked. She said they discussed their childhoods, school, and family customs. It amazed her how similar their childhoods were, including the rules their parents had for them when they were growing up. She found her to be very much like her best friend at home. Presha regretted the time wasted, not trying harder to become acquainted.

Greg responded to Presha, "Perhaps we humans sometimes find it much easier to stick with people most like ourselves and not attempt to venture too far from what is familiar. I am thrilled you already, within an hour, found you may have wasted time not meeting sooner. We designed the program to educate by enabling you to meet people you normally would not, and learn about each other. Then you can decide whether you would like to continue becoming better acquainted.

"Without this opportunity, you and Marsha might never have realized what you missed; now, you are doing so. Thank you so much for sharing with us."

Greg and his staff had given all of them very detailed notes regarding the connections needed, which enabled them to complete their assignments in ten minutes.

They were ready for their second round. Greg announced they would have thirty minutes to become acquainted with their new partner.

While the students and staff got into the second round of introductions, Greg sought President McGuinness. His observation of the process taking place in the conference center amazed him. He thought bringing students together would always be just a dream. He told Greg they could never thank him enough.

Greg made it back just before the final buzzer, announcing the end of the thirty minute extension.

A young white student stood up and requested a microphone. He stated, "Hello, my name is Steven, I thought I could imagine what it would feel like to be on the receiving end of racial discrimination until I met with Abioye, who is from Yoruba, Nigeria. He told me his name means born into royalty. Upon his arrival, he met with incredible opposition because of his race. It caused Abioye to stay close to his friends from Nigeria. He never even attempted to become acquainted with white students or any other minority. He thought they would all judge him as the first student did and not accept him for himself. We had a pleasant conversation. We plan to introduce our respective friends to each other and attempt to expand our friendships. I am so grateful you came here to open our eyes and hearts to what others may have felt in theirs. Thank you so much."

"Thank you, Steven, I am thrilled you got so much out of your meeting and conversation with Abioye. I hope you continue introducing him to your friends. We will break for lunch, then resume in one hour. Please take this opportunity to speak with people you haven't spoken to during the lunch break."

Greg and his team made tremendous progress. They encouraged people of different races and from various countries to listen to each other without anger or violence, with their hearts.

Students and staff members proceeded to their next match. Greg and his team met with President McGuinness to discuss the university, continuing to offer their training to future students and staff members. Conducting training would ensure prospective students' education in the awareness of related discrimination and its causes.

Greg stated, "It thrills us you will continue our work here daily, and not lose ground. I did not realize it would come to this point when we scheduled the program here today. We will work with you and your staff to ensure a smooth transition and in-depth training for your chosen instructors. I cannot thank you enough for your interest in this important work."

Another session had ended.

Greg suggested a light conversation before beginning the next match, saying, "Let's stop for a few minutes before you all move on.

Would anyone like to comment or ask a question? Whatever you share will be welcome. Would anyone like to start?"

"I am Margo. I came today because I've had a desire for a very long time to become acquainted with students other than those I have known my entire life. When I saw this program advertised, I realized I must attend. We discussed childhoods, parents, customs, and also discrimination because of some people looking different from us. I felt their pain, and it made my heart ache. I apologized for their unfair treatment and gave them a bit of hope the future will be better for all of us, now that we are learning through this beautiful program. Please accept my thanks for bringing this hope for today and the future to all of us."

Greg responded, "Margo, my eyes are tearing, hearing your beautiful words. You found the answers you sought here today. You have also been able to share hope with others. Thank you for including all of us; we've all gained."

An older man stood and identified himself. "I am Professor Halstead. I must admit I have not always been easy to reach with racial differences. As you can observe, I am white, and I never had many ethnic friends. Other than my students, I never became well versed in their plight until today. I attended because I realized the time had come for me to learn what others had known for years. I, too, met some fantastic students. After spending a while with them, I realized how pleasant they were, and their issues are very much like mine. Then the color of their skin seemed to fade, and I only saw and heard the actual person I was fortunate enough to meet. Thank you so much for teaching me; it is never too late to open your heart and learn."

"Thank you, Professor Halstead, for sharing your experience with us. Would anyone else like to say anything before we resume?"

Most of the attendees asked that the program continue, at which point Greg instructed the staff to move forward.

Greg acknowledged that accepting the university's invitation to speak and bring their presentation to the professors and students was one of the best decisions he had ever made.

It had been so busy he had forgotten Laura and Ellen were also participating in the program, which pleased him on many levels. Not only would it benefit them on a personal note but also as physicians. They shared how much they enjoyed taking part.

President McGuinness announced they would continue to offer the program at their university, making it part of the curriculum. Staff members would connect it to any classes currently being taught addressing such issues. When the president concluded his announcement, everyone cheered.

The day had ended, but Greg and his staff were thrilled to know their work would continue, hopefully for years to come at the university

* * *

Greg arrived home exhausted yet exhilarated. He had no doubt they were on the right track. He played it over in his mind, allowing it to penetrate. Their program would carry on at the university. It was beyond amazing!

Sylvia immediately knew and said, "Good day?"

"Wonderful!" Greg responded.

They had decided to hold the graduation party for both girls at the Peaceful River Country Club. Ellen's parents and her brother would arrive days before their graduation. They hadn't realized Ellen's family had never visited America, making this visit even more exciting. Ellen's dad was a neurologist, and her mom, a surgical nurse. Both of them spoke excellent English, which would be a real plus. It would make life much more comfortable for them during their visit.

Greg recalled he had never asked Ellen what her parents and brother's names were, but had learned during a conversation. Her father's name was Abeo, nicknamed Abe; her mother's name was Abayomi, nickname Yomi; her brother's name Ike, and his nickname Joe. Their last name was Adebisi. Ellen's actual first name was Monifa, but she always used the nickname Ellen.

Greg and Sylvia planned to take some time off during the three weeks Ellen's family would visit them. Sylvia looked forward to taking them to the hospital to show them around. They had many fun things planned, but they would leave it up to Ellen and her parents to decide what interested them the most.

Chapter Twenty-One

Revisit the Past

Greg needed to compile the list of people that deserved an apology for his past behavior. It would be quite an undertaking to face the people from his past, one at a time, and share how sorry he had become. Knowing he had to make amends for his life to be complete, Greg picked up the phone and called Alan.

"Alan, I need your help. I must apologize to every person I have ever offended or victimized. To make right the wrongs of my past and find peace within myself. You've worked with me for many years; if you can, please make a list of all you remember; then, we can compare them. Hopefully, you won't mind helping me with this. There is some sense of urgency in completing my list and making the calls as soon as possible."

"I'd be happy to help you in any way I can. Of course I'll compile a list."

Greg thanked him and hung up.

He was not able to shake the sense of urgency that continued to build. Greg drove to his office to begin the tedious and emotional work of compiling his list. To list them, he had to relive them. To revisit the experiences became much more painful for him in the present than it would have been before his transformation.

Greg began straining to remember as far back as possible, to when he first became abusive toward other people. He realized he had blocked

160

out many people, choosing not to recall the pain and distress he had caused. He remembered John, who worked for him when Greg first became the Attorney General. John was white, but Greg believed not on his level. He made several mistakes in his attempts to please Greg and never seemed to measure up. Greg remembered belittling him. John resigned, saying he wanted to find a job closer to home. Recalling it now became downright painful. Why hadn't he made more of an attempt to improve relations between them? He showed no patience with John.

His next memory was of Tonya. She was a lovely black lady, passed over for promotions because of her race. She met with Greg and complained they had promoted many other women instead of her. Greg denied her claim, saying she should deal with things the way they were. Tonya tried several more times to convince him it was racial discrimination. She was the only black woman in their department; he refused to see it. Tonya became depressed and quit her job. At the time, Greg felt relieved she had left, along with her problem; he never pursued the issue. Now, he became sick over it.

Greg had mistreated many other people in similar situations. Since his transformation, Greg no longer believed anyone deserved better than another. He continued to work on his list until he could remember no one else. Greg hoped there were no more.

He called Alan. As soon as Alan answered, he asked, "How many people have you been able to remember?"

Alan recalled twenty-seven people. Greg only remembered twenty-five which he had abused.

Greg asked, "Can we please set aside some time as soon as possible to review this list; I do not think it can wait."

When Alan sensed a reason for Greg's impatience, he suggested they meet for breakfast the following morning, which Greg agreed to without hesitation, hoping it was twenty-five, not the twenty-seven people Alan remembered. They would know soon enough since he was approaching the restaurant where they would meet.

Greg realized just how fortunate he had been to have Alan ever by his side. No matter what the issue. It meant the world to him. Loyalty such as theirs was rare.

The men reviewed their menus, ordered, and got right to the point. As they compared their lists, it became apparent Greg had blocked out two of the people he had hurt the most. Alan's recollection was correct.

Alan shared with Greg his memory of a white woman named Edith, who worked for Greg when he first became Attorney General. She was a delightful person. Edith annoyed Greg daily, and he fired her without cause. She cried like a baby, begging Greg to reconsider, but he refused. Edith had two young children and had just lost her husband. Greg announced she had to go! Alan bled for her. He attempted to reason with Greg, but even he could not get through to him.

As Alan spoke of Edith, all of those painful memories came flooding back. Greg wondered how he could have done something so heartless to such a lovely woman. How would Greg ever explain himself to Edith?

Alan's last memory was of a black man named John. He had appealed to Greg to sponsor him for citizenship, so he, his wife, and his children could remain in the United States. Greg refused. Instead, he told him he would have to go home and return when he prepared to take the test. John collapsed, after which he and his family returned to Africa. Greg never heard from him again and didn't know whether they returned at a later date. He hoped they had.

The memories of his earlier cruelty saddened Greg. Had he not experienced such extensive therapy himself, he would have collapsed right there on the spot. He never ceased to wonder how he had gotten to such a point in his heart and soul. It allowed him to destroy lives without ever looking back. He wasn't that man any longer. Now, he must organize a plan for contacting and meeting with all the people on his list. He had to do everything within his power to undo the pain he had caused them and somehow make it right. His soul required earning their respect, no matter how long it took.

The two men spent about two hours discussing the list of people Greg had to meet. When Greg and Alan had finished reviewing the file, Greg knew where he would begin.

His chief hope was they would meet with him. It would take some convincing. He would begin making telephone calls to schedule appointments immediately!

Greg made a list of people he needed to contact and the order in which to meet with them. He listed all the old contact information he had on file and began making his calls. He would adjust his schedule to meet whenever they were available.

His first call had to be to John, the man Greg felt not his equal. Greg belittled him until John resigned.

His old telephone number still worked, and John answered the phone.

For a second, Greg couldn't speak, but composed himself and responded with, "Hello John, this is Greg Hastings. I am hoping you will meet with me and allow me to apologize to you for my poor treatment of you so many years ago. John, as you've heard, I've gone through a lot of changes in the last few months. One of them has been some deep soul searching along with lots of therapy. I am attempting to correct the wrongs of my past, and you are the first person on my list. I hope you will consider my request and agree to sit down with me, for lunch or dinner, or just a meeting if you prefer. It is up to you."

Nothing but silence on John's end of the phone, as though he were thinking. He answered, "I must be honest with you, Greg. So, I must admit I am thrilled to hear from you and am looking forward to speaking with you soon. How about over lunch?"

Greg told him it sounded great and asked how his schedule looked for the next few days. They would meet on Thursday at a lovely restaurant close to Greg's home, at noon. Greg breathed a sigh of relief, realizing all he did was be honest with John.

Greg's next call would be to Edith. He realized why she annoyed him so much: she was too sweet! He found it hard to believe anyone would ever be that nice or so genuine. Seeing Edith reminded Greg he had become an underhanded bigot, so Edith's presence made him uncomfortable. He prayed life had been gentle with her, and she would somehow find it in her heart to forgive him.

Greg called the old number in his file, but couldn't reach her. How would he find Edith? Perhaps his staff could assist with a compiled list of those people who appeared to be unreachable. He hoped he could make things right with her.

Tonya was the next person on Greg's list. He dialed her old number, and she answered. Greg inhaled and said, "Hello, Tonya, this is Greg Hastings."

Complete silence on the other end of the phone!

Greg continued, "I imagine you know about the changes in my life over the past several months. They included a complete change of personality and heart. I must meet with you after everything I did so many years ago to hurt you. Please meet with me and grant me the opportunity to explain and apologize for the wrongs I did back then. We can meet for lunch, dinner, coffee, or just a meeting; the choice is yours. I am just praying you will grant me the opportunity to meet with you, in person, as soon as possible."

The silence on the other end continued. Tonya replied, "Now why in the world would I ever want to meet with you, Greg Hastings? You destroyed my life back then, even though I pleaded with you to reconsider. I appealed to you for consideration. You rejected me for promotions, which I felt was because of my being black. You would not bend, so I quit. I loved my job working for you, and I never wanted to leave, but being treated as though I were invisible broke my heart and spirit. I had to get away from you. Just for that reason, Greg, I will meet with you. I am curious about what you believe you can say to me to change my feelings or opinions. I will have lunch with you any day next week. How about Lisa's Lunchroom, next Wednesday at noon?"

Greg agreed to Wednesday and looked forward to the opportunity. After thanking Tonya for agreeing to meet with him, they hung up. Greg was grateful for the chance to explain how he could have been such a cold-hearted, unyielding bigot.

John was the African attorney that had appealed to Greg to sponsor him for citizenship, so he, his wife, and their children could remain in the United States. Greg had regrets he couldn't forget. He must find them.

Greg had hurt many people with his actions over the years. These four were among the worst cases. Greg knew he had to see all of them to enable him to achieve peace within himself.

Greg called Alan to request help with a few people. "I need more clout from within our office to track them down, if even possible." He shared all the information he had in his old files.

Alan told Greg, "We will find them!"

The next few days passed, until it was Wednesday morning. When Sylvia entered the kitchen, she knew why Greg had become so quiet: Tonya was occupying his mind. She, too, prayed that Greg could reach her and explain his behavior of so many years ago.

Sylvia reached over and kissed Greg on the cheek as she said, "I believe in you."

Greg looked up and smiled, responding with, "I love you, Sylvia; you always read me so well."

Greg told her he was nervous about their meeting that day at noon. He wasn't sure he could explain everything to Tonya's satisfaction, but he would find the solution. He drove to meet Tonya at her favorite restaurant, Lisa's Lunchroom. Wow, the years had gone by so quickly. Tonya had worked for them as a senior stenographer and did a remarkable job.

Greg arrived and waited inside for Tonya. He gave his name and sat down. She arrived right on time, straining to provide him with a brief smile, but did not shake his hand. The waitress directed them to their table, and they took their seats. Tonya remained silent, so Greg began the conversation.

"Tonya, thank you for agreeing to meet with me. You will never know how sorry I am for my past behavior toward you. I needed to meet with you today. Please tell me how your life has gone since I last saw you if you would not mind starting there."

"I'd heard you had gone through a DNA transformation. Still, it is incredible to sit with you here today, as a black man. You were white when I worked for you eleven years ago. It affects my heart to see what you have experienced, but I am very grateful to see it has changed yours. I believe you are not the same person who hurt me all those years ago. I have never been so happy as when I worked for you."

"Would you be willing to tell me what amount of salary you are receiving and what your benefits package is like?"

"I have no benefits package, and I earn less than what I did eleven years ago, which was $38,000 per year."

"I cannot make up to you for what happened in the past beyond offering you my sincere apology. However, I received a call on my way here this morning informing me we have an opening for a senior/manager stenographer. The starting salary is $82,000 with a full benefits package, which I am sure you will find attractive. Now I am sure you must feel resentful toward me, but I am also aware you stated you have never been so happy as when you worked for me. You can see I have changed. Ask anyone in our department at the DOJ. Now I would like to offer the job to you if you would take it, and we will work together until retirement. What do you say?"

Tonya's eyes filled with tears. She could not answer.

When she regained her composure, she replied, "Yes, I would love to take the job, for so many reasons, I must ask, though, are there any black people working there other than you?"

They both laughed and ordered their lunch.

"Yes, there are several black people along with other races working for the DOJ."

"How soon would you like me to start?"

"As soon as you have given adequate notice to your present employer and taken a week off to breathe," Greg answered.

Tonya could not believe it; she had arrived for lunch, dreading the entire experience, but would leave with a new outlook. As the two walked toward the door, Tonya hugged Greg and thanked him for giving her back her life.

"Thank you for helping me to recover mine. I will see you in three weeks at eight thirty. If you have any questions, please call me."

On the drive back to the office, Greg noted an incredible sense of relief. He was able to help Tonya secure a much better job to enable her to live her life. Greg felt tremendous.

The following day Greg left the office in time to meet with John at the restaurant, which would be the second lunch meeting of vital importance to Greg within two days. He would not miss it. He did not know how to explain his behavior to John once they got there.

As Greg approached the entrance, he saw John waiting for him just inside the door. He walked in and reached for John's hand, shaking it as he said, "Hello John, it is a pleasure to see you again."

John remained reserved, which he understood.

Greg told the hostess he'd made a reservation, and she took them to their table.

"John, there is an impressive amount I need to apologize to you for and ask for your forgiveness. I am sorry for my behavior toward you so many years ago. I should have pleaded with you to stay. Instead, I accepted your resignation, knowing full well I was the one responsible for your leaving. I've changed an enormous amount. Not only my race, but also everything else about me. No longer am I a self-centered narcissist; now I am a decent human being with a very kind heart. The memories of my past behavior torment me. Unfortunately, I cannot explain any of it except to say I became self-absorbed and developed an incredible sense of entitlement. Not caring about how I affected others. Hopefully, you will be able to forgive me for my inexcusable behavior. My hope is you found a position that has brought you joy and happiness."

"Greg, I tried so hard to please you, but could never seem to measure up to your standards. I always felt so insignificant and was going down a path that diminished my self-esteem to where it was almost nonexistent. There was no choice. I had to leave for my survival. So, I told you I planned to secure employment closer to home. You never pressed me for an explanation, for which I became grateful. Leaving your supervision was the smartest move I have ever made for myself.

"After leaving, I realized without completing my college degree, I would never amount to anything. So, I returned to college and became an attorney and have pursued my career ever since. You did me a favor. Had you not pushed me into resigning, I might still work for you in my former position. So, it is I who owe you a thank-you. You were not a nice man back then, but I find I am grateful. Though, I appreciate your apology more than you can imagine. I always felt my quitting was incomplete, and seeing you now today makes everything right for me. I hope it does for you too."

Greg chimed in, "I cannot put into words how sorry I am for the man I became back then and how I treated you. You deserved my gratitude and admiration. Instead, I tortured you with my abuse and degradation. I will always be sorry. I cannot rewrite the past, but I can let you know how much I've changed. Rest assured, I will never mistreat another person, ever. I'm so sorry for what my treatment of you caused you to feel. Thankfully, you have done well for yourself; I am proud of you too. Unfortunately, I was not a contributing factor to your success. However, I am thrilled it turned out this way and pleased we are having lunch together today. Thank you so much for accepting my invitation."

"Shall we order?"

Greg and John talked for over an hour. They hoped to become friends for the rest of their lives. Despite what had happened, they always liked each other. The DOJ was still looking for a law firm that was above reproach.

When lunch ended, the men shook hands and hugged. Both men were appreciative; they had discussed the issue that stood between them. They promised to stay in touch.

Greg looked for Alan as soon as he arrived back in the office. He wanted to share the last two days with him. He had launched a course to reverse the wrongs of his past and attempt to make them right.

Alan was thrilled to realize how well everything had turned out after Greg's meetings with Tonya and John. He asked Greg, "Do you realize how very fortunate you are that Tonya and John would listen to you, and further, they were kind enough to forgive you?"

"Alan, I do not have the words to convey to you how grateful I am. My heart is so much lighter already, and I only met with the first two people whose lives I imploded. I pray every person I hurt will be willing to forgive me; then, I will find the peace I seek."

Alan stopped and stared at Greg; he had not realized how critical it was to Greg until then. He would continue to do everything in his power to help Greg find all the other people he needed to see.

"Do you remember when Tonya worked here?"

"I remember her. She was a fantastic worker who loved her job and got along well with everyone."

"Well," Greg shared, "she is coming back to work for us; she agreed to accept the steno-manager's job, beginning in three weeks."

"Greg, what fantastic news, she will fit in nicely. I'm thrilled that Tonya and John were receptive to your explanations and apologies."

Greg made significant progress. He was accomplishing all the duties of his office while searching for his missing victims, which was not an easy feat. He believed them to be his victims, knowing how he had hurt them. Greg had such a conflict playing out in his mind. He was aware of the depth of pain he caused all of those people. He was no longer of the caliber which a person would need to be to inflict such emotional pain on another. His personality shift made it difficult for him to fathom ever committing such acts.

Alan took the list from Greg to continue to exert all efforts to locate every person listed and free Greg to work on some high priority pending cases.

Chapter Twenty-Two

Extended Family

T he weeks flew by, and Ellen's parents and brother would arrive the
following day. They were ready. Sylvia and the girls prepared their
rooms with their favorite things, including fresh flowers and their
choice in towels. Ellen helped with the details.

Greg and Sylvia appreciated that Ellen could verbalize her prefer-
ence in picking her family up at the airport herself. They would all meet
back at the house for dinner.

The excitement reached a fever pitch at the Hastings home. Ellen
and her family were to arrive at any minute.

Laura saw the car pull into the driveway and yelled to her mother
and father, "They're here!"

Everyone rushed to the front door. Greg stepped up and opened
the door, smiling from ear to ear.

They all said, "Welcome!" in unison.

After all of the communicating before their arrival, they felt as
though they had already met. Sylvia asked Ellen to direct everyone to both
sleeping quarters to enable them to decide which they would like to occupy
for the next couple of weeks. Sylvia departed to the kitchen with Laura to
prepare lunch since it was almost that time.

After a brief period, Ellen came back and announced they had decided Joe would sleep downstairs, and her parents would take the guest

room upstairs. Ellen always found Joe's music loud, so they were less apt to hear it if he were on the lower level. He loved the idea; it felt like having his "very own" private place.

The families gathered in the dining room for lunch; it gave them a chance to exhale, enjoy lunch, and talk to each other. The first topic of conversation was Ellen's parents' thank you to Greg and Sylvia for inviting them to stay in their home; it was generous.

Greg spoke up, "We are all happy you agreed to stay with us. Please do not give it another thought. Having Ellen with us has been a joy; she is like a second daughter. Hopefully, being here will seem like home for her when she has to be away from you and her existing home while attending school. Also, there is the fact she and Laura are already like sisters."

Sylvia chimed in, "Our door will always be open to you whenever you can come. You are family, please always remember that."

Abe spoke as the head of his family, "We want you all to understand what a great sense of relief it has brought us knowing you welcomed Ellen into your home, and you love her and look after her as we do when she is at home. It gives us such peace, knowing she is not alone. Further, we are grateful you would invite us to join her and stay here while visiting in America. We would love to have you visit our home."

Greg and Sylvia thanked them for their generosity. The conversation flowed as they enjoyed their delicious meal. Yomi told Sylvia she would have to share her recipes. Sylvia acknowledged her willingness to do so.

Yomi added, "While we are here, I hope you will let me cook for all of you. I would love to bring some of our traditional African recipes to your dining room."

Everyone responded with a loud yes.

The girls' graduation day had arrived. They woke up exceptionally early on a gorgeous sunny day. Everyone felt the excitement accompanying the long-awaited graduation. After a quick breakfast, they followed each other to the university, a two-hour drive away. Fortunately, they were all set with reservations and assigned seating. The ceremony would begin at eleven, which would allow them time to stop for coffee on the way. At Laura's favorite restaurant, of course.

Abe and Yomi had tears in their eyes when they spoke of how exhilarated they felt to be able to attend the graduation of their eldest child, mostly since it was a world away from their home.

"I cannot express enough how grateful Yomi and I are to all of you for making this day possible for us. We would not have wanted to miss it for anything on earth. You have welcomed us into your home and allowed us to participate in such a loving manner. We will never forget this and always keep you in a special place in our hearts."

The ceremony was beautiful! Seeing their girls receive their diplomas was the thrill of a lifetime for all of them. Their fathers each took pictures of both of the girls for their memory books. They would undoubtedly fill them. It was a glorious day filled with a great deal of happiness.

They arrived back home exhausted, but with enough energy for coffee and cake before retiring for the night. It had been a glorious day, especially for Ellen and Laura. They were almost halfway through their education and could now enjoy their summer together, but first, there would be a most enjoyable graduation party.

The country club was beautifully decorated in blue and yellow, Ellen and Laura's favorite colors. Sylvia and Greg had asked them to do their very best for their girls. They wanted it to be a memory that would live within their hearts forever. All of their friends from school were invited, along with family and lifelong friends as well. The appetizers were terrific, along with the music, decorations, and delicious dinner. The chef went beyond his usual meals for them, which was much appreciated. Everyone was in awe. When it was time for the girls to dance with their dads, the band played, "I Did it My Way." They certainly did, both of them. There was not a dry eye in the building. They were all blissfully happy, and it showed.

They filled the following weeks with laughter, sharing, and beautiful moments. They were born worlds apart but might have lived next door to each other their entire lives. It proved to be a beautiful experience like no one had imagined. In addition to the girls' graduation, it encompassed day trips and visiting the Department of Justice and Sylvia's pediatric practice. They became acquainted with each other with no orchestration; it naturally occurred. The coming together of their minds and hearts was beyond expectation. They allowed others to see them as they were.

By the end of the visit, they had become family. Joe hoped to return in a few short years to attend college himself. He would stay with Sylvia and Greg in his new quarters in the basement. Abe and Yomi were much more comfortable with Ellen remaining in the United States, knowing she would be with Laura, Sylvia, and Greg. They invited the entire Hastings family to visit them in Africa and enjoy learning about their country.

Greg shared with Abe and Yomi how he had treated many people years ago. He explained what he was doing now to turn things around, hoping to reverse the pain he had caused so many people, including John. Greg had refused to sponsor him for citizenship and how much regret it had caused him. So far, he did not know for sure whether John and his family had returned to America.

"Greg, as soon as we return home, I will attempt to locate John for you. If I find him, you will come to Africa and meet with John yourself. I will not contact him for you. How does that sound to you?"

"Abe, that would be wonderful. I appreciate your offer. Thank you so much."

The days passed so quickly it was time to say goodbye, for the moment, to Abe, Yomi, and Joe. They all realized they had developed a lifelong relationship, with a deep love for each other that would carry across the world to Nigeria. Nothing would ever come between them. On the morning of their flight, everyone pitched in to make a delicious breakfast. They all sat together in the dining room, reminiscing about their beautiful visit. They were very fortunate, and they all knew it. Imagine; all because the girls became friends and then sisters in college!

Ellen chose, once again, to take her family back to the airport alone, to spend some private time with them. They all kissed and hugged and shared some tears before leaving for the airport. It was difficult for everyone to say goodbye to their new extended family, but they would all see each other again soon.

* * *

Laura and Ellen's summer amassed fun times at the beach and overnight trips to neighboring states. It allowed them to explore as they searched for the right place to locate their clinic. They knew it was premature. But realizing how quickly years pass, they did not want to wait until they became doctors to find a destination right for them. They wanted to work with the underserved population. People who could not afford the medical care they needed and deserved. Ellen and Laura realized it would require a substantial amount of research, so the sooner they began, the better.

Professor Williams informed Laura he heard about an area in Louisiana which might be perfect for their clinic. It was a beautiful place with warm and generous people. Their industrial earnings might drop off substantially due to the possible relocation of two of their most significant clothing manufacturers. If the companies moved, the area would give up their primary source of income. The relocation would take place within the next five years.

The girls went to Louisiana that week to check out the area. They booked a flight and made hotel reservations for the following day, planning to stay for at least four days. It was such an exciting time for them to be preparing for the next several years of their lives.

In less than two hours, Ellen and Laura landed in Louisiana. Laura noted it would not be a long flight home whenever they wanted to visit Mom and Dad.

They spent two days driving from city to city, concentrating more on rural areas. The results of their prior research made them aware the Bureau of Primary Care and Rural Health was dedicating itself to improving the health status of Louisiana residents in rural and under-served areas. They offered many incentives to entice physicians to move to Louisiana. Which pleased Laura and Ellen since they would be just starting their careers in medicine.

They checked on two clinics and met with the doctors, to get their opinions on whether they would be a good fit for Louisiana and vice versa. They received more information than they thought they would. The majority being positive. They came away both in favor of considering Louisiana as their target location.

They found the people welcoming and loved what they saw in the area, making them feel at home right away.

Laura told one doctor, "It must seem premature since we do not even begin medical school until the end of August. Yet here we are checking out the area to move and begin our practice."

"I do not think it is premature at all. I'll always wish I had done something similar before I started med school. It became a two-year search before finding the right fit for me. I'd worked at a clinic in an area I had lived in all of my life, not doing what I wanted. When I found Louisiana, I knew I had found the perfect place. Please stay in touch with us."

Laura and Ellen thanked them and assured them they would be in touch, then drove to a lovely restaurant for lunch. They both enjoyed their experience. They were pleased with their decision to scope out the area while they had the time to do so.

They could return home and concentrate on beginning medical school, knowing they very well may have found the ideal place to relocate to after graduation to begin their careers as primary care physicians.

Chapter Twenty-Three

Actual World

After waiting for so many years, Laura and Ellen were about to realize their dream. They would leave for medical school that morning right after breakfast. Sylvia and Greg were elated for them, but they were a little sad for themselves.

Greg announced, "We realize you are starting medical school, but you will both always be our girls, no matter how old you get. So, if there are times when we get to be a bit overprotective, we hope you will try to understand. It will always be out of love for both of you."

They knew how busy the girls would be and how seldom they would make it home. They would try to visit the girls for lunch, dinner, or whatever time they had between classes. It was not a realistic plan since they kept so busy themselves, but they would try to do so.

Sylvia cooked a lovely breakfast before the girls departed for their new apartment. It was a mere two-hour drive from home, which would enable frequent visiting. Time would pass, and they would be home for Thanksgiving. With lots of hugs and kisses and good wishes, they were off. Laura and Ellen laughed and joked the entire drive to their new apartment. They would be within walking distance of their school. They both felt as though they had been attending school forever, but they were now almost halfway.

Everyone had helped Laura and Ellen with their move; now, they could relax for two days before their classes started.

* * *

On Monday morning, Greg sat across the breakfast table from his beautiful wife. He would soon leave to drive to his office to do a job he loved, for which the president had chosen him. What more could a man want? Life was good to him, and he realized it. His level of gratitude was high and always would be. They would miss Laura and Ellen. They were pursuing their dreams; they put a smile on his face and pride in his heart.

He prayed with all he had Abe could find John somewhere in Africa. They could not locate him anywhere in the United States. He did not understand how he would make it up to John and his family, but he wanted to try.

Greg shared his thoughts with Sylvia. "I thought of the word gratitude, and immediately thoughts of Ellen and her family came to mind. Ellen is now a crucial part of our family along with her parents and her little brother, Joe. Ellen has become a sister to Laura and a second daughter to you and me. I feel like my heart will burst with happiness when I remember the fantastic times we've experienced over the many months since she came into our lives."

Sylvia agreed. "I feel the same way; we are so incredibly fortunate."

* * *

Greg sensed some concern on Alan's part and asked, "Is something bothering you this morning?"

"Greg, I cannot imagine being this happy in my entire life; we've accomplished so much already. I just received word the remaining ethnic groups want to start meetings at their locations too; it is so incredible I almost cannot breathe."

Greg's smile became fuller. He was joyful for Alan, too; he had been such a vital part of this program.

"That is fantastic news Alan! I thought we had reached the peak, and now you share this with me, there is no guessing how far it might go. Perhaps, worldwide?

"Now I would like to ask you a question. Would you consider leading this program and beyond, if it goes to that extreme? Then oversee the planning, staffing, etcetera, necessary to move this forward?"

Alan sat speechless for a moment before responding to Greg.

"You'll have adequate staff under your guidance to guarantee the additional locations will be functional as soon as possible. You're my right arm, and I will continue to need you by my side. If it is overwhelming, say so, and we will search for someone else. Also, if you would like to take some time to consider it, please tell me. Or you could get it started, then appoint someone to oversee it at that point; the choice is yours."

"I would like a few days to think about it, but in the interim, we could call upon our program staff to gear up for more locations. What do you think?"

"It's a magnificent idea. Would you like to notify Jim and Bob?"

Alan said he would take care of it right away.

Greg did not want to overwork Alan, but he trusted him and his judgment, like no other person he had ever known. Alan was not only a valued employee but a dear friend, like a brother to Greg. He had an idea and called Alan back into his office. Alan responded. Greg motioned him to please sit down and buzzed the receptionist for some coffee.

"I have an idea that I would like to propose to you. What if we offer a significant promotion to both Jim Stacy and Bob Richards to supervise the programs in the field and report to you? They would need to hire support staff to assist them, and you would need people to supervise them. It will take a lot of the burden off of you if you accept the additional responsibility. If not, you could assist me in finding the right people to oversee this program; we do not even know whether Jim and Bob would accept the challenge. We will resolve it to everyone's satisfaction."

Alan thanked Greg for his latest suggestions and said he would let him know within two days. Greg prepared a chart of duties without filling in names. No one would blame Alan not being thrilled with more responsibility than he already dealt with daily. Greg relied on him for everything, and Alan had always stepped up. He never disappointed him for any reason.

* * *

Cindy announced to Greg, "There is a woman named Edith on the phone for you. I sensed it might be personal."

When Greg answered her call, she remained reticent for a moment, then said, "Hello Greg, this is Edith. I understand you are trying to contact me. Why don't you leave me alone?"

"Edith, as you know, I am no longer the same person who hurt you so many years ago. It is important to me that I speak to you in person. I must attempt to explain my behavior and beg for your understanding and forgiveness. Edith, I cannot go forward with my life until I make amends to everyone I've ever hurt. You are the first person on my list. Please allow me a few minutes to meet with you for coffee, lunch, or dinner; the choice is yours."

"Why is it so important to you? I've carried the pain with me until this very moment. I'd give anything to have it gone forever, so perhaps we should meet. You should have a chance to explain. It may relieve me of this weight once and for all."

Greg shared a few things with her, then said, "Edith, please meet me for lunch next Wednesday at noon, at the old sandwich shop. They still serve the best lunches around."

Edith agreed but added, "This is against my better judgment, but I will be there at noon on Wednesday. See you then."

Greg sat and stared out the window. He had tears in his eyes as he remembered the pain Edith endured so many years ago at his hand. Could Greg ever make it right? He prayed he could somehow turn things around with both of them in whatever time remained.

Many issues were pending at the AG's office. Greg and Alan had scheduled to meet in half an hour to discuss them. Greg needed to take a walk; he thought the fresh air would help clear his mind enough to move on to their issues with more clarity.

* * *

Greg was very nervous as he pulled into the parking lot. He had destroyed Edith many years ago. Greg had many questions whirling

178

around in his head, but he had few answers, and wouldn't until he met with her.

Greg got out of his car and walked toward the door just as Edith entered. He caught up with her as she approached the desk. She saw Greg and managed a half smile; he greeted her with, "Hello, Edith, it is so nice to see you after all this time."

Edith did not respond.

Greg motioned to her to walk ahead and follow the waiter to their table, which she did. She chose her seat and sat down. Greg sat across from her. At first, neither of them talked. Edith looked long and hard at Greg.

"Do you remember what you did to me back then? How much you hurt me and trashed my life? I had two children to feed and take care of, had just become widowed, and you fired me without consideration. I begged you, but you just wanted to get rid of me with no explanation. Why did you do it to me? I never hurt you or betrayed you in any way!"

"Edith, I wish with all of my heart I could take back my behavior, but I cannot. I'd become a ruthless person then, with such a sense of privilege, truly intolerable. I've thought about how I treated you. You somehow put me in touch with just how evil I had become. I could not stand to be around you because it became too complicated for me to remain that way. I thought perhaps I had become ill and could not stop myself. Since my DNA and personality transformed, I now have a terrible time reliving my behavior with everyone back then, especially you. You are the sweetest and kindest person I ever had the pleasure of meeting. I destroyed you."

Edith cried as she listened to Greg.

She spoke up, "Greg, I heard about what happened to you. Despite all the pain you caused me. It pained me to hear the details. I am sorry for you and your family for having to experience all of this pain. Perhaps it saved your life and brought out the kinder, more humane side of you before it became too late.

"Greg, I do not know what you are hoping will come from our meeting today, even though I can now understand a little better. I can never forgive you for all you did to our lives. We lost our home because I could not find a job to support us in time. I found it necessary to move my kids away from the school and friends they loved, so soon after losing their dad. We had to survive! It took me years to recover, both financially and emotionally. I cannot just forget about it, and I do not imagine they could either. So as much as I appreciate you meeting me here today to make things right, I am afraid I cannot get over it as you might."

Greg asked Edith if she would stay for lunch with him, which she agreed to do. He motioned to the waiter to please bring them some water while they reviewed the menu.

They had a peaceful lunch together, after which Edith thanked Greg for contacting her. She thought it would help her find the closure she had needed for a very long time.

She told him, "It was nice to see you today. I am not attempting to be hateful. I am grateful I can now put you and this issue behind me. I wish you and your family well. God bless you always, goodbye Greg."

Edith waved to Greg as she left the restaurant. He would have to find relief with the level of peace they had attained during their lunch.

Greg relived the experience as he drove to his office. It made him sad, but also relieved to find Edith and her family were doing well. They would both be able to move on with their lives.

As soon as Greg arrived at his office, Alan walked in and asked to talk for a minute. Greg agreed.

Alan told him, "Greg, I've given your request that I take over senior leadership of the ethnic groups across the country an impressive amount of consideration. I called Jim Stacy and Bob Richards; they both agreed to supervise the new ethnic groups. They are beyond thrilled to do so. They are putting together a graph of what they believe their staffing needs will be to do the job.

"I decided I would like to be the senior person in this endeavor, but possibly, only until we organize it, then someone else may fit into the slot. We can access it as we go along. I already have so many duties here with you. I do not want any of my assignments to suffer from neglect. So, if it's acceptable to you, I will go forward?"

Greg was pleased that Alan would be in charge, knowing how conscientious he had always been. He agreed Alan's plan would work out fine and informed him if he would like, he would assign both Janice and Cindy to the project full time.

"I hoped that would be the case; they are both familiar with these programs, having started at their inception. Thank you so much for recognizing that."

Greg told Alan about lunch with Edith, which ended bittersweet, but he understood it could not have gone any other way. Alan agreed. They departed, going their separate ways.

Greg called Jim Stacy and Bob Richards to both congratulate them and welcome them aboard, once again. He reminded them staff would be what they would require to accomplish the task and do it right. They would need some top-notch employees they could count on and trust to assist them. Both men agreed and expressed gratitude in being offered the positions. They assured Greg they would assess their needs and locate the proper employees to accomplish this monumental task.

Greg hung up and breathed a sigh of relief. He still found it difficult to believe they had already made such incredible progress.

Mission accomplished: Greg had come full circle. His gratitude exceeded words for all the fantastic people who had assisted him and their phenomenal success.

Greg became tired, thinking it might be because of the emotional component of his lunch with Edith causing him not to sleep well the night before. Since their lunch, Greg had a sense of relief, allowing him to experience his fatigue. He tried to fight it to obtain some much-needed concentration with pending issues. It worked for a while, but Greg had to leave in desperate need of a nap. He experienced a familiar, yet uncomfortable feeling, but ignored it.

It relieved him to pull into his driveway. The rest would keep until tomorrow. Awakening in a fog, he realized he had gone home to rest. Experiencing difficulty bringing his thoughts into focus caused him concern. He'd never been one to nap.

Greg called Sylvia to ask what she was planning for dinner, wondering if he could start it for her. Sylvia had intended to make the homemade macaroni and cheese she had frozen a few days before. He could put it into the oven for her. Sylvia would finish the dinner preparations when she got home. Greg agreed, and they hung up.

Sylvia could not get their conversation out of her mind; she kept going over it. What caused Greg to be so tired he had to go home? Could he be sick again, she wondered. It might be just a fluke, a part of the effect of his meeting with Edith. Sylvia would watch over him.

When Sylvia arrived, Greg seemed well-rested, so she decided not to bring it up. Instead, she thanked him for starting dinner and for the delicious dessert he created while waiting for her to arrive. He enjoyed baking when he had the time.

Sylvia and Greg shared a lovely evening. They discussed Alan's accepting the senior leadership role for the entire minority program, including the newly created locations. Sylvia could not believe the formation had occurred so fast. Now it would be a matter of quickly staffing and fine-tuning the operations, which she knew they would complete soon.

"I am astounded to learn you created such an impressive number of program locations so soon. It is wonderful and beyond my wildest imagination. I am so happy for you, Greg!"

Greg was sure his experience was all part of a larger plan. He believed it an opportunity to give back for that which he had unleashed on unsuspecting victims because of his selfishness. He found himself grateful.

Sylvia understood and agreed with everything he had said.

Greg stared at Sylvia, then responded, "You understand, don't you?"

Sylvia assured him she understood how significant the changes were that Greg had experienced. They were not dreaming or imagining them.

Greg shared the day's events with Sylvia, elaborating on the entire day, including the dialogue between himself and Edith.

When he had finished, Sylvia looked up at him with tears in her eyes and told him, "I am sorry, Greg. But I understand Edith's behavior, and I do not blame her at all. Did the result surprise you? At least you met, and you talked; it gave both of you a chance to voice what you had been feeling, and for you to apologize to her."

"You are right. I did not expect a different outcome. I am relieved we met, had lunch, and shared our feelings."

Sylvia and Greg retired early that evening, with a much more peaceful expression on Greg's face as he climbed the stairs to their bedroom.

"Since Ellen has come into our lives, I see my patients for themselves. When I worked with them previously, it created a longing within myself to have the other child—the one we missed having because I could never conceive a second time. Since Ellen has become like a stepdaughter to us, I no longer require another child. We are sharing Ellen with Abe and Yomi, and it thrills me."

Greg felt happy for Sylvia, himself, and Laura. Ellen had made such an enormous difference in all of their lives.

Greg told Sylvia, "I love you, and I am thrilled that Ellen has become a part of our lives. It is a joy having a stepdaughter and Laura having a sister. I will see you in the morning."

Chapter Twenty-Four

A Step Back

Greg awoke with vivid memories of the previous day's fatigue, although it had subsided by morning. He called his doctor to discuss it with him, but he would not talk to Sylvia about it yet. He needed to reassure himself since it wasn't his first experience, although it had become the most pronounced.

When Dr. Berkin took the phone, he responded, "Hello, Greg, is something wrong?"

"I've been experiencing severe bouts of fatigue, but I must clarify: the work I am doing is deeply emotional, which may be a contributing factor."

"I would like to recheck your blood work. How does that sound?"

"Good, I will drive over. Sylvia is unaware of my visit to you. I do not want her to worry, unless it is necessary to do so."

Greg arrived and met with his doctor, whom he hadn't seen for quite some time, to begin the testing. The preliminary results looked excellent except for two numbers being off. Dr. Berkin reminded Greg he had been going at a driven pace for quite some time. His body might just be reacting to driving himself so hard. Pacing himself would be a better idea. His next appointment would be in two days.

Greg drove to his office, preoccupied. He'd had a sense of an impending storm. He hoped it was not his health or the health of anyone close to him. If he was candid with himself, he had been feeling a bit off. He wasn't sure why.

The days passed quickly, and Greg found himself back in Dr. Berkin's office to discuss his test results.

"Well, Greg, we've run a series of blood tests, done an EEG with various other minor tests, and everything seems okay. The only exception is two items in your CBC are off. If you continue with the fatigue issue, I want you to call me back right away, and we will test further. In the meantime, please try to pace yourself and avoid stress as much as you can. You returned to being the powerful and healthy former Greg, but you must remember you may tire more easily. If there are any concerns, please never hesitate to call me. I am always here for you whenever you need me."

The months flew by. Alan had all of his extra staff in place, with the latest programs operating throughout the country. Jim Stacy and Bob Richards had completed their hiring of the regional, district, and local managers, with support staff for the new locations. They reached a point where they had everyone they needed to run a reliable ethnic program, with offices throughout the country. A staff member could go from one state to another and run each office; they were all duplicate copies. It was an endeavor to be proud of, worth all the work it entailed. Janice and Cindy had traveled as integral members of the organization and would remain involved to a significant degree.

Greg could relax. He thanked Alan; he was proud of him and grateful to him for the work and hours he dedicated to this fantastic project.

Alan told him, "I enjoyed every minute. I began unsure at first. As we progressed, I realized, yet again, just how important the work we were doing was to our country, and I loved it. We've combined an outstanding, knowledgeable staff, who are as ingrained into this as we are. It is their life. So it is I who must thank you for the opportunity to supervise this extraordinary work. I will always be grateful for having completed it."

"Alan, I am so proud of you and what you helped to create across this beautiful country of ours. Imagine, there is now a way to encourage people of all ethnic backgrounds to associate and become acquainted!"

"It is the most rewarding assignment I ever had the pleasure to take part in. Thank you for offering it to me; it has changed my life."

"It's great to hear that, Alan. You were the best person to oversee it. I'm thrilled you have been the major force behind this assignment and happy for Janice and Cindy for their involvement. It will be wonderful for their careers. Thank you again, my dear friend."

* * *

Laura and Ellen were close to graduation from medical school. How did the time pass so fast? Greg assumed it happened when you are busy living life. The girls specialized in primary care medicine, which had been their goal from the beginning. Both Laura and Ellen had enjoyed their medical school experience. However, they were ready to move on to the actual world, heading to Louisiana to begin their new careers.

Ellen's brother Joe had been considering attending the same university in the fall that both girls had attended. Sylvia and Greg invited him to stay with them if he did. He would be with them during vacations, holidays, and over the summer break. One of the big pluses would be the opportunity to see more of Ellen and Laura, which they all loved.

Laura spoke to Professor Williams often. He was ecstatic for Laura and Ellen to be realizing their dream. They planned their future years ago, when they visited Louisiana and met the group of doctors they would now join. They had both worked hard, but their efforts were about to come to fruition.

Chapter Twenty-Five

Finally

Breakfast was bittersweet for Ellen, Laura, Greg, and Sylvia. They relaxed, and it was delicious. However, everyone realized the girls would leave that afternoon for Louisiana to begin their new profession as primary care physicians. One could sense the air of excitement. Ellen and Laura would start work in the practice they had waited five years to join. Sylvia and Greg would wish them well while hiding their tears. The conversation flowed, as they discussed last-minute items they didn't want to forget and made quick notes to accompany them on their flight.

Greg and Sylvia had met the doctors they would join, who had also helped them to find an apartment. They were both very comfortable with their choices, but unhappy they would be so far away. They realized it made up developing one's destiny, and their parents would never stand in their way. They would, however, pray a lot and keep in touch as much as possible.

Laura and Ellen were all packed, except for some extra luggage. Their belongings were shipped and had arrived the previous day.

The girls both experienced such conflicted feelings as they said goodbye to Greg and Sylvia, through tears and laughter. They were eager to get on the plane and begin their future. They boarded the plane and waited for takeoff, both so excited they became almost giddy.

Before they realized it, they were landing; it wasn't a lengthy flight by any means. They claimed their luggage. Then joined their new colleagues, loaded their suitcases into the van, and were off to their new apartment. They had taken the same trip five years before, when they met these fantastic doctors and made the most necessary arrangements they would ever make.

They were not due to start work at the clinic until the following Monday. Since their schedules would be so similar, they intended to rent one car while looking for two used cars. Even car shopping excited them. It should be fun.

The guys carried their luggage in for them then left them alone. They'd had their rental car dropped off as soon as they arrived. The landlord arranged for everything at that end. They had directions to the closest market, drug store, and restaurant, so for the moment, they were all set.

Before doing another thing, Laura called home to let Sylvia and Greg know they had arrived and were at their apartment.

Greg answered the phone with, "Where are you right now?"

Laura laughed as she attempted to respond, "Hi Dad, we are at our apartment, we just got here. We just wanted you and Mom to know we are fine, just unpacking and getting settled; we did not want you to worry."

Sylvia took the phone. "Hi Laura, thank you for calling. As long as we know you arrived, we won't worry. Talk to you when you have a minute. Enjoy; we love you both."

Laura told her they would talk soon and hung up.

The girls' new home came furnished. They agreed if they loved the apartment, the owner would remove their furnishings as the girls purchased new to replace them. It would make it much easier for Laura and Ellen. It would afford them time to get settled and decide what they would like to keep, realizing they might live with everything there.

They unpacked, then drove around the neighborhood to familiarize themselves with markets, stores, etc. They even drove out to the nearest beach, about twenty miles away. It was fabulous to see the ocean. They planned to squeeze a lot into the next few days, considering once they started on a regular schedule, they might not get time off for a while.

They were up at 5:00 a.m. drinking coffee and reading the Louisiana newspaper.

Ellen stated, "Look at us, reading the paper, checking the happenings around us before we start our new jobs. When we get settled, we will be more familiar with how much time we will need for our morning rituals. We certainly have plenty of time this morning, don't we?"

Laura and Ellen were about to begin their beloved careers as primary care physicians. Never wavering, they held on to their hearts' desires and would now realize the fruits of their labor.

They arrived ready to see their first patients. Since they had been seeing patients before graduation, it made their first day much more relaxed. Most of their patients at the clinic would be meager income families with children.

All the doctors they joined forces with were very dedicated and loved what they did every day. They adjusted to their hectic schedules as part of the job. It had been an incredible first day.

Chapter Twenty-Six

Call from Abe

Greg reached for his phone, glancing at it before answering. He responded, "Hello, Abe, it is so nice to hear from you."

Abe said, "I believe it will please you when I explain the reason for my call. I located John. He is still here in Nigeria and has been since leaving the United States. He is now a senior partner in a prestigious law firm here in the city. I will text you all of his contact information, including the best time to reach the firm. I would be more than happy to help you arrange for your flight. You will stay with us while you are here. Do you know whether Sylvia will come with you?"

"Wow," Greg responded, "I am still in shock over receiving your call, I have not processed it yet. I do not know whether she will accompany me, her schedule has been tight.

"Abe, I am so grateful to you for finding John. Thank you, too, for inviting us to stay with you in your home. I do not know how John will respond to my request or whether I should call him before I arrive there or show up."

Abe told Greg to show up. It would be a definite sign to John: It meant enough to Greg to fly to Nigeria to see him. He would be more open to discussing the past with him. Greg agreed. He would check his schedule and talk to Sylvia to determine whether she could accompany him and call him back.

Abe responded, "Wonderful, and whenever you can make it, you will both be welcome. We are looking forward to having you here with us for however long you can stay."

Greg thanked Abe again, and they hung up.

Greg had a hard time containing himself. He called Sylvia to share the news with her and check her schedule to determine whether she could accompany him to Nigeria. Sylvia was thrilled, knowing how vital contacting John was for him. She had already been out for such a long time during Greg's illness. She promised to review her schedule and discuss it with him when they got home.

Greg and Alan spent the afternoon in talks with the president behind closed doors. They included an impressive amount of positive information involving racial progress, with all ethnic groups. None of the men could entirely fathom the immense numbers of people now included in the program.

Greg and Sylvia reviewed their calendars after dinner; she determined she could take time off. Greg was relieved knowing Abe had located John. It excited them, the mere thought of seeing that part of the world with Abe and Yomi. Staying with them for a few days would be most enjoyable.

Sylvia reminded Greg it would be his most challenging task to date, attempting to repair all the pain he had caused their entire family when they had to leave the US and return to Nigeria without Greg's sponsorship. She told him he should think long and hard about explaining his behavior to John and his family.

Greg had never forgotten his cruelty toward John, and through him, his entire family. It was the reason he had tried so hard to find them! He must make it right, somehow.

Greg and Sylvia determined they could leave in three weeks and be away for ten days. Greg called Abe and told him they would both come and asked him to check the flights landing closest to their home three weeks from then. Abe sounded very excited knowing they were both coming; he would make their reservations, then get back to them.

When Greg ended his call to Abe, Sylvia hugged him and said, "I am thrilled to accompany you to Nigeria and be there with you, and for you, when you meet with John. He will see you, and somehow, you will reach him. It is a guess whether he will forgive you, but I think you will at least be able to find peace. I'm praying for both of you."

"Thank you for understanding and agreeing to go with me. It will be so much more enjoyable visiting with Abe and Yomi if we are together. After I meet with John, we will have a wonderful time and make more amazing memories to add to our scrapbook. The girls will be happy to know we will visit Ellen's family. We have a lot to do before we go, preparing to be away for ten days."

Sylvia was pleased that she could accompany Greg to Africa. She had fabulous friends who would cover for her while she was away. They were doctors too!

Three weeks flew by, and the day of their departure arrived. Greg and Sylvia were both up early. The trip would take over eleven hours. According to Abe, the airport was about forty-five minutes from their home. They should arrive at eight o'clock at night, at least in their time zone of origin.

Packing was easy since the temperatures are hot in Nigeria, and the clothing lighter. They closed their suitcases and were ready to go just as the taxi arrived to drive them to the airport. Henry agreed to oversee the watering of their garden. It was his baby!

Greg and Sylvia boarded their plane with no stress. They were looking forward to a fantastic time with Yomi and Abe in Nigeria. The airplane turned out to be relatively spacious, which was nice since they would fly for quite a while. They flew first class. It provided so many more enjoyable amenities than business class would. Their seats were lounge chairs, so the foot raised and the back reclined, allowing for actual sleeping on the plane. Their area was comfortable.

They put on their seatbelts and prepared to land—very smooth landing!

They walked toward the baggage claim area, then customs before being cleared to enter Africa.

Abe and Yomi were waiting for them in the incoming passengers' area. They were not so tired anymore. Both Sylvia and Greg got enough sleep on the plane.

It became a grand reunion with hugs and kisses and an incredible amount of warmth and love between them. They talked on their way to the car and their home. They lived in a lovely, spacious house with colors and furnishings they might have chosen themselves, showing just how similar their tastes were. Yomi led them to their bedroom and left them alone to unpack. Yomi announced they would meet in the kitchen in about an hour for coffee. Greg and Sylvia were thrilled to be there with them and to see their beautiful country.

They talked over coffee and caught up, discussing the girls' progress. Joe had changed his mind about where he would go to college. Yomi made an incredible dessert, which they enjoyed while they talked. Joe had gone to a school conference, so it was just the four of them.

Abe suggested Greg call John the following morning. Making John aware of his trip to Nigeria to meet with him might make John more agreeable to see him. He also thought Greg should tell him he would meet with him wherever he was most comfortable.

Greg agreed to do so and told Abe, "I would like to do this as soon as possible, I cannot wait. I must learn the outcome."

"I have a powerful feeling John will meet with you. John will see your situation for himself when the two of you meet."

Greg got up early the following morning. He wanted to call John and hoped he would have a telephone conversation with him, leading to an in-person meeting. He could only tell the truth and pray John would listen long enough to enable him to ask John to meet with him. His contact with John would be his most challenging call to date, and without a doubt, one of the most important.

Greg ventured outside to take a walk and clear his head until John's office opened. He walked around the entire area and noticed how lovely it was, with exotic foliage and beautiful flowers everywhere. He knew they could enjoy their visit after he met with and talked to John.

Abe and Yomi lived at the edge of a lovely park-like area. Greg found a bench and sat down, waiting for eight thirty, when John would arrive at his office. He couldn't concentrate. How would Greg explain what he did to John and his family?

At 8:45 a.m., Greg dialed John's number and held his breath.

His phone rang three times, and was answered with, "Good morning, this is John."

Greg responded, "John, this is Greg Hastings. Before you say anything, I have come here to Nigeria, hoping to meet with you. I need to do so. I'd like to see you as soon as possible to have a long overdue conversation and issue a heartfelt apology to you and your family. I've gone through a complete DNA transformation and am now a black man with a much kinder heart and an incredible change of personality. I've visited with every single person I ever abused, except yourself, because I could not locate you until now. You do not owe me anything, but I pray you will allow me to meet with you, wherever you are most comfortable. We could meet for coffee, lunch, dinner, anywhere you choose."

John could not speak, as expected. Eventually, he squeaked out, "I cannot believe you came all this way just to see me, why didn't you call me?"

"I had to meet with you in person. John, please consider meeting with me today so we may discuss what happened between us and why it occurred."

"Since it meant so much to you that you flew all this way, I will not refuse your request. Yes, I will meet with you today. How about lunch at the Cactus Grill, right across the street from my office, at twelve thirty?"

"Thank you, John. I will see you then."

Greg walked back to the house to share his experience with Abe, Yomi, and Sylvia.

Yomi and Sylvia had made an excellent breakfast for everyone.

Abe suggested he drop Greg off at the restaurant to meet John at lunchtime, then pick him up after their meeting. Greg became relaxed and somewhat hopeful.

Chapter Twenty-Seven

The Moment of Truth

Greg approached the front door of the restaurant as John was coming up the walkway. He turned to greet him. Reaching out his hand as he said, "John, I am so happy to see you and apologize and explain myself. Thank you so much for agreeing to this lunch; you cannot imagine how much it means to me."

John responded with, "You told me, Greg, you are now black, but I would never have believed it had I not seen you myself. How did this all happen? I think explaining is important to help me understand all of this."

The two men entered and found a quiet table where they could continue their conversation without being disturbed.

Greg asked John, "Would you like to order first? Then we can talk in greater detail."

John agreed it would be the best idea.

Greg explained to John all the stages he had gone through related to his transformation. "I also experienced a complete change in personality and demeanor. I am no longer the person you met so long ago."

"Greg, I am having trouble wrapping my head around any of this; it is unbelievable. You devastated my entire family and me by refusing to sponsor me and allow us to remain in the United States. We so wanted to become American citizens. For me to give up and return here with my family created a sense of complete failure. I had promised my family a wonderful fresh life in America, then had to bring them right back here. Seeing the disappointment in the eyes of my wife and children almost killed me."

"John, I am sorry. I'd like to take away the pain I caused all of you. Back then, I suffered from such a sense of entitlement and false importance. I'm unable to even explain to you what prompted my attitude. All I know is it grew to be the monster in Greg Hastings. I've become so ashamed. Beyond the shadow of a doubt, I know I will never be that person again. I was even close to losing my wife and my daughter because of my insufferable behavior. My question to you now would be: is there anything I can do for you today to make your lives easier? Can I bring back the hopes you had for yourselves? Are you still interested in becoming American citizens? If so, I will help you accomplish your goal."

"Greg, I am at a loss for words. Now to be sitting here with you listening to all you've said to me, it is beyond belief. It will take time to process everything. I'm an attorney who prepares legal documents and weighs out data every day. Here and now, my experience is not helping me one iota. Why don't we enjoy our lunch and see what comes together?"

After lunch, they had a lovely conversation discussing all that had transpired in both their lives over the years. John became intrigued by the fact Laura's best friend lived in Nigeria. What a coincidence. He found the entire story fascinating and told Greg his life had not been dull.

John asked Greg for the time to discuss applying for citizenship with his family; then, he would get back to him. It would be difficult to explain the changes Greg had gone through. Then he would have to convince his family to consider what Greg had suggested. John said it might be an excellent time for them to move since his twin sons were about to apply for colleges. He must even question employment opportunities.

The feeling among the men had improved by the end of their lunch. John admitted he liked Greg until the end of their relationship. He admired his professionalism and friendliness, along with his charisma. It all added to his disappointment in the man he had called his friend.

Before the men parted, John turned to Greg and announced, "You don't look bad as a black man, Greg!"

Abe arrived, which enabled Greg to introduce him to John. John promised to get back to him.

Greg shared the day's events with everyone, which included his relief after meeting with John. He had a firm sense John would call him back while they were still visiting with Abe and Yomi.

Greg suggested, "Let's go out to a pleasant restaurant for dinner, our treat, what do you say?"

Abe and Yomi accepted Greg and Sylvia's dinner invitation for the four of them. Since Greg could breathe a lot easier than before his lunch with John, he could concentrate on their hosts and their beautiful country. They discussed the many places they would like to visit with Greg and Sylvia, which all sounded exciting.

They were entranced with the beauty of Abe and Yomi's home. They hoped to visit again soon.

John called Greg two days after their lunch, saying, "Greg, I needed time to digest all of what we discussed. My family and I talked about the possibility of us returning to the United States at substantial length. Once we got beyond the anger, everyone still cared about you despite our past trauma. You've come back into our lives at the perfect time. I no longer believe this is the best place for us to live out the rest of our lives. We would still like to become American citizens and have the boys educated in good colleges in America. There are a lot of details we would need to check on before even coming close to a decision of this magnitude. Greg, you are now offering us the dream we have continued to hold on to, and with you as our sponsor, it just may materialize."

"As you know, I have a lot of great connections. Together we can help to point all of you in the right direction. Perhaps we could all get together for an enjoyable dinner and discuss this further, which we would enjoy."

John thought it sounded like a beautiful idea and promised to discuss it with his family and let him know.

They spent the next few days becoming acquainted with some more beautiful spots in Nigeria. Abe and Yomi escorted them from one to another, ending up at a fantastic spa for the weekend. Everyone enjoyed their stay. Sylvia and Greg would head home within a few days, allowing Abe and Yomi to return to their jobs. They had taken time off to be with Sylvia and Greg during their visit.

Greg received an unexpected call from John. They accepted the invitation to get together for dinner, but they insisted on hosting at their home. They asked that Abe and Yomi accompany Greg and Sylvia for dinner. Everyone looked forward to a lovely visit and dinner with recent friends.

The evening was delightful. Everyone was cordial and pleasant, but Greg acknowledged they were always amiable people. The boys had grown so much since Greg last saw them. They were young children then. Now they were almost ready for college.

As soon as they returned to America, Greg would check on citizenship guidelines for everyone, as well as employment possibilities for John and his wife. And colleges, which would offer their sons the best education in medicine and engineering. Abe and Yomi promised to be in touch with them soon. Abe and John's wives were both nurses, providing them with a significant commonality.

When they arrived back at Abe and Yomi's, it was still early enough for coffee and an excellent discussion about their recent friends and girls.

It had been a delightful and productive visit. Greg and Sylvia felt such gratitude to Abe and Yomi for their hospitality, but also their friendship. It became so much more in-depth, too, back to them bonding over their girls' relationship, with them becoming like sisters.

Greg had been a monster, but his present person was so far from those memories. It enhanced everyone's respect for Greg. He never denied how he lived and what he had gone through to transform. Abe and Yomi were proud too of the program he had developed across the United States.

Time had passed; they were already at the airport saying goodbye to Abe and Yomi, but just for the moment. They believed they had now become friends for life. There would be a tremendous amount for them to share with Laura and Ellen about their joyous time in Nigeria.

It was a long flight home, giving both Greg and Sylvia time to nap before lunch. They held hands as they both drifted off to sleep.

* * *

As Greg drove to work, he reviewed what he must do first to assist John and his family in becoming United States citizens. He knew his first discussion would be with Alan, to determine the time frame involved and how Alan might help.

As soon as he arrived, he asked Alan to come to his office to discuss an important matter.

Alan arrived and said, "Greg, it is terrific to see you back. How did it go with John?"

"It worked out better than I ever dreamed it would. After explaining everything to John and him seeing, for himself, the color of my skin, he softened a bit. I explained everything to him and apologized for as much as possible. He agreed to discuss it all with his family. Everything worked out. Now I must ask you to help me get all the information needed to assist them in coming to the US and becoming citizens."

"I would imagine it wasn't easy to make the call to John or meet with him the first time. I give you so much credit."

"Thank you, Alan. That means the world to me. No, it was not easy, but an excellent experience for everyone. John and his wife got along well with Abe and Yomi. Their twin sons are almost ready to attend college, which is another reason to accomplish this as soon as possible."

"I will gather all the information you need to start the immigration process quickly."

"Both John and his wife are hoping to secure employment. As you know, John is an attorney. He has remained current on all legal changes and regulations for practicing law here in the US. I wonder if John who worked here many years ago, might have room in his practice for this John. Sylvia will see if they can hire his wife as part of her practice since she is a nurse."

"It may all come together."

Greg knew he could rely on Alan to gather information for John and his family to begin their immigration process. If anyone could find all the answers, it would be Alan.

He had renewed happiness within himself, to have reached the people he had hurt and made amends to every one of them. Greg now had a lighter heart. The memories had tormented him. It appeared his present self would not do those things, but he had to make it right. Now he must forgive himself. He visited his parish priest for a conversation regarding forgiving one's self.

Chapter Twenty-Eight

Forgiveness

F ather Muir and Greg hugged when he entered the meeting room at the rectory. Greg explained what had transpired with all of the people he had met and discussed John at great length. Father Muir told him, "Greg, I am so happy to hear everything went so well for you meeting with all of the people you had offended over the years. You accomplished such a difficult task with empathy, kindness, and love. I am sure God felt your pain and granted you the relief you are now feeling."

Greg found great comfort in Father Muir's words and could finally forgive himself. He had become another person, in almost every sense. Greg never denied responsibility for his past actions, but had turned his life around. It was so freeing it brought tears to his eyes. He enjoyed the pride he carried within himself. It was genuine, no longer created by his self-indulgence.

Greg called Sylvia to share how rewarding he believed his conversation was with their pastor. She had relief for him, knowing it to be his last stumbling block to being whole once again.

"Greg, how about celebrating this momentous occasion with a nice quiet dinner out, just the two of us?"

"Yes, that is a wonderful idea. I'll reserve a table right away. I love you."

"See you soon. I love you too." All was right with their world. He realized there would be the daily problems life always has in store, but they were on the right path together.

Greg had not spoken to Jim or Bob since Alan worked with them, so he checked in short of their report time on Fridays. He reached Bob first, glad he had when he learned what Bob had to report.

"Greg, we have excellent news for you. We will need more staff and a larger building to do our weekly program meetings. The response has multiplied; we almost can't keep up, which is terrific."

"That is great news, Bob! It goes to show how people wanted this change to come about and how much everyone needed it."

"You are so right! Greg, we are seeing such a surge of congeniality overall with everyone that attends, and much less anger and violence."

"I am thinking. For now, the best and fastest way to find more space for meetings would be to check out the conference centers in your surrounding area. Check hotels, etcetera, see what might be available every week. Thank you, Bob, for all of your diligence; I appreciate it. I will talk to you soon."

Chapter Twenty-Nine

Plans

Greg sent word to John in Nigeria. They were all working on getting them answers regarding their next step toward US citizenship. They would soon provide him with the information he needed.

The programs continued to grow using local hotel conference areas for meetings while the entire country seemed to take on a much more peaceful aura.

Laura and Ellen became more comfortable with their positions. They adjusted to living in Louisiana. It differed from what was familiar to them in Virginia, but they loved it. They were realizing their dream together, as they planned for so long. Perseverance had paid off once again.

Greg and Sylvia enjoyed the peace in their lives. Things were going along at Sylvia's practice, and Greg found himself on a rewarding path with race relations throughout the country.

Greg realized he had not checked in with Dr. Berkin as he had promised to do when he returned from Nigeria. He had been tired, but again, not stopped to rest as the doctor had advised him to do. They could determine his levels when he was tested the following day.

Greg got up and dressed very early, eager to determine whether it was a health issue or just fatigue. He had an uncomfortable feeling something was wrong, but he did not want to acknowledge it. It became much more comfortable to deny the reason existed. He did not want to allow his health to be their prime concern. Denial can sometimes be a splendid thing—until it isn't!

Greg became so familiar with the drive to the hospital he could almost do it in his sleep. He had to accept, long ago, the hospital and his doctor would be a permanent part of their lives. Greg wanted to think his health had become stable enough not to require constant monitoring. He realized he was luckier than many people with chronic health issues.

After parking his car, Greg sat for a moment, wondering whether this might be a recurrence. Could he be sick once again? It had been several years since his transformation. No one could be sure how or why it happened, so how would they answer in-depth questions regarding his health now?

He wouldn't panic yet, although he would not deny how strong and unrelenting his internal feelings had become regarding the issue.

Greg reported to the lab for blood work, after which he would meet with his doctor. He sat down and pulled up his sleeve, almost feeling the needle piercing his flesh before the phlebotomist had even punctured it. It amazed him; his memories remained so vivid!

Greg walked toward Dr. Berkin's office. He picked up on the doctor's concern.

"You seem concerned, is there a reason?"

"You may be harboring a virus of some sort. I am not comfortable with the readings we are getting. I asked that they send your samples out for a more extensive workup. I think you should share this with Sylvia. Not Laura just yet, but talk to Sylvia, so she will be aware we are checking."

Greg agreed to tell Sylvia as soon as they got home that evening.

"How soon should you have the results?"

"Some are time-consuming; others will be back soon. We should know by mid-next week. I promise to call you the minute I receive your results. Please try not to panic."

Greg assured himself he felt nothing like he had years ago when he first became ill and began his transformation. He remembered hearing he might get sick like anyone else in the world, but it did not need to be terminal.

Greg waited until after dinner to discuss his testing with Sylvia. He told her he had gone through a previous blood test a few weeks before. They had a minor concern about his blood work at the time and suggested Greg retest when they returned from Nigeria. He assured her they were not worried, just being cautious. Dr. Berkin had suggested he tell her they were conducting an intensive workup which they had sent out for processing.

Sylvia realized they did not send blood samples out for no reason at all. She asked Greg several questions about how he felt. He confirmed the only real symptom he had been experiencing was fatigue and nothing like previously.

Sylvia told Greg, considering what he had experienced years ago, they erred on the side of caution, which she concluded was the safest route to take. She would not want them to be lax with Greg's health.

On the way to his office on Wednesday morning, Greg received a call from the doctor. He answered, then held his breath and just listened.

"Greg, we've begun receiving your blood test results, and I must admit, I am becoming concerned with what I see so far. Your full blood count shows you are anemic, and you are showing infection of some sort in your system. The more sophisticated test results will provide a more intensive look at your overall health. How are you doing now?"

"Other than tired, I seem to be fine. I wake up in the middle of the night, and my mind goes at a hundred miles an hour, trying to figure everything out. That is an enormous part of the reason I am tired."

"Yes, Greg, it very well may be the reason. Do not panic yet. We should have your remaining test results in the next couple of days. I will call you the minute I get them."

Greg thanked him and hung up. His thoughts had gone to his previous experience. Now the worry began building. Dr. Berkin said all the right things, but somehow, Greg didn't believe it himself. It was too soon to allow himself to go down that road.

Greg pulled into his parking space and exhaled; he always felt a sense of peace when he arrived there. He looked into his mirror before leaving the car and noted he looked tired once again.

Greg tried very hard not to regress in time. Back then, as he exited the vehicle, he lost his balance and almost fell. Then proceeded to panic. Most of which he had forgotten, but the memories resurfaced when anything even slightly familiar occurred.

Greg was careful as he exited his car to maintain his balance, avoiding the appearance that there could be a problem. It had come on suddenly, reminding him of a similar experience years ago, which did not play out to that extent. He could not conjure up any other explanation.

Greg entered his office and shut the door. He checked with Laura to see if she and Ellen were free that weekend. His condition seemed to escalate. He wasn't sure what would happen next. It would be marvelous to spend some time with them in their new surroundings and see them in their clinic.

He called Sylvia, and she answered. "Hi, honey, what's up, you seldom call me in the morning! Are you already in the office?"

"Yes, I just got here. I would love to visit with the girls this weekend if you are free, and perhaps they can spare some time for lunch or dinner with us either together or separately. Can you do it?"

Sylvia was excited at the suggestion and said she would love to.

Greg said he would call the girls and get back to her as soon as he reached them.

When they hung up, Sylvia wondered what precipitated Greg's desire to see the girls so suddenly. She would love to see them, too. But Greg had not mentioned a word of it before this phone call. Sylvia decided not to say anything to alert Greg. She would pay close attention to see how he seemed to do.

Chapter Thirty

Déjà vu

G reg called Laura, hoping she would be free to answer during lunchtime, forgetting a busy clinic does not endorse what one would consider a lunchtime break. Greg left her a message and one for Ellen: Sylvia and I have a few hours free over the weekend and wondered if either of you is open for lunch, dinner, coffee, or just a hello and hug.

He hoped they'd get back to him soon.

Greg wanted to see both of them before his condition worsened. If his memory served him right the last time, he deteriorated quickly. He knew it would be great to spend some time with the girls before it became apparent he was revisiting the past.

Could it be déjà vu? Greg had been there before, and it did not prove to be a fun experience.

He already felt himself losing ground. His strength waned. If he were anemic, that would account for the fatigue, balance, and also breathing issues. He prayed the cause was something else. Something quickly explained and cured. Greg had a unique sense of this experience.

His phone rang. Laura returned his call.

"Hi, Dad, are you experiencing Laura and Ellen withdrawal already?"

"Yes, I am. I missed you both and hoped you might spare a little time over the weekend for your mom and me to stop by."

"Dad, that is hysterical. It sounds like we are just two miles down the road from you. I checked with Ellen before I called you back. We would love to have lunch with you and Mom on Sunday if you can arrange it. It was such a pleasant surprise to receive your message. I cannot talk long."

"Okay, I will check on flights and leave you a message. Please give our love to Ellen. I love you, Laura, with all my heart! Talk to you soon."

"I love you too, Dad, give our love to Mom. Talk to you soon."

Greg sat looking at his phone, wondering: How many more times would he talk to his little girl? How much time would there be? He hoped Dr. Berkin would soon call him to say everything would be fine.

Greg called Sylvia to inform her that the girls were open for lunch on Sunday. He got them a flight out at eight on Sunday morning, with a return flight on Sunday afternoon at half past four. Sylvia had missed them and was delighted to know they were going. They were fortunate the girls were not far away, which allowed them to visit often.

The office phone interrupted Greg's thoughts. It was regarding the progress made in Michigan. Stanley Motley called to invite Greg to a dinner scheduled in his honor, giving him a three-month notice to save the date. Greg did not want them to go to all the trouble to thank him, which he expressed to Stanley.

"Stanley, it is unnecessary. I am pleased you've made so much progress in Michigan, and that's all I need. Please save the money to use in your center for something else you may need to purchase."

"That is very nice of you, Greg, but I am afraid the members would be disappointed if you did not attend. They want to thank you in person, so please note the date and plan to be here with us."

Greg thanked Stanley and told him he would save the date.

Alan asked, "Greg, are you okay, you look tired and pale!"

"I am fine, just a little excited. Sylvia and I are flying over to see the girls on Sunday."

"What excellent news! I am sure it must seem like a long time between visits. How are they doing?"

"We are so glad they didn't move too far away."

Greg told him they were becoming incredible doctors and seemed thrilled about working in Louisiana. Alan had stopped in to share some news with him. He had received some new totals, and the enrollment for the ethnic programs had continued to grow at a shocking rate. Every week remained high.

"Imagine, Greg; we thought it might drop off after a brief period. It is continuing to flourish. It is like a miracle! Well, my friend, I must go back to my office. I, like yourself, still have a lot of work to do this afternoon. Talk to you later."

"Yes, we will talk later."

Their lives were at a fantastic point, stable and happy for the first time in years. Greg could not be sick now. Sylvia and Greg wanted to be around to watch Laura and Ellen develop as doctors and marry someday and have families. He longed to become a grandfather, too. He hoped they would get beyond having his health be the primary focus of their lives.

He returned to their parish for another discussion with their parish priest.

Greg shared his problem with the priest, saying, "Father, our lives have improved so much with God's guidance. Now, I believe he chose me for this mission for a reason, and I must complete it. I'm afraid I may be sick once again, and I may not survive this time. We are just beginning to make an incredible difference bringing together people of all races."

Father Muir asked him, "Greg, did you come out and ask God to restore your health to complete your work for people of all races? Have you talked to him the way you are talking to me? Did you thank him for allowing you to experience this complete DNA change, to enable you to relate to people of all races on a more personal level?"

"No, Father, I didn't do it as you are asking me. I thanked him for allowing me to experience a change of races and thanked him for allowing me to see and correct—most times—the error of my ways. I have not asked him to restore my health to allow me to continue our work, his and mine."

"Yes, Greg, God needs you to ask him to grant you renewed health to enable you to continue helping all of those people around the United States and the entire world. You are an extraordinary man, Greg. I, too, believe God has chosen you to assist him in bringing together people of all races. You've already accomplished this in incredible numbers, but if you believe you have more work to do, ask God for the time and the guidance, he will respond to you."

"Thank you, Father; I'm so grateful for your guidance. I will ask him right away. I felt he had blessed me in so many ways I did not have a right to ask for more than he had already given me."

"Greg, you are not asking for yourself; you ask for all the people you have touched so far, and all of those you continue to guide. Please speak with Our Lord whenever you want to. Never be afraid to ask for whatever you need, he will respond. Remember, Greg, God's answers come in his own time, not ours; it may not be immediate."

"Thank you, Father, for listening and guiding me today. I am most grateful. I will be in touch with you again soon, if it is okay with you?"

"Greg, I look forward to hearing from you whenever you would like to talk with me. Be well, and God bless you always."

Greg walked from the rectory to the church, went in, and sat in a pew close to the altar. He knelt and prayed, asking God once again to forgive all of his prior sins. To allow him to go on with the mission he believed God had assigned to him.

Aloud he said, "Please, dear Lord, grant me the time to complete your plan for me. Please let me achieve my contribution to humanity. Thank you again, you have allowed me to connect with and apologize to all the people I had hurt as a white man. Thank you for enabling Sylvia, Laura, and Ellen, to love me after all the pain I thrust upon them for so many years. Please guide me in being the best Christian possible from now on."

Greg exited the church feeling a renewed strength surge through him. As he drove home to see Sylvia and share his experience with her, he realized he was still waiting for a call regarding his latest test result. It was difficult continuing to keep it from her. Sylvia waited for Greg with a much-needed hug. He relayed his entire conversation with their priest, and she cried. Sylvia felt so grateful Greg had spoken with him and had faith in his wise advice. She attempted to calm Greg's fears relating to his health issues and told him they needed to temper their concerns until they received the last word from his doctors. They may go through a rough patch, but Sylvia thought everything would be okay.

They boarded the plane with two carry-ons. Their flight to Louisiana ended up being about two hours. They'd no sooner gotten up into the air than they were landing. They picked up their rental car and stopped at a lovely bakery on their way. Sylvia chuckled. Greg could not hide his sweet tooth for very long.

Laura and Ellen were a quick drive from the airport, which allowed them more time together whenever they visited. They were elated to be spending the day together.

Everyone enjoyed their conversation over coffee and pastry, which had become the habit for them when they got together. The girls were always aware of how many new programs Greg's group had operating. They were amazed at the incredible progress he and his group had made.

Laura told them, "We read the articles in the Louisiana newspaper daily, about the ethnic community meetings. All positive feedback; it is beautiful to read."

Ellen announced to everyone, "Attention family, I met someone! He is also a doctor, working at the city hospital. We met while discussing a complicated case we worked on together. Laura has met him, too, and likes him. I discussed it with her and arranged for her to meet him. He is also black and about three years older than I am."

They wished her good luck, thanked her for telling them, and asked whether she had told Abe and Yomi. Ellen had mentioned him in a letter to them, which pleased them both. Everyone asked whether she had a picture of him to show them. She did!

Lunch gave them all a chance to relax, which they appreciated. They all found relaxing difficult unless someone else did the actual work; they were grateful for the waiters and waitresses.

Greg felt stronger while he and Sylvia visited Laura and Ellen, so they did not realize he had any health problems.

Their time together flew.

Back on the plane, Sylvia and Greg both smiled; they had their daughter fix and could tackle whatever came next. Thankfully, the girls had not moved across the country; the present distance worked, even for just a Sunday afternoon.

The telephone broke the silence as they drove to Hot Chocolate, their go-to restaurant when they desired great pancakes and some peace.

"Hi Dr. Berkin, do you have some news for us?"

"Yes, Greg, I do. Have you discussed this with Sylvia?"

"Yes, I did. I told Sylvia everything to date. We have been waiting for your call. What have you determined so far?"

"You have an infection somewhere. I would like to run another blood test, which should give us a more accurate breakdown of where it is. Any new symptoms?"

"A slight balance issue twice."

"Ok, it could be anything. I do not find it a major concern."

"Perfect, try not to panic. There is more checking to do, and we have seen no outstanding results of concern. I will see you in the morning."

"That is fine, Greg, I will see you then. Try not to worry; we will figure this out."

Greg turned to Sylvia and said, "Well, I am sure you figured out his end of the conversation."

"Yes, I did. Let's try not to get concerned until we get some definite news."

Chapter Thirty-One

Truth Is Stranger than Fiction

Greg woke up early, eager to get beyond his blood testing with answers in his hand. He attempted to bolt out of bed, but he stopped in his tracks. He felt so weak he had to proceed cautiously, afraid he would pass out or collapse on the bedroom floor. Sylvia had already gone downstairs to start the coffee. His attempt to stand failed; he lost his balance, falling back onto the bed. Determined not to give up, he tried three more times. The inability to stand and walk on his own continued. Being too weak, he called down to Sylvia and asked her to come upstairs.

As she came through the doorway, she asked, "What is wrong—Greg, you are still in bed?"

"I cannot stand by myself; I am too weak. Every time I try, I fall back onto the bed. I need help, Sylvia, and I am terrified! This weakness has come on so fast."

"Let me try to help you; maybe together, we can get you up to stand."

Sylvia could not help Greg stand up. Greg was aware he would have to call his doctor right away to inform him of the latest development. He dialed his number, and Dr. Berkin answered.

"Something has happened to me overnight. I can't get out of bed and stand; every time I try, I collapse back onto the bed. Sylvia attempted to help me, but I am too weak, and she cannot support my weight. What should we do?"

"I will send an ambulance to bring you here so we can attempt to discover what has happened. Please try to remain calm. I will see you soon."

Greg thanked him and hung up.

Sylvia already knew what the next step had to be. Greg needed help, and she could not lift him. She helped him to wash up then change his clothes. Her heart was pounding! She could not stop shaking but got herself ready. Sylvia tried her best to be reassuring and reminded him there could be a simple explanation. She brought to his attention his test results already showed anemia. Perhaps it had escalated and could be causing the weakness.

They heard the ambulance approaching. Laura dreaded them having to take Greg to the hospital once again. The men in the ambulance were gentle with Greg. Sylvia called her office and Alan on the way. There wasn't very much she could share with anyone. She would follow up with more information when it was available.

Greg's doctor directed the rescue staff, getting him into an exam room to begin the testing. He ordered blood drawn and whisked off to the laboratory and processed STAT, and an EKG, which they performed, along with additional blood tests. The doctor was concerned about Greg's current state. He did not understand what had happened to him. Based on the previous testing, he decided, on a whim, to order sophisticated blood tests to check certain levels not explored. They had already completed all the routine blood testing with no revealing results.

He looked pale and in a weakened state, which had become of significant concern to his doctor and Sylvia. Realizing the press would get wind of Greg's hospitalization, Dr. Berkin suggested that Sylvia contact Laura, Ellen, Alan, and other family members. It puzzled the doctor. Whatever Greg was dealing with had progressed too quickly.

Sylvia left the exam area to call Laura. To her surprise, Laura answered the phone right away, saying, "Hi, Mom, is everything all right?"

"No, honey, I am afraid it isn't. Your dad could not get out of bed this morning. Dr. Berkin sent an ambulance to pick him up and bring him to the hospital for testing. He's exhausted. He thought it could be the pace he has been keeping. The doctor directed him to rest, and he had not done so. At this moment, they are conducting a sizeable group of tests. We cannot tell in which direction his health will progress. When he wanted to see you and Ellen this past weekend, I should have realized. It didn't seem to matter if it was only for an hour; he had to see you. Now I understand. He wanted to spend some time with you before his condition worsened, as he thought it would. For a few days, he kept it from me too."

"Mom, I am petrified! I do not understand; he seemed pale on Sunday. It sounds strange to say a black man looked pale, but he did."

"I agree with you, he looked pale, so I know what you mean."

"No thinking necessary, I will be on a flight as soon as I can make the arrangements for someone to cover for me and get my ticket. I love you, Mom, please hug Dad for me and tell him I am coming."

Sylvia assured Laura they would talk soon. When they hung up, Sylvia cried; she had held up as any professional would until that moment, then Sylvia, the wife, broke down. She tried to pull herself together, knowing she had more calls to make.

"Hi Alan," Sylvia said as he answered the phone. "Alan, I am sorry to call you this way, but they took Greg to City Hospital this morning. He could not get out of bed. The doctor has ordered extensive testing. Please inform everyone that needs to know. I will call you back as soon as they receive more test results. We realize the press will hear about this since he is here under his name, and someone may have seen the ambulance at our house this morning. It is serious Alan; they do not understand what is happening to Greg, but it's progressing rapidly. Prayers would be most welcome."

"I didn't know Greg was having an issue again. Please call me as soon as you hear anything."

"I promise. Thank you, Alan, as always. Talk to you soon."

Last, Sylvia called their families and repeated what she had said to Alan and Laura. She had no more information. Nothing seemed to make sense. She promised to keep everyone informed when she had more knowledge. Sylvia also called their parish priest, Father Muir, to tell him of Greg's plight. He promised to pray for Greg and relate it to their earlier conversation. Father Muir knew Greg's heart after speaking with him and would share that with God.

The doctor sat with Sylvia and tried to reassure her, but couldn't do so. They didn't know what was happening to Greg. Sylvia asked him to pray with her and walked to the chapel.

Alan released a statement to the press after speaking with the president. Alan reported Greg Hastings's health had declined because of an unknown cause. He was in City Hospital, with unexplained weakness and breathing difficulties, and on oxygen. Alan asked everyone to pray for Greg's recovery.

Many ethnic groups across the country scheduled candlelight vigils for that evening, with services to follow, to pray for Greg's healing. They were appreciative of all he had done to bring ethnic groups together since his transformation. No one would believe they might lose this man who had worked to aid them in developing empathy, to relate to each other in a way that had allowed them to come together as friends. They no longer saw each other as unique races. The movement spread from state to state at rapid speed, enriching and enhancing the lives of millions of people. He guided people in racial relations everywhere. The numbers increased. The ethnic centers experienced a problem keeping up with them until they began holding their weekly meetings at hotel conference centers.

Laura and Ellen took a taxi to the hospital from the airport. They wanted to be with Sylvia, and by Greg's side, as he battled through whatever had taken over his body and his strength. They loved him and would not give up the battle or believe he wouldn't overcome this demon once again!

People arrived at the hospital to sit outside and pray for Greg and their family. They did not enter the hospital. They sat outside and prayed harder than they had ever prayed.

His family told Greg millions of people were praying for him all over the country. He had helped them and instilled everyone with fresh hope for the future. He was thankful. They were not giving up. Greg had asked God to restore his health to allow him to continue their work. Father Muir told him his answer would come in God's own time, not Greg's, so he still had faith. God would answer him before time ran out.

Greg woke up to find Father Muir praying beside his bed. He smiled and pulled back his oxygen mask enough to speak.

"Father, you will never know how grateful I am to see you here praying for me. I've asked God to bless me and to restore my health, to allow us to continue our work with ethnic groups around the country and the world. God will listen to you Father, thank you so much for coming."

Father Muir asked Greg, "How are you right now?"

"Father, I am fragile, I can't move. I have developed a breathing issue, which is quite concerning to the doctors and me. Most of my test results came back fine. If they do not discover the cause soon, it may be too late for me."

"Do not lose faith, Greg, continue to pray and ask God for your health. Sylvia told me millions of people would pray for you tonight at seven, all over the country. I am sure God will hear their prayers alongside ours. Miracles happen, you already know that. God will answer you. Try to rest now. I will return tomorrow, but I will pray for you until then. Goodnight, Greg, and God bless you."

"Goodnight, Father."

Sylvia, Laura, and Ellen sat with Greg for hours without saying a word. They, too, all prayed for his recovery. Dinner arrived, but Greg could not eat. It was difficult to chew and swallow when he couldn't breathe. They added another IV bottle to ensure he received enough fluid. Greg napped while they had dinner. His doctor stayed there too, not wanting to leave the hospital until they had more of an idea of what direction Greg's health was moving in.

The hospital's director of hematology, Dr. Angelli, appeared, looking for Dr. Berkin.

"Well, I must tell you I am puzzled. I went over Greg's file with a fine-tooth comb. I am shocked to say Greg appears to be going through another DNA transition, as painful as it may be to believe and wrap one's head around. His numbers are all returning to what they were before he completed his last DNA transition. It is such a shock to his immune system it is overpowering and crippling him. I would not even venture a guess at this moment whether he can survive this. We must continue to monitor him and make sure we do everything known to medicine to build him up while this transition drains every ounce of strength."

"I noticed he is becoming pale, or his color is returning to what it was. Do you think it is possible? Let's not say anything to his family just yet. We will have more results within the next couple of hours, and then we can discuss it more."

"I agree with you. Let's meet here again when the next results arrive, just text me and I will come right away."

A special news broadcast announced that candlelight vigils would begin simultaneously in every state across the country, starting at 7:00 p.m. Eastern Standard Time. After the candlelight vigils, they would hold Masses in churches to pray for Greg's recovery. Millions of people would take part. It would be a powerful and prayerful event for the man contributing to changing history with race relations within the United States of America.

Greg could not believe what he heard, all of those people coming out to pray for his recovery. How would he ever thank them?

As the nurses helped him back to bed, he saw his reflection in the mirror. His color seemed to fade, but how could it? He had become black. He assumed he hallucinated because of weakness. He could not stand alone if his life depended on it. The nurses helped him back into bed.

When the girls returned from the cafeteria, Greg told them what he had heard; they, too, were overwhelmed. It staggered the imagination to comprehend so many people praying for Greg at one time. Greg noticed everyone looking at him, as if he puzzled them, so he asked.

Sylvia said, "Greg, I may be imagining it, but your color seems to be fading."

"It must be your imagination," Greg responded. "How could my color fade? I am a man of color."

"Yes, you are, so it would have to be that everything your body is going through is causing you to be pale," Sylvia responded.

"What do you ladies think is happening?"

Neither of them would guess without having the final test results.

Laura spoke up. "Dad, we do not have the answers yet. Why don't we wait until the results come back then we can discuss this? Besides, the candlelight vigils are about to begin."

They showed state after state, and the enormous number of people carrying lighted candles in Greg's honor. The vigils lasted an hour until every group had entered their respective places of worship, then the services began. Videographers recorded people in churches across the nation and carried a glimpse of the Masses. At nine, people began exiting their churches. Several people spoke, sending messages to Greg and his family.

Encouraging them not to lose hope, reminding them God had listened to all of their prayers.

He was shocked at the generosity of the people, their prayers, and the love they shared. Greg suddenly experienced a surge of energy passing through his entire body. Without thinking, Greg pulled back the covers and stood up. He didn't even realize what he had done until Sylvia asked him where he was going.

Greg looked down at himself and responded, "I did not even realize I stood up. I could not help myself. I feel terrific, better than I have in my entire life. It had to be all the prayers. God heard them, and he cured me. There is no other explanation. Thank you, God!" He ran to the mirror in the bathroom and stood to stare at his reflection. He was as white as he had been when he was born! Could this be God's reward for him completing his mission?

Greg cried and thanked God. He asked Sylvia to please call Father Muir; he needed to see him right away! She also ran out to the nurse's station and requested that they call his doctor.

Sylvia said, "Father Muir, this is Sylvia Hastings. Please come to City Hospital, Greg needs to see you as soon as you can get here."

Father Muir responded, "I will be there within ten minutes."

Dr. Berkin arrived as Sylvia walked back into Greg's room. He found Greg sitting up in the chair; the shock showed on his face and inability to speak. As he stood there staring at Greg, Sylvia talked to him.

"Yes, Doctor, Greg is sitting up. Your eyes are not deceiving you; he is also white, once again. As the millions of people praying for Greg exited their churches across this nation, Greg pulled back his sheet, stood erect, and walked without aid. He was breathing and talking to us. Unless you have another explanation, we believe it to be the prayers of millions of people praying for Greg. It is a miracle! It appears our Lord has also chosen to return Greg to his birth race after completing his enormous mission, on behalf of ethnic people everywhere."

Dr. Angelli was thrilled for Greg and his family.

"We just received the remaining test results; I came to find Dr. Berkin to tell him the tests were conclusive. I expected to find him in bed, on oxygen, and still weak. There is no question; it is Divine Intervention! There is no other explanation possible."

Father Muir arrived. He already knew, in his heart, Greg had survived and improved. The two men had an excellent understanding which required no words. Father Muir hugged Greg and told him how happy he was for him, his family, and all the people in the world he was yet to help. Greg told him how grateful he felt for all of his help and guidance.

Father Muir stated, "We will talk soon, God bless you, and goodnight," as he disappeared down the hallway.

Greg picked up his phone and called Alan.

"Alan, it's Greg. Thank you for your prayer requests, and for the millions of people who responded to pray for me and us. Please come to the hospital. I am in Room 327; can you come right away?"

Alan told him he would be there in about fifteen minutes and asked if Greg needed anything.

"All I need right now is my dearest friend, and when you arrive, I will have everything I need."

The mood in Greg's room was exhilaration! Everyone was overwhelmed by the evening's happenings. Greg asked the doctor if this would be his last DNA transition. He could not imagine anything ever coming between Greg and his DNA again.

Sylvia, Laura, and Ellen were floating. Knowing Greg would survive, all became right with their worlds.

Alan arrived and rushed into Greg's room to find everyone smiling and Greg at the center of the conversation. He had just finished watching the candlelight vigils, Masses, and wrap-up interviews on television, praying for Greg. Then he arrived at the hospital to find Greg looking well and very similar to his old "white self."

"I believed I might lose my dearest friend; how did this turnaround take place? Please explain all of it to me, I am bewildered."

Alan hugged Greg.

Greg attempted to explain the evening's events and what he experienced as the people began exiting the churches.

He told Alan, "Without a doubt, it was the most powerful feeling I ever had in my entire life. It was like what it must feel to have an electric energy charge through your entire body. Then I could walk and breathe. I guess you have noticed my coloring. That was God's decision, not mine. I was content to remain black for the rest of my life."

Alan told Greg, "I must call the media and issue a tremendous thank you to send across the airwaves. Otherwise, people will not grasp the intensity of this outcome. They would love to hear from your doctors, your parish priest, and you, Greg, along with Sylvia, Laura, and Ellen. I realize it is getting late, but to issue the thank-you will carry a tremendous amount of weight. It will allow millions of people to rejoice right along with all of us. Will you allow me to make the call?"

Everyone in the room agreed, so Alan called the media. They did not waste any time arriving; they were there within thirty minutes.

Greg thanked the reporters for coming, then explained he would like them to record a critical message as soon as they had their equipment up and running. He had essential news for everyone across the nation who were so kind as to take part in the candlelight vigils and attended Masses to pray for his recovery and family. He took the microphone and began.

"Good evening ladies and gentlemen, I asked to speak to you this evening to thank the millions of people who took part in the candlelight vigils and Masses across our nation tonight, to pray for my recovery. Just two short hours ago, I lacked the strength to stand or breathe on my own. My condition escalated, so my doctors weren't able to predict whether I would survive. When all of you exited your churches across the country, I experienced a bolt of energy surging through my entire body. I stood up without giving it a thought. At that point, I was breathing on my own and could speak without being fatigued. May God bless every one of you for this amazing miracle I experienced tonight. Without your prayers, I would not have survived. Together we made incredible progress in bringing ethnic groups together. However, we are far from finished. I will now pass you on to my doctors. They will interview my parish priest, Father Muir, at the rectory, and his statement will follow. Again, I thank you!"

Everyone present commented on the events of the evening and expressed their feelings about Greg's experience. Drs. Berkin and Angelli gave their medical opinion. In the final analysis, they believed it was the millions of people praying for Greg, and our Lord, as being the source of the "miracle."

In the last statement, a reporter said, "Greg, I would be remiss if I did not address the fact that you are once again white. You were not a few short hours ago. To what do you attribute this unexpected occurrence?"

"It is all part of this incredible miracle. It had to be God's decision to return me to my birth race. I was content to remain a black man for the rest of my life. One thing I can tell you is I will never forget how it felt to be black. It has helped me to be much more empathetic to all races throughout the world. I thank God for allowing me to do so."

Taking part in such an interview was an incredible experience. Greg was thrilling the media along with everyone else. One reporter called Father Muir, who stated he was still up and ready for an interview. Could someone stop by the rectory soon? The media honored his request. The interview was nothing short of inspiring.

"I've come to know Greg Hastings well over time. Now, being sure of his genuine kindness and honesty, I am grateful to have lived the experience. He was chosen for this mission to improve race relations across our nation."

His doctors asked him to remain in the hospital until morning, to monitor him for a few more hours. He agreed, which left Sylvia, Laura, and Ellen free to go home and sleep. No one would ever forget the incredible miracle they had witnessed.

When Laura and Ellen were sure Greg had recovered, they returned to their beloved clinic in Louisiana. Sylvia continued taking excellent care of her little patients. Greg moved forward, creating more new programs to touch every ethnic group possible within the United States. They soon expanded, beginning programs in many other countries, eager to remove the stigma for people of all races and the name, "minority."

Greg returned to his birth race, but never forgot the valuable lessons he learned during the years he lived as a black man. Teaching people to communicate on racial issues, he helped to bring people of all ethnic backgrounds together throughout the world.

Thanks to God and all the people who prayed for his miracle, Greg survived to complete his mission.

Contact the author at:

paintzel@aol.com

www.MaryLByrne.com

www.ingramcontent.com/pod-product-compliance
Lightning Source LLC
Chambersburg PA
CBHW061447030726
47503CB00005B/1602